This Is So Not Happening

THE HE'S SO/SHE'S SO TRILOGY

kieran scott

SIMON & SCHUSTER BFYR

New York   London   Toronto   Sydney   New Delhi

ALSO BY KIERAN SCOTT

She's So Dead to Us
He's So Not Worth It

SIMON & SCHUSTER BFYR
An imprint of Simon & Schuster Children's Publishing Division
1230 Avenue of the Americas, New York, New York 10020

SIMON & SCHUSTER BFYR is a trademark of Simon & Schuster, Inc.
For information about special discounts for bulk purchases, please contact Simon & Schuster Special Sales at 1-866-506-1949 or business@simonandschuster.com.
The Simon & Schuster Speakers Bureau can bring authors to your live event. For more information or to book an event, contact the Simon & Schuster Speakers Bureau at 1-866-248-3049 or visit our website at www.simonspeakers.com.
Also available in a SIMON & SCHUSTER BFYR hardcover edition
Book design by Krista Vossen
The text for this book is set in Andrade.
Manufactured in the United States of America
First SIMON & SCHUSTER BFYR paperback edition June 2013
10 9 8 7 6 5 4 3 2 1
The Library of Congress has cataloged the hardcover edition as follows:
Scott, Kieran, 1974–
This is so not happening / Kieran Scott.
p. cm.
Summary: Told in two voices, Ally and Jake, back together and both "Cresties" again as senior year begins, are shocked when Chloe tells Jake he is the father of her child.
ISBN 978-1-4169-9955-3 (hardcover)
[1. Babies—Fiction. 2. Teenage mothers—Fiction. 3. Teenage fathers—Fiction.
4. Social classes—Fiction. 5. Dating (Social customs)—Fiction. 6. High schools—
Fiction. 7. Schools—Fiction. 8. Family life—New Jersey—Fiction. 9. New Jersey—
Fiction.] I. Title.
PZ7.S42643Thi 2012
[Fic]—dc23
2011041612
ISBN 978-1-4169-9956-0 (pbk)
ISBN 978-1-4169-9959-1 (eBook)

For Matt, Brady, and Will

august

So Jake Graydon and Ally Ryan are officially together?
Bummer.

Oh, please. I bet he cheats on her before
homeroom tomorrow.

You think?

It's Jake Graydon! He puts the "play" in "player."

Yeah, but he's never had a serious girlfriend
before. You have no precedent on which to base
your hypothesis.

Since when did you start speaking Thesaurus?

She's been studying for her AP exams.

Well, whatevs. I promise you. Jally or Ake or Gryan or
whatever stupid name the sophomores come up with for
them . . . they won't last a week.

ally

"Chloe's *pregnant?*" Jake blurted, pushing himself up off the ground.

There was a grass stain on his cargo shorts from where he'd fallen on the edge of the lawn in front of Connor Shale's house, and some gravel embedded in the skin of his calf. He touched the blood on his lip with his fingertips and flicked it away just as Hammond Ross grabbed him by the front of his shirt and pulled his monster-size fist back again. Jake's arms flew up to protect his face, but I got between them and shoved Hammond as hard as I could with both hands. He stumbled back, surprised, and I took the two-second reprieve to whirl on my boyfriend.

My boyfriend, Jake. He was finally my boyfriend. We'd been officially together for five weeks and they'd pretty much been the most perfect five weeks of my life. So much for that.

"You had *sex* with *Chloe?*" I choked.

Jake's incredible light-blue eyes said it all. He somehow looked scared and ashamed and apologetic at once. The sensation inside my chest was like nothing I'd ever felt before. It was as if first the air in my lungs, then the blood in my veins, then the life in my heart, were each getting sucked down a thirsty drain one at a time. *Slurp, slurp, slurp . . .* gone.

Jake opened his mouth to speak. "I . . ."

It was the longest syllable ever uttered by man.

"When?" I said. I was shaking from head to toe.

"It was one time. Over the summer. We weren't together, I swear."

I should have been relieved by this. I knew I should have. It wasn't like they were a couple. It wasn't as if they'd been humping like bunnies all summer while I was hanging out down the shore, clueless and pining for him. It wasn't like he was in love with her.

Thank God he wasn't in love with her.

But still, my stomach clenched over and over again, telling me it didn't matter. Telling me it sucked either way. Because I'd kind of thought *he* was pining for *me*. I thought we had both wanted to be together, and only circumstances and stubbornness had kept us apart. But now I find out he had sex with my popular, stunningly hot former best friend. Pining? Not so much.

"Unbelievable," Hammond said. He was standing behind me now, and I could feel his hot breath on the back of my neck, could hear how ragged it was. His adrenaline was on high alert. "That's all you're gonna say? You . . . my best friend . . . you go behind my back and you fuck the girl I was with for two years, and that's all you're gonna say?"

I hugged my own arms, even though the late-summer-evening sun was warm on my skin. I might not have agreed with the vehemence or the language, but honestly, I couldn't have said it better myself. Chloe had been with Jake in a way I never had. She'd seen things, done things, touched things . . . things I had never done or seen or touched. I felt like an iron fist was trying to push its way up from my stomach, through my throat, and into my mouth. Jake was mine. I had thought that he would one day be my first, and just thinking that was a huge, *huge* deal for me. But clearly, not so much for him. Didn't sex matter to him at all? Didn't *I* matter?

Jake clenched his jaw. "Where is she?"

I flinched. Right. This wasn't about me. It wasn't even about Jake, really. Or Hammond. It was about Chloe. Chloe was pregnant. Chloe Appleby, princess of perfection, queen bee of Orchard Hill High, she who had never stepped a pinkie toenail out of line in her life, was going to have an actual baby. This was what I like to call a holy-crap moment.

The sinking sun winked off the wall of windows at Connor's house, not fifty yards away, where partiers danced in their skimpiest summer clothes, relishing our last night of freedom before school started tomorrow. I stared at them, choosing to be mesmerized by their carefree rhythm, instead of trying to breathe.

Images from *16 and Pregnant*, which our sort-of friend Shannen Moore had spent half the summer watching, flitted through my mind. The nonstop crying and fighting and cursing and heartache. This wasn't happening. It could *not* be happening. Not to me. Not to us. Not here. Not now. Not ever.

But it was.

"She's at her house bawling her eyes out, thanks to you," Hammond spat.

"I have to go," Jake said.

He started past me, and my hand shot out to grab his arm. His tan skin was warm, as if holding on to the summer sun we had basked in that day in his backyard, jumping in the pool whenever we got too hot, slurping down fresh lemonade, cuddling in one lounge chair and kissing whenever his brother went inside. It seemed like a million years ago. Then the thought of us kissing brought up an image of him and Chloe doing much more, and I let go.

"You're just gonna leave me here?" I said, tucking my fingers under my arms.

"I'm sorry." He didn't look at me. His head was so far bowed it must have been straining his neck. "I'll call you later."

Then he turned away and took off through the woods, headed back toward Vista View Lane, where he and Chloe both lived. Slowly I leaned back against my mother's car. Hammond eyed me warily, like he was expecting me to burst into tears or shove him again or throw some kind of hissy fit. But I just stood there and stared.

For a long time, neither one of us said a word. A car screeched up a half block away, parking behind the others that lined the street, and a pack of loud, laughing people headed into the party, oblivious to our existence. Slowly, Hammond's breathing began to normalize, and soon he leaned back next to me.

"Bet you're wishing you'd kissed me now, huh?"

My head snapped around so fast my neck clicked. "What?"

"That morning when you turned me down cold?" Hammond said. His tone was joking but his blue eyes were angry. A few weeks back we had passed out on the couch at my old condo while watching a movie, and when we'd woken up, he'd tried to get physical. As daydream-worthy as he was, I'd managed to resist. At the time I'd been hoping to get back together with Jake, and knew hooking up with Hammond would be a bad idea. "You wouldn't even kiss me, and meanwhile Jake and Chloe are going at it like dogs in heat."

"Ugh. Stop it. Just . . ." My stomach turned as fresh images of Jake and Chloe assaulted my brain. Naked skin and sweat and tongues and fingertips. Why did I have to have such a vivid imagination? "I can't deal with this."

I started around the car, shaking the keys out of the pocket of my jeans.

"Join the club," Hammond blurted. It was almost like he was mad at *me*. Like I'd done something wrong.

I paused with my hand on the door handle. Why was he so pissed off, anyway? He and Chloe had broken up at the beginning of the summer and he'd spent half our time down at the shore flirting with me and trying to kiss me. But then, Jake and I hadn't been together all summer, and I'd spent half *my* time at the shore making out with Cooper Lane, even though I was in love with Jake. I guess nothing was that black-and-white.

"Wait a minute," I said, looking at him over the roof of the Subaru. "You called her your girlfriend. When you first got here . . . you said Jake knocked up your girlfriend." I tasted bile as I said the words "knocked up" and had to swallow a few times to clear my throat.

Hammond blinked. "So?"

"So are you guys getting back together?" I asked.

"I thought we were, but now . . ." He shook his head and scoffed.

"So . . . what? She's pregnant and now you don't love her anymore?" I demanded, suddenly and oddly defensive on Chloe's behalf.

"No! It's not that. It's just . . ." He pushed his hands into the roof of the car and leaned forward, hiding his face on the other side. He let out this guttural growl of frustration that I felt in my toes. "She had sex with my best friend!" he said, lifting his head. His skin was mottled as he pushed his hands into his blond hair, freshly shorn for the first day of school. "I mean . . . are you still in love with *him*?"

And that, right there, was the worst moment of my night. Even with the punching and the shoving and the horrifying revelations. Because in that moment, I didn't have an answer.

jake

I stared up at the columns around the front door of Chloe's house and couldn't make myself move. This wasn't happening. It couldn't actually be happening. Not to me. This was the kind of shit that happened on bad CW dramas, or on those Lifetime movies my mom was always watching, then denying she'd ever seen. Chloe couldn't actually be pregnant. She'd just told Hammond that to piss him off, right? Yeah. That had to be it. She was still mad at him over what happened last year and she was just trying to mess with him. I was going to go in there and we'd have a big, fat laugh about it.

I took a step toward the door, then stopped. What if it was true? What if it was true and she'd told her dad? That guy was, like, a linebacker in college or something. Yeah, he was old and stuff, but that didn't change the fact that his hands were the same size as those hugemongous hams his wife served up at every other Sunday dinner. I was pretty sure he could flatten me with one punch. I stepped back again and looked over my shoulder toward my house across the street. Maybe I should just go home. Pretend I didn't know anything. I could ignore her at school tomorrow and let her make the first move.

But no. I was not a wuss. I wasn't going to chicken out. And besides. There was no way I was ever going to chill until I knew for sure what was going on. I had to know.

I walked around the side of the house, cut through the rose garden, and climbed the trellis. Just like I did the night that we . . .

Yeah. I couldn't even think about it.

My arms shook the whole way up, like I was climbing the rope in gym class with two other guys clinging to my back, when it should have been as easy as scaling a ladder. When I got to the top, I wiped my palms on my shorts and took a breath. My head was pounding but felt weightless. Like it was trying to float away from here. Like it wanted to avoid this moment.

I knocked on the glass door. The curtain was pushed aside. Chloe looked like shit. Her light brown hair was stringy around her face, hanging half out of a ponytail. Her nose looked double its usual size. I'd never seen anyone's eyes so puffy. Not even my mom's after my grandma died.

"What're you doing here?" she said as she opened the door a crack.

The word "pregnant" was lodged at the back of my mouth. *Pregnant, pregnant, pregnant.* I cleared my throat. "I saw Hammond."

"Oh."

She walked away, letting the door swing open. I followed her inside and closed it as quietly as possible. Chloe went to her queen-size bed—which was covered in crumpled tissues—and sat on the edge. She was wearing gray sweatpants and a white tank top. She didn't look pregnant. In fact she looked skinnier than ever. Tiny even. I felt a surge of hope.

Maybe she *had* lied to Hammond for some reason. But then, why did she look like her dog had just died?

Chloe picked at her fingernails. I pushed my hands into my

pockets. An hour could have passed like that; I had no idea. It definitely felt like one.

"Aren't you going to say anything?" she asked finally.

"Is it true?" I demanded.

Chloe nodded, looking down at the wood floor. "It's true."

My heart shriveled up and died. She sounded like she was drowning. Like there was water clogging her throat.

"How do you know it's mine?" I asked.

Her head popped up. Her mouth was open in this sort of ugly, silent cry of pain. Part of me wanted to take it back, but it was a valid question, right? I mean, right?

"How could you ask me that?" she blurted, standing.

"Chloe, come on. I know you and Will Halloran were, like, a thing this summer. And—"

"Oh, so now I'm a slut or something?" she cried.

My mind reeled. This was not going well.

"No! It's just . . . I don't know what you did with him. And we used a condom! How could it possibly be mine?" I said, turning out my palms.

"Well, I guess it didn't work," Chloe replied, crossing her arms over her flat stomach and pacing away from me. "And Will and I, we never had sex."

I scoffed. "Yeah, right."

"Oh my God! What's the matter with you?" she demanded, bending at the waist. "Did you just come over here to make me feel like shit?"

I was pretty sure I'd never heard Chloe curse before. And she was looking at me like she wanted to spit in my face. I took a step back and tried to think. Tried to figure out how to make sense of this without being even more of a jerk. But I had to know the truth. This was too important to just crawl away with my tail between my legs. She'd gone out with Will for at least a month. At *least*. And I knew he'd been over here in the middle of the night a couple of times. I'd seen him through my window, sneaking off. Was I really supposed to believe she didn't give him any all that time, but all I had to do to get in her pants was show up on her doorstep once?

"You are unbelievable, Jake," she said, pushing one hand into her hair as she walked back and forth from her flat-screen TV to the end of her four-poster bed. "I haven't seen you or heard from you or gotten even a text from you since that night and now you come over here and accuse me of being a lying whore?"

My jaw hung so low I swear it scratched against the wool on her pink throw rug. "I didn't . . . I just—"

"You'd better not tell anyone I was going out with Will," she continued, her voice gaining strength. "Because if you do, I'm gonna look like a slut and you're gonna look like an immature jerk who couldn't take responsibility."

I pressed my lips together. There were a million questions in my head. Desperate, awful questions. But I couldn't ask a single one of them or I knew she'd take my head off again. But I couldn't just stand there and say nothing, could I?

"So what are you . . . I mean . . . what are we . . . supposed to do?"

Chloe's scrawny arms fell limp at her sides. She looked away. "I don't know."

And then she burst into tears.

"My parents are going to kill me," she wailed. "Hammond hates me. You hate me. I can't deal with this. I just can't."

I hated watching girls cry. My arms twitched to hug her, but I hesitated a second. Was hugging her a bad idea? Would she think I wanted to be her boyfriend or something?

Suddenly Ally popped into my brain and I wanted to run. Get the hell out of here and never look back. But that wasn't an option, was it? I lived right across the street. We went to the same school. We had the same friends. It was either man up now, or commit to being the biggest asshole in Orchard Hill.

I took a step toward Chloe, and she basically fell against me. My arms wrapped around her small shoulders. She was so little I probably could have wrapped them around twice.

"It's gonna be okay," I said, my voice flat. "I don't hate you."

She sobbed into my shirt. "What are we going to do?"

My whole chest tightened. We. She'd said we. We were a we now, no matter what. And there was going to be a baby. She was going to be Mom and I was going to be . . . I was going to be . . .

Run, man. Run now.

I gritted my teeth and didn't move. "I don't know. But we'll . . . we'll figure it out."

Chloe held on to my shirt and cried and cried and cried. I stood there and stared over her head at the double doors to the hall. The doors to freedom. I wished I'd never stepped foot in this room in my life.

ally

As soon as I shoved open the door of the Dunkin' Donuts, the air-conditioning blasted the hot humidity of the outside right off my skin. Annie Johnston looked up from her ever-present laptop and arched one eyebrow like she was sizing me up for the first time. I was so nervous, both from seeing her and from what I had to tell her, that I practically fell into the plastic chair across from hers. There was an open box of Munchkins on the table, and one glance told me she'd already eaten every last chocolate.

"Hey," I said.

"Hey."

I couldn't even believe she'd finally answered her phone, but I guess dialing her ten times in fifteen minutes was some kind of record. And then, when I'd told her I had serious news, she'd been, in her words, "mildly intrigued." Of course now that I was here, I wasn't sure I could tell her, or that I even *should* tell her. But I needed to talk to someone and even though we hadn't spoken since our stupid, drunken—on my side, at least—fight the first week of August, Annie was still my best friend. I just wasn't entirely sure if I was hers.

I chewed on the inside of my cheek. She picked at her black nail polish. Her look had gotten slightly Gothier since the last time I'd seen her. She'd cut her hair into a straight-banged bob and wore cat-eye eyeliner. Her shirt was black and baggy, but her skirt was baggier, and her legs were covered in holey fishnets. There were about a million colorful bracelets on each of her arms, the ones that had gotten supertrendy over the summer.

"Nice collection," I said, nodding at her wrists.

"I've started stealing them from little kids," she deadpanned. "I think it's important to teach them, from a very young age, the evils of hoarding."

I managed a laugh. "Ah."

"So what's your news?" Annie asked, leaning back in her chair.
I cleared my throat. "It's about Jake."

Annie blinked, as if surprised. "Trouble in paradise already?"

"Kind of," I said, ignoring the twinge of annoyance I felt over her lack of sympathy. She almost sounded amused. I took a deep breath, grabbed a cinnamon Munchkin, and popped the whole thing in my mouth. "He got somebody pregnant."

Doughnut clogged my dry throat and I coughed, showering the table with cinnamon. Annie sat up at full alert.

"I'm sorry. Could you repeat that in dough-free English?" she requested.

I chewed, then swallowed with a significant amount of discomfort. Kind of felt like a rock going down my throat and lodging itself in my esophagus.

"He got somebody pregnant," I said.

"Holy shit. Is it Chloe?" she asked.

I felt my face flush with color and tried not to cough. "What? No! Why would you think it was Chloe?"

The look she gave me clearly said, *Don't insult my intelligence.* She knew they'd hung out a lot this summer. She was the first one to tell me, actually. But she hadn't been sure if they were hooking up. Well. Now we were sure.

I drew the back of my hand across my dry and cinnamony lips. My tongue was grossly gummy. "You can't tell anyone."

"Omigod, this is *huge*!" Annie said under her breath. She gripped the edge of the table with both hands. "Chloe Appleby is pregnant? This is the biggest scandal to hit the Cresties since Josh Schwartz's dad ran off with Connor Shale's housekeeper!"

"Shhhhh!" I whispered, glancing warily at the two other patrons and at the middle-aged dudes behind the counter.

"Could you please take the glee-factor down a notch? This is my boyfriend we're talking about, remember?"

Her face went slack and she released the table. I saw her glance once at her computer, and knew she was itching to log on to Twitter and spill the deets in 140 characters or less, but instead she laced her fingers together in her lap.

"You're right. I'm sorry," she said. Her eyes focused on mine and she did look sympathetic, like it was just sinking in. "Wow. God. Are you okay?"

"Not exactly," I replied. The rock-hard Munchkin slid slowly from the base of my throat down through my chest, and I felt it the whole way.

"What did he say? I mean, were they, like, together for a while or—?" Annie asked.

"He says they only did it once," I replied quietly.

Annie shook her head, staring off into space. "I can't believe he cheated on you."

My stomach turned. "Well, not really. We weren't together, and I *was* with Cooper—"

"That's such crap. You and Cooper didn't have sex," Annie interrupted.

"So what if we had? Would we be, like, even, then?" I shot back. Why was I defending him?

"Uh, totally," Annie said, like the logic was so obvious. "The point is, you were with this hot guy for weeks and you guys were completely into each other, but you didn't have sex. Why? Because you knew deep down you weren't over Jake."

I knew where she was going with this and I didn't like it. "Well, that wasn't the *only* reason . . . ," I said, fiddling with an empty and torn sugar packet.

"But it was the main one," Annie said in a know-it-all voice. "Meanwhile he wasn't even *with* Chloe and he didn't think twice about hooking up with her. How could you not be more pissed?"

"I *am* pissed!" I snapped. The pair of old men nursing coffees on the other side of the shop looked over, making me feel about two inches tall. I stared at the pink tabletop, my cheeks on fire. "But I don't know. Does it matter how I feel? This has nothing to do with me."

"Dude. Of course it matters how you feel," Annie said, her voice low. "And if you ever say it doesn't, I'm gonna smack you upside the head."

We sat there for a long time in silence. For some reason I couldn't make myself look her in the eye. It was like I was afraid she was ashamed of me or something.

"Well, if you want my advice," she said finally, breaking the silence, forcing me to lift my head. "And I'm assuming you want my advice or you wouldn't have offered to pay me back for my coffee and Munchkins."

I narrowed my eyes. "I don't remember offering to pay you back for—"

She pushed the fresh receipt across the table. "It was implied. Anyway, what you need to do, like, yesterday, is figure out how much crap you want to deal with for this guy. 'Cause there's gonna be a lot of crap. *A lot* a lot a lot of crap."

She took another Munchkin and studied it for a moment before biting into it. Jelly oozed out onto her chin. She swiped it up with her fingertip.

"So the question is, do you really want to spend your senior year shoveling up this guy's crap?" she asked matter-of-factly, pointing at me with the bright red finger. "That's what you need to figure out." She sucked the jelly off to punctuate her point.

"That is a disgusting image," I said.

Annie tossed the second half of the doughnut hole in her mouth and smiled, raising her eyebrows merrily. "Isn't it though?"

My body collapsed and my head hit the table. She and Hammond were basically asking me the same thing, and they were both right. Did I still love Jake, and if I did, did I love him enough to deal with the massive crap-storm that was about to engulf us?

Outside, the sky was finally black. In a few hours, school would start for the year. In a few hours, I'd either be walking through the front doors of Orchard Hill High alone, or holding hands with Jake. I needed to figure this out, and I needed to figure it out fast.

jake

I tripped over a sprinkler and took a header into the wet grass in Dr. Nathanson's side yard. Fuck. Just what I needed. I shoved myself up off the ground. The whole front of my shirt was soaked and I looked like I'd peed in my shorts.

Fucking great. Ally was gonna love me now. Why hadn't I just gone to the front door? Ally's mom didn't know anything. What was the matter with me? I had to stop sneaking around girls' houses like some kind of dumb-ass cat burglar. Clearly it got me nowhere good.

I made it to the backyard without breaking any bones and

stood under Ally's window. The light was on. I took out my phone and texted her.

SRY 4 BAILING. AM IN YARD. CAN I COME UP?

Her face appeared at the window. I lifted a hand. She held up one finger. Not the bad one, thank God. She was telling me to wait.

So I did. The crickets were so loud back here it was like they were assaulting my brain. I tried to wring some of the water out of my shorts, but all I managed to do was wrinkle them. When it was clear that I wasn't making myself look better, I tipped my head back and stared up at the stars. There were thousands of them. Millions. I wondered if there were any other planets out there with alien people on them, looking up at me. If only I could be wherever *they* were instead of here.

I heard a door click and slide open, and I squinted. Ally stood at a side door I'd never noticed, waving me down. I jogged over and slipped past her, stepping inside a small room with dozens of shelves, a work desk, and boxes piled everywhere. Luckily it was pretty dark, so she didn't notice my muddiness. Yet.

"Where are we?" I asked.

"It used to be Quinn's mom's gift-wrapping room or something," she whispered. "We have to be quiet. My mom and Quinn are in the theater having a wedding-movie marathon. She's trying to get ideas."

Ally's mom was getting remarried in the spring, to the guy they were living with, Gray Nathanson. Quinn was his hot, but kind of annoying, daughter. "You want me to go so you can hang with them?"

She shook her head. "I watched *Sixteen Candles* with them last night, so I did my daughterly duty," she whispered.

"Yeah, but you love that movie," I said.

Ally's eyes flicked over me, surprised. She'd told me once that her mom made her watch it with her every year on her birthday and that she secretly looked forward to it.

"I can't believe you remember that," she said.

I remembered everything she ever told me. Because I was in love with her. I just hoped she was still in love with me. Finally she broke eye contact.

"Come on."

I followed her out the door. She held up a hand to stop me and listened for a second. I didn't hear a thing. Then she turned, tiptoed through the kitchen, and raced up the back stairs. I followed her quickly, my heart pounding. She didn't look at me again until we were finally inside her room.

"What happened to you?" she asked, her face scrunched.

"I tripped."

I sounded like a caveman.

"Oh." She sat down on the edge of her bed, almost exactly like Chloe had before. "So. What happened?"

"I went to Chloe's," I said, pressing my fist into my palm. "She's a wreck."

"I can't believe this is happening," Ally said. She hugged herself hard. "I can't believe you had sex with her."

"It was one time!" I whisper-shouted desperately.

Ally swallowed.

"And I used a condom, I swear," I pleaded.

She looked away.

"It was so, so, stupid, Al," I said, walking over to her. I almost actually knelt at her feet to get into her line of vision, but stopped myself. "I didn't know what I was doing. I was pissed off about you and Cooper and she was upset about . . ."

About Will, I'd almost said. But then I remembered what Chloe had told me. That no one could know about Will.

"About something else," I said. "And it just happened. I couldn't stop myself. I couldn't—"

"Oh my God. Stop!" Ally said, holding her hands up in front of her face as if I was trying to pummel her. She got up, forcing me backward, and walked toward her desk. "I just can't believe you actually did it with *her*. Why her?"

"But it was just one time," I said, sounding whiny. "And it's not like I cheated on you. We weren't together."

Ally let out this laugh that sounded more like a snarl. "Okay, fine. What if I told you I slept with Hammond?"

My face burned to a crisp. "What?"

She took a couple of steps toward me. "What if I told you that down the shore this summer, Hammond and I were hanging out a lot and one night it just sort of happened? He started kissing me and I just couldn't stop myself. What if he—"

I closed my eyes and my fingers clenched into fists. "Stop."

"But we weren't together, Jake," Ally said, mocking me. "It's not like I cheated on you."

"Stop!" I shouted, glaring at her.

She flinched. "See? Doesn't feel so good, does it?"

I swallowed a few times and tried to blink away the mental image of Ally and Hammond doing it. Of him getting to see her naked.

"You didn't actually . . ."

She sighed. "No." She almost sounded disappointed.

Thank God. The images of her and Hammond started to fade. And then I realized, I could maybe forget about it, because it hadn't happened. But Ally would never be able to. Because what happened between me and Chloe . . . it *had* happened.

"I'm so sorry," I said. "But what am I supposed to do? I mean, I can't take it back. And it's not like it was the first time I ever . . . I mean, it was the first time with her, but I've had sex with other—"

"Omigod, stop talking! You're making it worse," Ally snapped. "I don't need the gory details of your sex life!"

She stormed across the room and started refolding a stack of clothes she had on the window seat, but she was just making them wrinklier. There was a huge lump in my throat and I didn't know what I was supposed to do or say. This had to be the worst night of my life, hands down.

"It's not like I thought you were a virgin or something," she rambled, shaking her head as she basically balled up a T-shirt. "I mean, you're Jake Graydon. You've hooked up with, like, every girl in school, right?"

Well, not every girl.

"So . . . what?" I said, frustrated. I mean, what was I being accused of? Having a life before I met her? "Like you've never . . . ?"

"No, okay? I haven't."

Ally dropped the clothes in a messy pile and faced me across the bed.

"Feel better now? You get to walk around knowing that no guy has ever gotten past third base with your girlfriend, while I get to imagine you screwing every hot girl who struts by in the hall."

I'd never seen her look so angry. So hurt and so small. There was something breaking inside of me.

"You're going to break up with me now, aren't you?" I asked quietly.

She didn't move or blink. Part of me wanted to beg her not to leave me. How pathetic is that? But I couldn't help it. I loved her. I'd never felt this way about anyone. And the idea that I could have messed it up so bad made me want to throw myself out the window.

And part of me needed her. Part of me realized that there was no way in hell I was going to get through this without her. How was I supposed to deal with Chloe? With Hammond? With Chloe's parents? With mine? With a baby? I couldn't figure this shit out on my own, and Ally was the smartest person I knew. And pretty much the only person who cared about me. Or she did. Before tonight.

Most of the summer I had been without her, and every day had sucked worse than the one before. I couldn't live like that again. I just couldn't.

"I don't know," she whispered.

I walked around the end of the bed and over to her. I almost died of relief when she let me touch her. I put my hand on her shoulder, and when she didn't pull away, I moved it so that my thumb was just touching her cheek.

"Ally, I love you, okay?" I said. "I love you more than anything. I never loved her. It meant nothing."

Ally took in a broken breath. "Apparently it meant a baby."

I looked at the floor. At her feet in her favorite Converse. I really did want to die.

"I think you should go."

Fear filled my chest.

"No. Come on. Please. Let's just—"

"I want to be alone," Ally said.

My hand dropped. I couldn't just leave. I needed more. I needed to know this wasn't it. So I leaned in to kiss her, but she turned her head. My lips bumped her cheek.

"Okay," I said hopelessly. "Okay. I'll go."

I turned around and headed for the door. Then something Chloe had said suddenly hit me and, as much as it sucked, I had to turn back.

"Don't tell anyone, okay? Chloe hasn't even told Shannen or Faith or her parents. I mean, I told her you already know, but . . . she wants to wait until she figures out what she's gonna do."

I expected Ally to yell or throw something at me for asking her to do me a favor—do Chloe a favor—but instead she just nodded. "Okay."

Then there was nothing else to do but turn around and walk out.

jake

I lay on the floor of my room, knocking the back of my head against the carpet over and over again in the dark. On my desk, my computer was set to Ally's website where Ally kept scoring the winning shot in the Chestnut Grove game over and over and over again. I kept hearing my own voice cheering for her in the background as the ball sunk through the hoop, and I wanted to climb up the bleachers and punch that guy—that guy I used to be. He was such a clueless idiot, living in his own clueless idiot bubble. I wanted to punch him in the face and maybe weld his zipper shut, too.

A baby. Chloe pregnant. I couldn't even imagine it. I'd never even held a baby in my life. It couldn't be real.

How was I supposed to be a father? What was I going to do, quit school and work at Jump, Java, and Wail! full-time? A wave of cold terror went through me at the thought. But wait. Stop. No. I might not even have to be a father. Chloe could have an abortion. Or she could put the baby up for adoption, right? I mean, she wasn't going to want to, like, marry me or some shit, was she?

My eyes squeezed closed. Probably I should've asked her a few of these things when I was at her house. What was wrong with me?

More cheers from the computer. I pressed my lips together and stopped breathing. Ally and I had worked on the website over the past couple of weeks, uploading videos of her playing basketball so scouts and coaches could check her out. I'd had one since the middle of last year. My dad had gotten some guy at his office to throw it together for me with clips of soccer games, swim meets, and lacrosse matches. Anything to try to get me into a good school, because we knew my grades weren't gonna do it. Most of the athletes at OHH had one, but Ally had no idea people did this until I told her, and now she'd had over a hundred hits. I'd been so proud of myself for helping her out, but now it seemed so stupid. So, like, trivial. Because now I'd ruined everything.

I'd killed my relationship with Ally. And now yeah, maybe she'd be going to a good school, but where the hell would I be going? Nowhere. If Chloe did want to keep the baby, I'd be going exactly nowhere. Not Fordham, where my parents wanted me to go, not Rutgers, where the lacrosse team was calling my

23

name, not to any of the zillions of schools constantly sending e-mails and catalogs and letters. The dream of getting out of here, away from my family, being free to do whatever the hell I wanted? It would all be over. Just like that.

In his room next door, my brother, Jonah, laughed, talking on the phone with one of his friends. For the first time in my life I wished I was him. Nothing to worry about except whether or not he was gonna make the varsity team this year.

I slung my arm over my eyes in the dark, blocking out the colors from the video that reflected on the ceiling. Squeezing my eyes shut as hard as I could, I went back to that night. That night with Chloe. That night that going over there had seemed like such a bad idea, but I'd gone anyway.

Why had I gone? Why, why, why?

Because of Will. Because I'd seen Will leaving there and I was jealous. But why? I didn't like Chloe. Not the way I liked Ally. Why did I give a crap that Will had been over there in the middle of the night?

I bit down on my tongue because I knew the answer and it sucked. I'd been jealous because I'd thought Chloe wanted me, and I'd liked it. Because when we'd driven home from the movies earlier, she'd looked so hot and seemed so willing that I'd actually thought about kissing her. And it pissed me off that I was wrong. That apparently she had a thing for Will and not me. So I'd gone over there. . . . I'd gone over there to prove that I was hotter than Will Halloran. To prove that she actually did want me.

I was going to be a fucking father because I couldn't deal with the fact that a girl could like someone else more than she liked me.

I flung my arm out, punching the floor so hard I saw stars. My teeth ground into my lip as I bit back tears. There was no way I was going to cry. I was not going to cry over the fact that I was an ego-crazed asshole with no self-control. I would not I would not I would not.

I pushed the heels of my hands into my eyes and saw myself rushing down the stairs and out the front door that night.

"Don't do it don't do it don't do it," I whispered in the dark.

I saw myself cross the street and creep through the rose garden.

"Don't don't don't don't don't."

I saw my hands on the trellis, felt the thorns brush my arms, heard the new floorboards of Chloe's deck creak under my feet.

"No no no no no."

But as hard as I pressed, as tightly as I clenched, as long as I held my breath, I couldn't stop what happened next. I couldn't take it back. Within thirty seconds I was kissing her and within three minutes we were on the bed and within ten minutes it was over.

And now I was completely and utterly screwed. For life.

september

I can't believe Ally and Jake didn't show up at the party last night.

Maybe they think they're too good for us.

Or maybe they had something cooler to do.

Probably. Now that Ally's a Crestie again, those two are gonna be the power couple to end all power couples.

Unless they were off somewhere breaking up. Maybe he doesn't want to be tied down by one girl this year.

You think? You think Jake Graydon is single again?

A girl can dream.

ally

The first day of school was all blue skies, bright sunshine, and balmy breezes, like Mother Nature was mocking us for having to sit inside all day. But I was so nervous as my mother and I walked up the steps toward the junior-senior entrance of Orchard Hill High that I barely noticed the weather. My vision homed in on all the important players like I was sizing up a battle scene.

Chloe was chatting with Faith Kirkpatrick on one of the stone benches outside the door, Chloe in brown linen shorts and a white top, Faith sporting her requisite minidress. God, I could barely even look at Chloe. She'd had sex with Jake. She'd seen my boyfriend naked. Or, at least partially naked. How naked had they actually gotten? Had it been short and fumbly and awkward or lingering and breathless and—

"Ally, don't forget we're tasting cakes after school today."

I blinked at my mom, trying to replace the image of sweaty skin with pink-icing roses.

"Right. Okay."

My attention immediately returned to Chloe. If she was upset, she was doing a fab job at hiding it, flipping her hair, waving to friends, shrieking over some text Faith showed her. A group of football players stood nearby in maroon and white jerseys, and one of them, Will Halloran, kept angling toward Chloe like he was trying to hear what she was saying. Shannen was nowhere to be seen, but Hammond stood next to the double glass doors with his arms crossed and a glower on, like he was a bouncer intent on keeping pasty dorks out of his exclusive club. The glower, of course, was directed at Jake, who stood a few feet away, laughing with Connor, Josh, and the Idiot Twins. He had a small, purple-pink bruise next to his left eye, which hadn't been there last night. Had he gotten in another fight after leaving Gray's house, or had I just not noticed it?

I paused a couple of steps from the top. My mom looked back at me. Her dark brown hair was up in a loose bun and she was wearing a colorful plaid pencil skirt and blue button-down shirt. I saw Connor Shale check out her butt and just knew what he was thinking: *Hot librarian.* Made me want to gag. But she *had* been working out a lot for the wedding and even I'd noticed she was looking prettier than ever lately.

"Everything okay, hon?" she asked.

My eyes flicked to where the guys were standing. Jake hadn't noticed us yet.

"Yeah. I guess I just feel a little old to be walking into school with my mommy."

She smiled and tilted her head. "So I guess no kiss for luck, then?"

I smirked. My mom had never been one for humiliating public displays of affection.

"Not this year," I joked back.

"Shucks. And I even wore my new red lipstick for the occasion."

"Hilarious Mom. *Hilarious,*" I said.

"Have a good day, Ally," she replied with a wry smile. Then she turned and walked inside, pretending she didn't notice Connor practically falling over for a better look.

With a deep breath I approached Jake. I could feel the junior girls watching me. I wondered how many people knew Jake and

I were together. I wondered if they cared. Then Jake turned and saw me, and nothing those people knew or thought or believed mattered.

He was completely beautiful and I was in love with him and he was mine. Whatever happened over the summer was in the past. Right now, this minute, he was mine.

I walked right up to him, slipped my arms around his neck, and gave him a long, firm kiss, pressing away the images of his body against Chloe's. Every inch of me relaxed and I felt like we were the only two people there. Everyone else faded into gray. That was when I knew for sure that I had made the right decision—that I was doing the right thing.

Jake broke away first. By that time, his friends were catcalling and laughing. Over his shoulder I saw Hammond roll his eyes and storm inside. I forced myself not to check for Chloe's reaction.

"What are you . . . I mean, are you . . . okay?" Jake whispered to me.

"Dude! Can you do that again?" Trevor Stein crowed. His brown hair was spiky, like he'd just stuck his finger in an electrical socket, and he wore a bright surfer tee over shorts. He tugged his phone out of one of the pockets and pointed it at us. "I want to get it on video."

"Do it with tongue this time!" his twin brother, Todd, added. He wore a similar T-shirt, but his hair was tamed, flopping over his forehead and making him look like a puppy dog.

As was often the best tactic with the Idiot Twins, I ignored them.

"Can I talk to you for a second? Alone?" I asked Jake.

"Definitely." He took my hand and flicked Trevor on the forehead as he led me away.

"Ow!" Trevor whined. Then he turned around and flicked Todd the exact same way. Before we'd gotten five yards toward the corner, the two of them were wrestling on the ground and everyone was gathering to cheer.

Welcome to Orchard Hill High.

Jake tugged me around the corner and laid another kiss on me. This one was slow and deep and definitely involved tongue. My brain started to filter in images of Chloe, but I pushed them back and repeated three words to myself.

I love him. I love him. I love him.

When we finally came up for air, Jake hugged me close for a second and I listened to his heart pounding beneath the soft cotton of his navy-and-white striped T-shirt. By the way he was deliberately slowing his breathing, I could tell he was relieved. He stroked my hair down my back and I smiled slightly, relishing the moment.

"So you're not mad anymore?" he asked finally.

I leaned back so I could see him. "No. Not mad." It was a lie, but a white lie. I felt less mad this morning, which gave me hope that I'd feel even less mad tomorrow morning. I bunched up a bit of his shirt, then let it go and smoothed it out over his stomach. "I thought about it last night, like, the whole night."

"Tell me about it," he said, rolling his eyes.

I chose not to ponder what part he'd been thinking about the whole night. He actually did look kind of tired. His skin was waxy and his eyes were a little bloodshot. But it didn't matter. He was the hottest thing I'd ever seen. Those junior girls who'd been watching us were probably plotting my assassination right now. Everyone wanted Jake Graydon. Even Chloe Appleby, apparently. That was just the way it worked around here. And I couldn't exactly blame them. But he was my boy-friend, and he was going to stay that way.

"And I realized I couldn't be a hypocrite," I said.

His brow knit, confused. "What do you mean?"

I looked away and lifted a shoulder. A school bus pulled up at the end of the long line of cars along the drive. The door opened with a hiss, spewing forth laughing sophomores and timid-looking freshmen.

"I mean, I did . . . *stuff* with Cooper this summer too," I said, fiddling with my own fingertips. His jaw clenched, but he said nothing. This sort of icky triumphant feeling bubbled up inside of me, which made me feel like a total jerk. But is it that wrong that I thought he deserved to feel jealous too, on some level? Just this once? "You were right. We weren't together. So unless you're gonna hate me for Cooper, I can't hate you for Chloe."

Jake nodded, looking less than pleased. I bet he was wonder-ing what "stuff" I'd done with Cooper. Good. Let him wonder.

"I know this is gonna be complicated. Like, beyond compli-cated," I said. "But I love you. And I'm not going anywhere."

Jake blew out a sigh. "Thank *God*," he said dramatically, tip-ping his head back and leaning back against the brick wall. "I swear I thought I was going to have to kidnap you and make you run away with me or something. I had us living in a hut on the beach in Mexico by next weekend."

I laughed and grabbed both his hands, lacing our fingers together. "Is that what you were up all night thinking about? Your kidnapping plot?"

"Yeah. Why? What did you think I was thinking about?" he asked innocently.

The warning bell rang and a couple of kids shrieked as they ran for the sophomore/freshman entrance. Jake and I exchanged a look of dread as the last reverberations died away. I didn't want to go in there. I didn't want to deal.

"How were we going to get to this beach exactly?" I asked.

He smirked and slung his arm over my shoulders. "I was thinking private jet. If you're gonna kidnap someone, I figure you gotta go big."

As we made our way back around to the front of the building, our steps got slower and slower. But no matter how hard we tried, eventually we arrived. Chloe and Faith were just getting up from their bench and walking inside.

"Hey, guys," Chloe said, glancing at me uncertainly.

They were the first words Chloe had spoken to me since telling me off at Shannen's birthday party last year, after she found out I'd kissed Hammond once when we were freshmen. I guess she realized it wouldn't make sense to stay mad at me for kissing her man three years ago when she'd gone all the way and back with mine, like, last month. I thought about averting my eyes, walking away, giving her the cold shoulder, but I couldn't bring myself to do it. As much as it killed just to be near her, I'd never been good at being mean. It wasn't in my DNA, even though I sometimes wished it was. Just a little.

"Hi." I stared at Chloe's back as we followed her inside, trying to sort through how I felt. Who was she in this scenario? An unlucky girl who got pregnant by mistake, or the evil slut who went after my man? Was it possible to be both?

"I can*not* believe you guys skipped Connor's last night. Even Hammond and Shannen didn't show," Faith said, grabbing my arm. Her straight blond hair shone in the sun and she tugged down on the skirt of her plaid dress, which she'd probably be doing for the rest of the day. I couldn't exactly decide how I felt about her, considering she'd been a total bitch to me last year and then sucked up to me all summer. But at the moment, figuring out my friendship with Faith was pretty low on my priority list. "What were you guys up to, anyway? Having an orgy without me?" she joked.

Chloe turned green and practically flung herself inside. Jake's grip on my hand tightened like a vice. Faith giggled and skipped ahead of us, and Jake grabbed the door before it could slam into my shoulder.

"Thanks," I said, trying to sound normal and failing miserably.

"Anytime," he replied, matching my tone.

Our expressions were grim as we stepped over the threshold together, hand in hand. This was it. My senior year. It was gonna be superfun.

jake

Jump, Java, and Wail! was packed for a Wednesday night. A crowd of sophomores sat in the corner making ridiculous noise like they were the only people in the place. Probably drunk with freedom over being allowed out on a school night. I kind of remembered the feeling. Now here I was, *working* on a school night, whispering to my girlfriend about the girl whose oven I'd bunned.

I wished I was a sophomore again.

"So you didn't talk to her? Not once?" Ally was saying.

"Nope. We have, like, one class together and every time I even looked at her she looked away." I wiped out a wet mug with my towel and added the mug to the stack behind the counter. "I guess she's avoiding me."

"Huh." Ally toyed with a box of sugar packets, mixing the white in with the brown. I was going to have to fix that later. Her dad, my manager, was kind of OCD about the sugar. "I wonder if she—"

"So what's up, you two? How was the first day?"

Ally's father walked up behind me and grasped my shoulder. I instantly stood up straight. Ally stopped talking and her face turned red. But her dad hadn't overheard. Otherwise he wouldn't have had that big-ass smile on.

"Hey, Dad," she said, getting up on her knees on the stool to give him a hug over the counter. "It was . . . good."

"Soccer practice was rough," I added.

"How's the team this year?" he asked, glancing up as an older couple walked through the door. Chase, the sixth-year college "student" at the register, took their order, which wasn't that complicated, so I stayed where I was. Ally sat back down again.

"Good," I replied. I picked up another mug to dry, but my hand was shaking, so I stopped. "We're good."

"And, Ally . . . how's your mom? How's the wedding planning going?"

His smile twitched and his voice broke when he said "wedding." Guess he wasn't cool with his ex-wife getting remarried. But from the grin he had on, he was *trying* to be. Kind of like I was trying to act normal even though I'd spent ninety percent of the day feeling like I could heave.

"Good," Ally replied, shrugging. She looked at me instead of him. Ally wasn't that psyched about the wedding either and I knew talking about it with her dad was tense. As much as I liked Mr. Ryan, I hated that her parents had put her in the middle of their gross love-triangle. "I haven't really gotten that into it."

"Don't avoid it on my behalf, bud," he said. "This is a huge deal for your mom. You should be there for her."

She just stared at him. "If you say so."

Mr. Ryan narrowed his eyes. "Are you two okay? You seem out of it."

That was when Chloe walked in. Ally and I both froze. Chloe glanced around, and when she saw Ally, I think she almost backed out again. But then she changed her mind and came over. Then Keisha called Mr. Ryan over for some help with something.

"I'll be back," he promised, eyeing us.

"Great," I said under my breath.

Luckily he didn't hear me.

Chloe hung on to the strap of her bag as she stopped nearby. "Hi, guys."

Ally stared down at her hands. Now she was the one who looked ready to heave.

"Hey," I said.

I wiped my palms over and over on the towel. They were sweating like crazy.

"Um, Jake? Can I talk to you for a second?" Chloe asked.

Her eyes kept darting around. From me to Ally to Ally's dad to the loud-ass losers by the window. She looked like she wanted to be somewhere else. Anywhere else. From the corner of my eye I saw Mr. Ryan head back to his office. Once the door was closed, I found my voice.

"What's up?" I asked.

Chloe shot Ally a look. "Alone?"

My teeth clicked together. "Ally knows everything. We can talk here."

Chloe touched her face, then her elbow, then her stomach. It was like she was uncomfortable in her own skin. Finally she let out a sigh.

"Fine. Okay. I was just wondering . . . I have a doctor's appointment this Friday at five." Her voice was so quiet I could barely hear her over the gurgling cappuccino machine behind me. "Would you come with me? Please? I don't want to go alone."

I felt like somebody had just flipped on one of those bright police spotlights right in my face. "Why?"

Ally's eyes kind of bugged out. Chloe looked like she was about to cry. What? That wasn't a valid question?

"Sorry. I just . . . I have practice, so . . ."

Ally looked away. She went digging in her bag like a raccoon in a garbage can. Okay. Clearly I was doing something wrong here.

"You can leave practice a few minutes early, right?" Chloe said. "I just . . . don't think I can do this by myself and no one else knows, so . . ."

My stomach felt hollow. And even though this was about the last thing on the face of the earth I ever wanted to do, I couldn't say no. Not with Chloe looking so scared and sad.

"Um, okay," I said. "Sure."

"Thanks." Chloe put her keys down on the counter and pushed her hair back from her face with both hands. She sat down next to Ally and sort of slumped. Ally automatically put her hands up to steady her.

"Are you okay?" Ally asked.

"Yeah, I just . . . I need something to eat," she said. "I get hungry and two seconds later, I get dizzy." She looked at me. "Can I have a muffin or something?"

"Yeah." I rushed to get one for her, snatching it out of the pastry case with the metal tongs and dropping it in front of her like a grenade. Chloe picked one of the crumbs off the top and placed it carefully on her tongue. She chewed it so slowly you'd think I'd fed her snails.

Ally and I stared at each other. I could tell she wanted me to say something, but what? I was so sure I'd say the wrong thing—kind of like I just had when she asked me to go to the doctor—that panic started to rise up inside my chest, blocking everything else out. Ally finally saved my ass.

"How are you . . . I mean, have you been feeling okay?" Ally asked her.

I felt this warm rush, guilty that I hadn't been the one to ask, and grateful that Ally was being so cool. I clicked the tongs together at my side over and over again.

"Yeah. Just the dizziness," Chloe said, slowly putting another crumb in her mouth. "And I'm nauseous in the mornings, until I eat."

She reached for her bag and took out her wallet.

"What are you doing?" I asked.

"Paying for the muffin."

"No. It's fine. It's on me," I told her.

Ally kind of smiled, her lips tight and flat. At least I'd done something right.

"Thanks," Chloe said. "I should go." She slid off the stool, taking the muffin with her. "I'll pick you up at the field on Friday?"

"Um, yeah," I said.

Even though Hammond would probably kill me. I clenched the tongs together so tight I thought they might break.

"Actually, better let me meet you there," I said. "I'm gonna have to make up an excuse, and you picking me up would kind of kill whatever I come up with."

"Okay. I'll text you the address," Chloe said. She looked at Ally. "Thanks for being so cool about this. After what I said to you at Shannen's party and now this . . . I don't know why you don't hate me."

Ally cleared her throat. She shifted on her stool and rubbed her palms together between her legs. "Don't worry about it." She cleared her throat again. "If you ever need anything . . ."

She trailed off and let the thought die. I wasn't sure any of us believed it anyway.

Chloe looked at the floor. "Thanks. I'll see you guys at school."

Then she practically ran out. It took a second for me to start breathing again. The sophomores in the corner laughed suddenly and loudly, and I wanted to fling my tongs at their heads.

"That was cool of you," Ally said. "Saying you'll go with her."

"Yeah," I said, placing the tongs down on the counter. I leaned forward, my elbows on the marble, and put my hands over hers. "I can't believe you were so nice to her."

Ally's eyebrows shot up. "I was? I totally froze."

"No, really. You're amazing," I said, hanging my head. "And I suck."

"You don't suck," she said lightly. She took one of her hands out and put it on top of mine. "This whole thing sucks."

I nodded, and stared down at the mound of our tangled-up fingers. I was going to the doctor on Friday. The lady doctor. With the girl who was going to have my baby. I held on to Ally so tightly I was surprised she didn't squirm. We just sat there like that for the longest time. Me clinging to her, her letting me, until the line at the register got too long to ignore, and I had to let go.

ally

Life's just weird. One second there's tons of stuff that matters so much it's stressing you out like crazy. Like getting my recruitment website just right. Making lists of coaches and scouts to call once the season started. Figuring out which schools to apply to and whether I wanted to be close to home or far away. Last week, it was life-consuming.

But I hadn't thought about any of it since Tuesday night. Not once.

On Friday morning, I sat at the huge island in the center of Gray's kitchen, my Frosted Flakes getting soggier and soggier as I stared at the babycenter.com website on my computer. I'd gone there thinking I could maybe figure out what Chloe's options were, and the first thing I'd seen was a due-date predictor. They wanted you to put in the date of your last period, and then they'd tell you when the baby was due. Of course, I had no idea when Chloe's last period had been. When had they had sex? June? July? August? How pregnant was she, exactly? Did her baby look like a cell sac, or was it already the size of a walnut, like the picture in front of me?

Down in the corner there was a special section to click on for daddys-to-be. That was Jake. That was my boyfriend. I tried to picture him holding a baby, and when I did, he looked completely freaked out. But he might have to do it soon. He might have to actually take care of a human being. Him and Chloe. How were they supposed to do that? And wouldn't they have to be . . . *together* to do it? My heart felt like it was gulping for air all of a sudden. No matter how hard I tried, I couldn't figure out where I fit in that lovely domestic scenario.

"Hi, hon! Whatcha looking at?"

My mom breezed into the kitchen with a huge smile on, reaching back to tuck her hair up into a bun. I slapped my computer closed and almost took my fingertip off. My mother froze, suspicious.

"Ally?"

"I was just . . . looking for wedding presents," I improvised.

Gray and Quinn strolled into the kitchen right behind her. He was all coiffed in a gray pinstriped suit that probably cost more than Jake's Jeep. She was decked out in a cute tweed skirt, tall boots, and a high-collared shirt, her blond hair perfect and her makeup carefully applied. Honestly, I think Quinn actually believed a Hollywood talent scout was going to descend on Orchard Hill High out of nowhere and discover her on the FroYo line. I mean, who dressed like that for school?

"Oh. That's sweet, Ally, but you don't have to get us anything," Gray said, giving my shoulders a squeeze as he passed me by. He joined my mom at the coffee machine and they shared a kiss as he poured half and half in her mug for her. Which made me think of how my dad used to do the same thing. Which made me nauseous. I pushed my Frosted Flakes aside.

"Gray's right. Just make a good speech at the wedding," Mom said.

My mouth fell open. She couldn't be serious. "I have to make a speech?"

"Hello? You *are* the maid of honor," Quinn said, peeling a banana as she sat next to me.

I dropped my head onto my hand. "Just kill me now."

"Ally," my mom said in her favorite warning tone.

I sighed and rubbed my face with both hands. It felt dry and tight, like my eyes.

"Ally?" Now she sounded more concerned. She placed her hand on my back and I tensed. "Is something wrong? Is it the wedding?"

"No." I slid my laptop off the island and into its case. "I'm fine about the wedding."

"Liar, liar . . ." Quinn sang, tilting her head to the side.

"Quinn," her dad said in *his* favorite warning tone.

"What? I totally heard her on the phone last night telling someone all about how the wedding planning was stressing her out," Quinn said.

My face burned. "You listened in on my phone call?"

"Well, you could try dialing it down a notch," Quinn said, rolling her eyes. "They could hear you all the way in Newark."

"Mom!" I groaned.

"Girls, please." My mother held out her hands like two stop signs. She and Gray looked at each other over our heads and, surprisingly, smiled. "Well, they've got the sister thing down."

Okay, now I really was going to puke.

"I have to go," I said, gathering my stuff. "Dad's probably

outside already. I'm going with him to Jump before school."

I headed toward the foyer, but my mom followed me.

"Ally, hang on a second, please."

I paused in the center of the marble floor, next to the huge potted tree I'd never seen anyone water. Yet somehow, it was still alive. One of the many mysteries of the Nathanson household.

"Remember what we said," my mother told me. "At the end of the summer? You promised me that if there was ever anything wrong, you would talk to me about it."

I yanked my backpack strap onto my shoulder, feeling heavy with guilt. Looking back on the summer always made me feel awful. I'd been a brat, plain and simple. I hadn't liked the way things were going and instead of talking to anyone about it, I'd pouted and complained and acted like an idiot, trying to manipulate my mom into getting back together with my dad. After we'd had our long, *long* make-up talk, I had promised her I'd tell her if something was bothering me, but I'd also promised myself I'd be nicer to her. Which meant not complaining about her wedding and a speech I didn't know I had to make.

But I also couldn't tell her what was going on. It wasn't my secret to tell.

"It's just . . . there's so much, between the SAT and college applications and the recruitment thing," I told her. "I just want it to be over with already. I want to know where I'm going to be next year."

I'd actually kind of like to be there already, I added silently, wishing for a mode of escape from all the drama.

"I know. I know it's not easy," my mom said, smoothing my hair behind my ear. "But you're gonna do fine. You're amazing, Ally. Any college would be lucky to have you."

I smiled gratefully. "Thanks, Mom."

"So, listen . . . there *is* something else I want to talk to you about," my mother said as we walked slowly toward the double doors at the front of the house. "Gray wants to take me on a real honeymoon. Two weeks on the Amalfi Coast," she said with a grin. "But if we go, that means . . ."

With a start I realized what she was getting at. My birthday. If she was gone for two weeks after the wedding, she wouldn't be here for my eighteenth birthday. I took a breath, remembered my promise to myself, and lifted my shoulders.

"That's okay," I said. "We can just celebrate when you get back."

"Yeah?" Her voice was an excited squeak. "Are you sure?"

"Totally. It's no big deal." But inside, my heart felt heavy. She was already doing it. She was already choosing Gray over me.

"When we get back we'll do our traditional birthday dinner," she told me. "It'll just be a few days late."

"Okay," I said, backing toward the door. I saw my father's newly leased Taurus idling in the driveway. "Cool. But I should go. Dad's here."

"Okay. Tell him I said hi!" my mom said awkwardly.

"I will."

Outside I jogged to the car, feeling the weight of the conversation tug free from my shoulders. My father had the radio on, tuned to a classic rock station.

"Tell me you have those cinnamon roll things at the shop this morning," I said, buckling my seat belt.

He chuckled, scratching at the stubble on his cheek. "Rough morning in the Palais du Nathanson?" he said in a French accent.

"Something like that," I said.

My dad pulled out of the driveway and we cruised down the hill, past all the mansions and gated driveways and skinny women jogging with their tiny dogs, headed for town. I was just starting to relax when I saw a woman with a jogging stroller, pushing a sleeping baby up toward the crest. I closed my eyes and sunk lower in my seat.

"Everything all right, bud?" my dad asked.

"Yeah." *Sure. Fine. Great.*

"I was thinking, if you want to go over your applications one night this week, I could help you narrow things down," my dad said, lowering the volume. "Maybe take some of the pressure off?"

I looked up at him. College. Applications. Visions of brick and stone buildings, fancy school logos, and happily smiling students hanging on lush lawns filled my mind, crowding out due-date calculators and gender predictors. The future. My future. Somewhere other than here, with people who'd never heard of Orchard Hill, of Chloe and Jake. And even though I felt a twinge of disloyalty, for thinking of a life beyond Jake, my chest filled with airy hope.

"Sounds like a plan," I said.

My dad smiled, and for the first time in days, I smiled too.

jake

The doctor's office smelled like lemon. No. Not like lemon. Like a lemon car air freshener. It had that synthetic fake-citrus smell that's so foul it makes the hairs inside your nose itch. Every time I breathed in, I wanted to heave. It didn't help that it was, like, five-fucking-trillion degrees in there and everyone was staring at me like I'd come to each of their homes and personally slaughtered their family pets. The pregnant woman in the corner with the graying hair. The couple that looked like newlyweds off some reality show with the leather, the dye jobs, and the bling. Even the janitor shot me a look on her way out, lowering her sunglasses so she could really give it to me.

What the hell was wrong with these people? Maybe me and Chloe were totally in love. Married even. Or maybe I was her brother. Yeah. Why not? God, they'd feel so stupid if they found out I was just her brother and I'd come here with her just trying to be nice. Jackasses.

"How long is this gonna take?" I asked Chloe, my leg bouncing nervously.

"I don't know." Chloe licked her lips and stared at my knee. "Could you please stop doing that? It's making me tense."

I opened my mouth to say something back—something probably stupid like "I can leave if you want me to"—but the nurse saved me.

"Chloe Appleby?"

Chloe cringed at the sound of her own name. I jumped up so fast the nurse looked confused and kinda disturbed. Like maybe I was Chloe Appleby.

"That's her," I said, pointing at Chloe.

From the look on her face, I'm pretty sure Chloe was coming up with ten different ways to murder me.

"Let's go," I said under my breath. All I could think about was getting out of that room and away from the Judgey McHolierthanthous.

"Right this way," the nurse said, giving us a smile. A real one. At least someone around here didn't hate us.

Chloe finally got out of her chair and we slowly followed the nurse. She weighed Chloe, took her blood pressure, and asked her way too many questions about her period. I stared at a pink calendar on the wall. On it was a stork dangling a wide-eyed, smiling baby right over the month of March.

"So your approximate due date would be . . ."

Chloe and I locked eyes. Due date? What? Already? The woman spun around a plastic wheel and smiled. "March twentieth!"

March twentieth. March twentieth. March twentieth. Suddenly I felt like I had about six and a half months to live.

"I'm just gonna have you pee in a cup for me and then you can see the doctor!" the nurse said brightly. She handed Chloe a plastic cup with a lid, sealed inside a plastic bag, and pointed her toward the bathroom. Seriously. Could this whole thing get any more effed up? Chloe ducked her head in a very un-Chloe-like way, and slipped inside. She started to close the door.

"Will your parents be joining us today, hon?" the woman asked.

Somehow Chloe's head ducked even further. "Um. No."

Then she shut the door. The nurse turned to me, grinning, as if this kind of thing happened every day and it was about as big of a deal as charging a cell phone.

"You'll be in room five. You can wait for her in there."

I glanced at room five. It was light blue and yellow and cheery, but to me it looked like the bowels of hell. I didn't move. My mouth tasted like dirt. The nurse stood there with her arm out.

"Um . . . are they gonna, like . . . is the doctor gonna go . . . you know . . . like in the movies?"

I made a gesture with my hand that turned her face red. God, I wanted to die.

The nurse recovered and tilted her head sympathetically. "Yes, the doctor will give her a pelvic exam to confirm the pregnancy," she said. "You can wait out here for that if you like."

"Thank you!" I said in an exhale. I dropped onto the plastic chair just as Chloe came out and handed a cup full of yellow to the nurse. The nurse placed it on the counter, right at my eye level.

I wondered if they did lobotomies in this place.

Chloe stepped to the threshold and looked down at me. "You're not coming in?"

My heart thumped. "Um—"

"You'll need to strip from the waist down, hon," the nurse said, handing her a paper sheet.

Chloe instantly got the picture. "Oh. Okay."

"I'll be right here," I said. "If you need me."

"Okay."

Chloe walked inside like she was in a daze and closed the door behind her. Other nurses and patients walked by, did their business, went into rooms. I kept my eyes on the floor, letting my leg bounce as much as it wanted, avoiding catching any more criticizing looks. Finally someone stopped outside the room, knocked on the door, and went inside. Had to be the doctor, but I wasn't sure. She said nothing to me, and I didn't look up.

Five minutes passed. Ten. Fifteen. Twenty million. I could hear murmuring voices through the wall but couldn't make out any words. In my mind I saw Chloe lying on a table, her legs open, the doctor coming at her with some scary instrument. My stomach turned. I finally lifted my head to breathe and noticed that from where I was sitting I had a clear view of the parking lot out the window. My Jeep was parked right in the middle, its army green paint glinting in the sun. Suddenly I saw myself jumping behind the wheel, gunning the engine, and taking off for the shore. Getting. The Hell. Out of here.

My fingers twitched toward the keys in my pocket. Then the door behind me opened.

"Are you Jake?"

I looked up at the doctor. She was thin, pretty, and young, with brown hair, green eyes, and a purple T-shirt under her white coat.

"Um, yeah?"

"I'm Doctor Muller. Come on in." She cocked her head toward the room like she was inviting me inside for a beer. Was she serious? I didn't want to see what was going on in there.

"Come on," she said again. "I won't bite."

It wasn't her I was worried about. I shoved myself up and, staring straight ahead at the far wall—past where Chloe was lying—walked inside.

"It's okay. I have my clothes back on," Chloe said, sounding annoyed.

I looked at her. Only her stomach was showing as she lay back on the table. Her perfectly flat stomach. There was no way there was a baby in there. Just no way. Was that why they had called me in here? To tell me it was a big mistake? I turned toward the doctor and she was holding this wandlike thing on a wire.

"What're you gonna do with that?" My hip hit the counter and I caught a glass bottle of Q-tips before they could smash on the floor. "Sorry. Sorry." I put it back on the counter with a clatter.

"It's okay," the doctor said, smirking. My jaw clenched. Glad she was enjoying this. "We're just going to listen for the baby's heartbeat."

My eyes widened. "It's got a heartbeat?"

They both looked at me like I'd just skipped A in a recital of the ABCs.

"Sorry."

The doctor sat on a tall stool and squirted some goo on Chloe's stomach. Then she put the end of the wand on there. Chloe's hand shot out toward me. I hesitated a second, but then held it. She squeezed my fingers crazy hard. This was so wrong. I shouldn't be here. Chloe should not be holding my hand. I'd never held her hand in my life.

Then, out of nowhere, this quiet thrumming sound filled the room. It was so fast it sounded like something panicked.

"There it is! That's your baby," the doctor said.

"That's it?" Chloe asked, lifting her head off the table.

"Yep. Sounds good and strong," the doctor said.

She put the wand away and handed Chloe some tissues. "To wipe your stomach," she explained when Chloe looked confused. As Chloe mopped up the goo with her free hand, the doctor clasped her hands between her knees. "So, is there anything else you want to ask me, Chloe? Or you, Jake?"

I couldn't think. My head was too filled with the sound of thrumming, even though the machine was turned off. I shook my head and let go of Chloe's hand. I couldn't stop staring at her stomach. There was a baby in there. An actual baby. I had the weirdest sensation. Like my head was emptying out from the back of my skull toward the top. The room tilted so fast I was shocked Chloe and the doctor didn't go flying. I pinned myself back against the wall and closed my eyes.

Don't faint, you pussy. Don't you fucking faint.

"Um, no. I think I asked everything I needed to ask," Chloe said. Her voice sounded small and high, like she was suddenly five years old.

"All right, then. You have my card and the pamphlets," the doctor said. "Please give me a call anytime if there's anything you want to talk about. Anything at all."

"Thanks," Chloe said.

She was staring straight up at the ceiling, her hands on top of her stomach, which was now covered by her yellow T-shirt. The doctor shot me this look as she walked out, like she was telling me to take care of Chloe, then she closed the door. Take care of Chloe? Did she not notice I was about to go down? I pressed my palms together—they were slippery with sweat—and tried to breathe.

"It's okay," I whispered. "It's okay it's okay it's okay."

"Are you *kidding* me?" Chloe sat up so fast it scared the crap out of me. "Omigod. What am I going to do? What am I going to do, Jake?"

Her eyes filled with tears and she clutched her stomach. Right. Clearly it was time to focus. I squinted at her, waiting for my brain to reset itself.

"Okay, okay, calm down," I said again. "It's gonna be okay."

"No! It's not! It's not gonna be okay. I can't have a baby, Jake! I'm seventeen!" Chloe cried. "But I can't have an abortion! It has a heartbeat! Did you hear that? It's an actual person."

"I know . . . I, yeah, I know." I had no idea what I was saying.

Wait. Did she just say she can't have an abortion?

"But, Chloe, we can't be, like, parents," I said, panicking. "I mean, can we?"

"No! No, no, no. We can't. We definitely can't," she replied, rambling. "We sooooo can*not* be parents."

"Well then, what're we gonna do?" I said, pressing the side of my fist against my mouth. I felt like if I didn't, I was gonna hurl.

Chloe did this groan-whimper thing that made her sound like a dying puppy. She turned sideways and slid off the table, pacing back and forth in the small room. "My parents are going to kill me."

"No, they're not," I said automatically. I wiped my hands on the butt of my jeans. But then I realized I had no idea what her parents would do. Some people were crazy about this kind of thing. They, like, threw their kids out of the house over stuff like this. "I mean, they're not actually going to murder you. Right?"

"Oh. God." Chloe covered her face with both hands and cried. Her shoulders bounced and she started making these scary choking sounds. Okay, clearly someone was going to have to hold it together around here, and it wasn't going to be her. I walked around the table, thinking of the doctor's silent look, and put my arms around Chloe.

"It's okay. We'll figure it out." I pressed my lips together and tried to think. What would make her feel better right now? What could I do or say to make myself feel like less of a prick? "What if we tell my parents first? Like a kind of test run?"

Chloe let out what I thought was a laugh. It was hard to tell with the snorting and blubbering. How the hell did I end up here? Chloe and I had always been casual friends, but until this

summer we'd never even talked much. How was it me here, holding her and talking about babies? It should've been Hammond.
It should've been Will. It should've been anybody but me.

"You can't be serious," she said.

"What?" I leaned back to see her face. Her nose was swollen, her eyes were puffed, and her lips were rimmed with red
blotches.

Chloe's hands dropped. "Your parents are way stricter than
mine. If we tell them, your dad will *definitely* kill you."

I swallowed hard as Chloe grabbed up her denim jacket and
bag. I wanted to tell her she was wrong, but she wasn't. In fact,
I was kind of thinking about hiding my dad's shotgun as soon
as I got home.

"I think we should wait," Chloe said, sniffling. She stared
at a painting of a sailboat on the wall, like she was talking to
it instead of me. "Yeah. I think we should wait to tell our parents until we figure out what we're going to do. It'll go better if
we have, like, a plan." She glanced at me then, and swiped the
back of her hand under her nose. "Okay?"

I nodded. "Okay."

As I trailed her out of the room I bit my tongue to keep from
saying what I was thinking. If we couldn't even get through a doctor's appointment without freaking, crying, and almost ralphing,
then how the hell were we going to figure out what to do?

ally

The metal soccer bleacher seat cut into the back of my legs as I
watched Hammond take the ball upfield toward the goal. I had

to remember not to wear shorts to these games from now on. When I stood up, I was going to look like I'd been sitting on a cheese grater. But then, it would be too cold to wear shorts soon anyway. It was so weird to think that this was our last fall in high school. That this time next year, I'd be cheering for some random dudes on some random college team. Last night over pasta at the Olive Garden, my dad and I had narrowed my choices down from twenty-five to ten, but the schools were still all over the country—everywhere from Stanford to Texas to UConn. Every time I thought about physically being somewhere else, living on my own, I shivered. In a good way.

Freaky.

"Pass it!" Shannen shouted, standing up next to me. "Come on, Hammond! Jake's wide open!"

Hammond did not pass the ball. Instead he took the shot, even though he had two defenders all up in his face, and it sailed way wide of the goal. Everyone in the stands groaned, even Annie, who sat behind me, unwilling as she was to share the same bench with Shannen and Faith. Claimed she was afraid of Crestie Cooties.

Faith looked up from her texting. "What? What happened?"

"We just *didn't* score a goal, thanks to Hammond," Shannen groused, plopping back down on the bench.

Coach Martz called time-out and the team jogged toward the sidelines, sweating and grumbling. They were losing one—nothing and looked lost out there, possibly because one of their captains was hogging the ball away from their other captain. The sun beat down on Jake's face as he jogged over to Hammond to ask what the hell he was doing, I assume. Hammond shoved Jake away from him and when Jake tried to grab his shoulder,

Ham whacked his arm so hard Jake almost fell over. My fingers curled around the edge of the bench, but Jake didn't retaliate.

The guys grabbed water and gathered around their coach while the backslappers, including Chloe, made a loose circle around the huddle. Chloe tried hard not to look at Jake as Jake tried hard not to look at Chloe, and Hammond gazed longingly at Chloe from behind. Yeah. Deciding not to do Backslappers this year? Best idea ever. That triangle was even deadlier than the one in Bermuda.

"Shouldn't you two be down there getting your rah on?" Annie asked the others.

"I decided to abstain from joining anything nonathletic this year," Shannen said, leaning back casually with her elbows on the bleacher seat behind ours. She crossed her long, semibare legs, and a pair of JV players a few yards away ogled her so hard I thought their eyeballs might combust.

"And I'm concentrating on drama," Faith said, twirling her blond hair around a finger as she read another text.

Annie snorted a laugh. "Isn't that what you're always concentrating on?"

Shannen smirked.

"Huh?" Faith said. Annie just rolled her eyes. "Whatever," Faith replied. "You can mock me if you want, but Ally's doing the fall play too this year."

"You are?" Annie and Shannen asked at the same time.

"I didn't think you were into that stuff anymore," Shannen added.

I shrugged. "It's *Midsummer Night's Dream*, which is, like, the only Shakespeare play I ever understood, so I figured I'd give it a shot. Tryouts are on Monday, so—"

"Auditions. We call them auditions," Faith corrected me.

"What about work?" Annie asked.

"I'll still have time to pick up a few shifts a week," I replied. Annie and I both had part-time jobs at the CVS in the downtown strip mall. "Just not as many as usual."

"Great. More shifts with Ancient Alice and Smelly Sal for me," Annie grumbled.

Faith's eyes lit up in a fake way and she turned to look at Annie. "Hey! Maybe you should join stage crew. Since you already have the uniform down," she added, flicking her gaze over Annie's black-on-black outfit with disdain.

"Oh, yeah. Nothing I'd rather do than spend more time with you," Annie shot back.

"No, no, no, no, no." Faith shook her head facetiously. "I will be on stage under the spotlights. The stage crew stays back behind the curtains, in the dark, where they belong."

I was surprised when Annie didn't yank out her laptop and break it over the top of Faith's head. But I'm pretty sure she considered it.

The whistle blew and the guys jogged back out to the field. Annie did take out her laptop, but instead of braining Faith with it, she opened it atop her knees, typing in some observation or another. She hit save and pressed her hands into the bleachers at her sides.

"I gotta say, Chloe looks unreasonably hot for someone in her delicate condition," she said casually.

I choked on my own saliva. Shannen and Faith both ceased to breathe. I could feel them staring at Annie and I slowly, slowly, closed my eyes, waiting for the explosion.

"Her *what?*" Shannen hissed.

"Chloe's not . . . you don't mean she's . . ." Faith watched from the corner of her eye as Chloe went back to the sideline with the other backslappers to cheer on the team. For the first time, I thought her butt looked maybe a teeny bit wide in her denim shorts. "She's pregnant?"

"Omigod. *That's* why she scarfed that entire bacon cheeseburger yesterday!" Shannen exclaimed, her eyes wide as she grabbed Faith's arm. "I thought she was just depressed."

Annie was almost transparently white. "You guys didn't know?"

I dropped my head into my hands. There was a crushed Wendy's cup in the dirt below the bleachers, Wendy's face mashed down the middle so that her eyes had combined to make one big Cyclops eye.

"How do *you* know?" Shannen demanded.

"Ally? A little help here?" Annie said.

Their heads swiveled slowly to look at me. So slowly I could practically hear their neck bones creaking.

"Ally? What the hell is going on?" Shannen demanded.

"Annie knows because I told her," I said quietly, checking around to make sure no one was listening in. "And I know because . . ." God. This was going to hurt. "Jake's the father."

"*What?*" they screeched in unison.

Now everyone in the bleachers was watching us, either intrigued or annoyed, depending on their age range. Plus some of the backslapper girls, the assistant coach, and a pair of grade-school kids playing tag. Chloe, at least, hadn't noticed us yet. She was too busy screaming for Connor, who'd just blocked a great shot.

"Can we just keep it down, please?" I said through my teeth.

"No. No way." Shannen's eyes darted around the field, the trees, the garbage cans, the fences, as if some inanimate object held the answer. "When? How has Chloe's father not killed Jake? How has *Hammond* not killed Jake? How have *you* not killed Jake?"

Out on the field, Hammond slammed into Jake's side as if he was blocking out the other team.

"Well, at least one of us is trying," I said, lifting my chin toward the action.

Hammond stuck out his leg, tripped Jake, then shoved him with both hands into the dirt. The ref blew the whistle, but then looked around, confused. Could he red card a player for fouling a member of his own team? Instead, Coach Martz shouted for Hammond to come out and replaced him with my friend David Drake.

"Yeah! Go, David!" I shouted at the top of my lungs, mostly because the inner tension was about to kill me. I had to let it out somehow. Jake had pushed himself up from the dirt and was dusting off his uniform. He didn't look hurt, but he did look pissed.

"What's she going to do?" Faith was so pale I was actually a little concerned she might faint. "She's not going to have an abortion, is she?"

"I love how you only turn religious when babies come into the picture," Shannen said snidely. "Of course she's gonna have an abortion. She's seventeen!"

"You guys, it's none of our business, so can we just drop it?" I blurted. The last thing I wanted to admit here was that I had no idea what Jake and Chloe planned to do, because he hadn't told me. This huge thing, and my boyfriend hadn't felt the need to clue me in. And I was afraid to ask him about it. I turned to narrow my eyes at Annie. "Thanks a lot, by the way."

She lifted her black-clad shoulders. "Sorry. I figured they knew by now."

I sighed and shook my head, feeling suddenly exhausted. Jake was going to be so mad when he found out Faith and Shannen knew. I wasn't supposed to tell anyone, but first I'd slipped and told Annie and now she'd slipped and told them. And I used to be so good at secret-keeping.

"Is he okay?" Shannen asked, watching Jake closely.

My heart was heavy as I tried to sit up straight. "Not exactly. He's gone into complete zombie mode the past week. He barely eats, I don't think he sleeps, he hasn't been studying, and he's skipped a couple of practices. . . . There are scouts coming next week, people he invited, and if he doesn't pull it together, he's screwed." I swallowed hard and looked over at Shannen and Faith. "I know he messed up. I mean, they both did, but . . . it's like his whole life is hanging by a thread. His entire future. And there's nothing I can do."

"Have you talked to him?" Shannen asked.

"Of course. But I can only give so many pep talks before I start sounding like my mother, and that is not attractive," I said with a pathetic smile.

Shannen hooked her arm around me and pulled me toward her side. Behind me, I felt Annie tense up and I wondered if it bothered her that much that a Crestie was giving me a hug. But then, I didn't care. At this point, I was taking the sympathy and the friendship wherever, however, and from whomever I could get it.

"We have to tell Chloe we know," Faith said quietly. "She has to know we're here for her."

"We'll talk to her after the game," Shannen said, letting me go. "As long as you promise not to get all preacher-girl on her ass."

Faith pouted her lips and crossed her arms over her eyelet tank top. "Fine. I promise."

I sighed and turned my attention back to the game. I supposed I was going to have to tell Jake they knew. That conversation was going to be a real laugh and a half. *Note to self: There's a reason why you never get your Crestie friends and your Norm friends together in the same place. Nothing good ever comes of it.*

jake

"I can't believe you told Annie!" I shouted, standing in the center of Ally's room.

"Shhhh!" She closed her door quietly and faced me. "I'm sorry, but I had to talk to someone. After Connor's I was totally freaking out, and you just disappeared! Besides, technically I told her before you told me not to tell anyone, so I didn't actually break my promise."

I stared at her. We both knew how lame that was. "And now Faith and Shannen know. . . ."

God, Chloe was going to kill me. No, she was going to torture me, then kill me. And then probably torture me some more. I sat down on the edge of Ally's bed, my palms sweating like crazy. First we lose the game because Hammond's too busy putting the beatdown on me to bother trying to score, and now this.

"Well, they were going to find out eventually, right?" Ally said.

"Not necessarily," I said quietly.

There was a long moment of silence. I could hear Ally breathing.

"What do you mean? Is she . . . I mean, are you guys gonna have an abortion?" she asked.

"No. I don't know." I pressed my fingertips into my eye sockets so hard I thought I might pop the suckers out and into my skull. "I have no idea what she's gonna do."

Ally sat down next to me carefully. Like I was a piece of glass and she was afraid to knock me over onto the floor. "You guys haven't talked about it?"

"Oh, we've talked about it," I said, flopping onto my back, making her bounce. "We just haven't decided anything. Every time it comes to deciding anything, we choke."

"Oh." Ally looked down at her hands.

"Yeah, and then one of us changes the subject, like 'So did you do the bio homework?' or 'Let's go get burgers!' and we pretend like nothing's going on."

Ally shifted, turning on her bedspread slightly so she could look down at me. "Well . . . what do *you* want to do?"

"I don't want to have a baby," I said firmly. "But it's not like I can make her have an abortion. And I don't even know . . . I don't even know if I could live with that. Like when you think about it and it's not about you, you think, 'Oh, yeah, just deal with it. Get rid of it or whatever.'" My throat nearly closed over the words "get rid of it." "But when it's reality . . ."

"It's not that easy," Ally finished for me.

I swallowed hard. I couldn't believe we were actually talking about this, but I was also *so* relieved we were talking about this. I'd been dying to spill it to her, but terrified she'd shut me down. I should've known better. I should've trusted her. "No, it's not."

"So . . . adoption?" Ally said.

"Yeah, but then she actually has to *be* pregnant. Like, in front of everyone. That's how she put it, anyway." I covered my face with my hands and groaned. "There's no answer."

"No good one, anyway," Ally said. She sighed. "You just need to be there for her. Whatever she needs. That's what I'd want if I were her."

I couldn't believe she'd just said that. I couldn't believe she didn't just hate us both. We sat there, quietly, for a long time. I didn't know what to do. I didn't know what to say to Chloe, what I actually wanted. I just knew I was so glad, so grateful, to have Ally right then. I slowly reached out and curled my fingers around hers.

"What would you do if it were me?" she asked, her voice practically a whisper. "Do you think you'd feel different about it?"

My breath caught in my throat. *I'd marry you* was the first thought that popped into my mind. And it was true, I realized suddenly. I would marry her. I would take care of her. I would do whatever it took to protect her. But what was I, insane? I was seventeen. I couldn't say that out loud. I sat up. Ally and I locked eyes. I could feel the heat coming through her fingers.

"I feel like ice cream," I said suddenly. "Wanna get some ice cream?"

"Totally," she said.

And we were out of there like the room was on fire.

ally

About halfway through my soliloquy on Monday afternoon, I finally stopped feeling like I had to pee, and started tuning in to what I was saying. Up until about five minutes before I was called in to audition for the play, I was questioning my sanity. I hadn't acted since the spring musical in Baltimore my sophomore year, and there were a lot of good actors at Orchard Hill High, vying for only a few good roles. Why even bother?

But then some random chick I'd never met had told me to break a leg, and Corey Hinds from my Spanish class had flashed me a thumbs-up from the wings, and I remembered why I'd decided to do this in the first place. I needed a distraction. I needed to be able to hang out somewhere where people barely knew me and definitely didn't know Jake. I needed something to do that he had nothing to do with. Faith was the only Crestie in drama club. It didn't get much safer than here.

So here I was.

Besides, if I had to make a speech at my mother's wedding, I might as well get used to performing in front of complete strangers again.

I finished my performance and stood there for a moment, the spotlight frying my face as I squinted out at Mrs. Thompson, the houndstooth-clad drama teacher.

"Very good, Ally," she said. "Thank you. We'll be posting callbacks tomorrow. Can you send Faith Kirkpatrick in next, please?"

"Sure. Thanks!" I said brightly.

I skipped down the stage steps and into the auditorium, experiencing that particular light-headed high I always get after finishing with something I'd dreaded. When I shoved open the heavy auditorium doors, the hopefuls in the lobby looked up expectantly. Faith was walking a tight circle in the center of the space, her mouth moving in silent recital.

"Faith. You're up," I said, hooking a thumb over my shoulder in a dorky way I never would have done if not for the high.

"How'd it go?" she asked.

"Good, I think. Who knows?"

"Oh, I always know," Faith said haughtily, flicking her blond ponytail. "Mrs. Thompson only ever smiles if you suck, because she, like, feels bad for you. So did she smile?"

I narrowed my eyes. It had been hard to see her face with the lights blinding my vision. "I don't think so."

"Yay! That's good, then!" She gave me a brief hug before slipping past me.

"Break a—"

She held up a hand. "I don't need it."

Then she disappeared inside, letting the door slam behind her. I shook my head at her ego and grabbed my messenger bag off the bench next to the wall.

"Hey! Are you done? Did you nail it?"

Annie was near the bottom of the stairs when she called out to me. Chloe was a few paces behind her. The two of them were coming from an *Orchard Gazette* meeting, no doubt. Chloe was editor in chief of the student news site, a fact that Features Editor Annie never ceased to resent.

"It was pretty good, I guess. I'm just psyched it's over," I replied.

"Cool. Wanna go get some food?" Annie asked.

"Sure."

Chloe was just walking by as we headed for the door. She paused and shot me a tentative look. "Hey, Ally."

"Hey," I replied. "How're you . . . I mean . . . how's it going?"

Annie stood next to me, her hands shoved tightly under her arms. I could actually smell the bitterness of her hateful scowl as she stared Chloe down.

"Good. I'm . . . good." Chloe shrugged. "How's Jake?"

Annie cracked her knuckles.

"He's fine," I replied, wondering why she was asking. We all saw one another every day in school. Although they'd been avoiding each other in the halls most of the time, I'd noticed. Almost like they thought if they were caught talking to each other, people would know their secret.

"Good. Okay. Well. See ya." Chloe turned and traipsed outside, slipping on a pair of designer sunglasses. She didn't look tortured or tired or conflicted, the way Jake kept saying she was. The way that most people would have been in her situation. She just looked like Chloe Appleby. Crestie Queen.

"How can you be so nice to her?" Annie demanded, turning on me the second the door was closed.

"Nice to her? I just asked how she was," I replied.

"The girl hooked up with your boyfriend!" Annie hissed.

I rolled my eyes. "He wasn't my boyfriend yet!" I shoved through the door and out into the sunshine, even as my heart tightened into a cold, dry ball.

"Oh please, everyone knew you were in love with him," Annie replied, scurrying to catch up with my long strides. "You know she only did it because she was pissed off you kissed Hammond. You do know that, right?"

I scoffed, even though I'd had this suspicion myself. I'd had a lot of suspicions about Chloe's motives. That's what happens when you spend half your time obsessing about something. *Was* she getting back at me for kissing Hammond freshman year? Was she getting back at Hammond? Was she just bored that night? Horny? Or did she—and this was the worst one—*like* Jake? "Please. That was a million years ago."

"Yeah, and she *just* found out about it in June and then suddenly developed the hots for Jake?" Annie paused at the edge of the parking lot. "Have you ever heard the expression 'There are no coincidences'?"

I frowned. "No."

"Well it's an expression because there *are* no coincidences," Annie told me. "I mean, did you hear her? *'How's Jake?'*" she said in a high-pitched, mocking voice. "It's like she's rubbing it in. Either that or she actually *does* like him, which would be a huge—"

"Stop," I said, practically choking on the word. "I don't want to talk about this anymore." I turned my steps toward my mother's car. It was parked in the faculty lot, waiting for me. Gray had gotten out of work early and picked my mother up for some kind of wedding meeting—flowers or limos or table linens or something. "Are we getting food or what?"

Annie sighed, her shoulders slumping. "Yes. We're getting food."

"Good." I opened the driver's side door and tossed my bag inside. "Try not to look so disappointed that I'm not as suspicious and negative as you are."

"You will be." Annie smirked. "Eventually."

I smiled, but inside I just felt sad. Because I had an awful feeling she was right.

jake

Okay, it was time to get my ass in gear. I hadn't done any homework in about a week. Not that my teachers were surprised. I'd never been a big homework-doer. But over the summer I'd taken this college class and I'd actually worked and I'd landed myself an A. And I'd kind of liked it. So I'd had this whole resolution to do real work this year.

Until I found out I was gonna be a baby daddy.

Now it was Friday afternoon and there was no practice because we had a game tonight, so I was going to spend the next three hours catching up. Pretending life was normal. I straddled one of the lounge chairs on our back patio, my pre-calc book open in front of me, and started to write down the first equation from Tuesday's assignment.

"Jake?"

My pencil point broke. Chloe had just stepped out from behind one of the flowering bushes. She was wearing sweatpants rolled at the ankle and a wrinkled Abercrombie T-shirt. There were tear streaks on her face and she had no makeup on. It was so weird. Every day at school she was just Chloe, all perfect hair, perfect body, perfect clothes. In fact she was so Chloe it was hard to imagine anything was off. But right now she looked nothing like herself.

"What's wrong?"

I stood up and my foot knocked my notebook closed over my broken pencil.

"I just . . . I can't do this anymore." Her flip-flops slapped as she walked over to me and pressed her face into my chest.

Crap. Crapitty crap crap. I put my arms around her and she cried for a minute or two, soaking the front of my white T-shirt. I never thought I'd look longingly at a math book, but I did right then.

"What happened?" I asked. "Can't do what anymore?"

She turned her face to the side so she could talk, but her skinny arms hugged me tight enough to crush my ribs.

"I'm starting to get fat," she whimpered with a sniffle. "My mom even noticed. And now that Faith and Shannen know, someone's gonna slip. I just know it." She pushed away from me and swiped under her eyes with her fingers. Her hands were shaking. For the first time I noticed she did look a little bigger than normal. "Every time the phone rings, my heart stops. I'm just waiting for, like, Mrs. Kirkpatrick to call up my mom and tell her everything. They can't find out like that. They just can't."

"Okay . . ."

"And every five seconds? It's like I know for absolute sure what I want to do, and then five minutes later I want to do the exact opposite." Her voice caught and she turned to hug me again. "I haven't slept in, like, weeks. . . . I'm totally losing it."

My throat was dry and my heart pounded so hard it hurt. "You can, like, talk to me about this stuff, you know. You don't have to avoid me in school all the time. If you're freaking out . . . you should tell me."

Chloe gave me this tight smile. "I don't want to bother you."

"You're not. I mean, we're . . ." I paused and cleared my throat. "We're in this together. We should be figuring it out . . . together."

Her eyes were so hopeful right then I knew I'd said the right thing. For once. "But what about Ally? Won't she mind if we're talking all the time?"

"Ally'll understand," I said automatically.

Chloe nodded and stepped back from me. "So, what do *you* want to do? If you had to decide right now, would you keep the baby or . . ."

My mind went completely blank. Here I'd just offered to be there for her and I had no answer to that question. I didn't want to be a father. I knew that. But ever since hearing that heartbeat, the whole abortion thing gave me the skeevs. So there was adoption, but if we did that, then everyone would know. What would it be like if everyone knew?

"God, Chloe, I have no idea."

She teared up again, but smiled. "Yeah. Me neither."

"Okay. It's okay," I said. "Look, we just . . . have to tell your parents. That way they won't find out from anyone else and they can help us figure out what to do."

"But they—"

"I know it'll suck at first, but your parents, like, worship you," I reminded her. "They'll be okay and they're gonna help you."

Chloe pressed her swollen lips together. Her whole face was wet. "You think?"

"Definitely. And if I'm wrong and they throw you out, you can totally stay here."

Chloe snorted a laugh and pressed her cheek against my chest. "Thanks a lot," she said sarcastically.

I hadn't been joking, but I figured I'd go with it. Her laughing was better than her crying. I smoothed her hair down her back.

"No problem," I said, shrugging. "You can sleep on the floor in your condition, right?"

Chloe laughed for real this time and looked up at me, just as the back door from the kitchen slid open and Ally came bouncing out with a big grin on her face. She took one look at us, Chloe smiling with her arms locked around me, me with my hand on her hair, and the grin completely disappeared.

"Ally! Hi!" Chloe said, pushing me away from her. She wiped her face again, then swiped her hands on her sweatpants. "Jake and I were just—"

"Chloe was upset about—"

"It's okay. I get it," Ally said.

She took a couple of steps toward us, fiddling with a small book. I awkwardly leaned in to kiss her hello. She turned her face so I got her cheek. Great. So maybe she *would* mind if Chloe and I started talking more. I cleared my throat.

"So . . . what's up?"

Ally had this look in her eyes. This look like she was trying really, really hard to like me, and it wasn't happening. She forced a smile onto her face and lifted the book.

"I got a part in the play," she said with some seriously weak enthusiasm. "I'm gonna be Helena . . . one of the two main female roles."

"That's great!" I said, hugging her for real.

"Congratulations, Ally!" Chloe said with a smile.

"Thanks." Ally looked back and forth between the two of us. She twisted her lips sideways, like she always does when she doesn't know what to do. "I can go if you—"

"No. It's cool. I was just gonna leave anyway," Chloe said, angling toward the side yard. "I'll talk to you later?" she said to me.

"Yeah," I said with a nod.

"Cool."

"Cool."

And then she was gone. I looked at Ally. She was watching me carefully, like she'd never met me before and was trying to decide if she trusted me.

"So . . . wanna help me with my precalc?" I joked.

"You're doing homework? Go, you," she said.

"I figured someone's gotta do it," I said, sitting down again. I stared at the closed notebook and suddenly felt very tired. I wished it was five minutes ago, when I'd actually felt like doing work.

"Well, I'll leave you alone, then," Ally said. "I just wanted to tell you about the play, so . . ."

"You don't have to go." But I had to turn around to say it, because she was already at the door. I was kind of dying for her to stay so we could get past the awkward. Plus I had a bad feeling I wasn't going to get anything done anyway. "We could watch a movie."

"No. Do your work. I'll see you at the game tonight," Ally said, halfway inside now.

"Okay," I said. "Hey, Al?"

"Yeah?"

It felt like there was a sharp rock stuck in my throat. "I love you."

She hesitated for a moment. "I know."

And then she was gone too.

october

Omigod. Jake Graydon and Chloe Appleby are totally hooking up behind Ally Ryan's back!

What? Who told you that?

No one. They didn't have to. Have you not noticed the extreme PDA?

You're making this up.

Nuh-uh. He waits for her every single day after first period, he's been jumping in front of her at volleyball during gym, and today I saw him run back up to the line at the cafeteria to get her a Diet Sprite.

Maybe she's helping him with his math or something. And all guys are ball hogs.

Then explain the Sprite to me. What about the Sprite?

Yeah. That is kind of telling.

They're so doing it.

Ugh. How rude.

ally

"Whatcha doin'?" Faith asked, dropping down next to me on the stage floor, where the cast of *A Midsummer Night's Dream* was gathering for our first read-through. She popped open a bottle of water, took a sip, and leaned over my shoulder to see my notebook. "'Love is patient? Love is kind'?" she read, screwing up her face like she was sucking on a lemon.

I flipped my notebook facedown. "I'm working on my maid of honor speech for my mom's wedding."

Faith settled back on her hands, looking around at the rest of the cast, who were slowly trickling in. "Isn't that, like, *months* from now?"

"Yeah, but believe me, I need months to figure out what the heck I'm gonna say." I shoved the notebook into my backpack and sighed. "How am I supposed to make it seem like I'm psyched about her marrying a guy who's not my dad? How could she even ask me?"

Faith shrugged. "Just fake it. *Act* like you're happy for them."

"Easy for you to say," I mumbled.

Faith got a text and pounced on her phone. "Chloe," she said with a groan. "She wants to know if I want to come over for ice cream after." She texted something back and shoved the phone under her thigh. "Ugh. This is, like, the third time this week. Pretty soon people are going to start thinking *I'm* pregnant."

"Faith," I said through my teeth, glancing around to see if anyone in the expanding circle of cast members had heard. Everyone was munching happily on their vending-machine chips and the conversation was growing louder and louder with each new arrival.

"What? I'm totally getting fat from hanging out with her, trying to be Miss Supportive," Faith countered. "And have you seen Chloe lately? I can't believe her mother hasn't figured it out yet. Her ass is drooping and her nose is, like, spreading across her face. Look at this picture I took of her at the mall last night! Look! It doesn't even look like her."

Faith shoved her phone in front of my nose until I had to look at it. Chloe was backlit by the awful lights of the food court and therefore looked, understandably, bloated and white.

"Could you find more unflattering lighting?" I whispered back.

Faith glanced at the screen. "True. But for reals. She has to tell her parents soon. Oversize sweatshirts can only hide so much."

"Faith!" I admonished again.

She gave me an exasperated look. "Ally!" she said in the exact same tone.

I looked at the girl next to me to see if she'd overheard anything. Luckily she had her iPod on, the cords dangling from beneath her thick black hair and pink-and-red knit hat, and she was staring up at the stage lights overhead.

"So have you and Jake, like . . . you know?" Faith asked. "Because, I mean, I would be terrified that he had some kind of, like, supersperm or something and—"

"Omigod!" I said through my teeth. "Can we please talk about anything else?"

She pulled her face back, offended, and turned away. "God. You'd think *you* were the hormonal one."

I closed my eyes and said a quick prayer for patience. I had joined this production so I could get away from this crap, but I should have known. I should have known that as long as Faith was a part of it I wouldn't be getting away from anything.

"Good afternoon, cast!" Mrs. Thompson called out, finally finished with the intense tête-à-tête she'd been having with our stage manager. "And congratulations on winning your roles!"

The girl next to me turned off her iPod as everyone in the circle applauded our mutual achievement. I clapped louder than anyone, because I was actually thanking Mrs. Thompson for distracting Faith.

"Today I'd like to do a line reading of the script so that everyone can familiarize themselves with who's playing which parts, and so we can start to get a rhythm down," Mrs. Thompson continued, removing her tweed jacket and tossing it over the back of a chair. Beneath it she wore a fitted black T-shirt and jeans, and suddenly she looked ten years younger. She sat down story-time style next to Faith and leaned over to take her copy of the script out of her battered leather bag. "But first, I'd like to shift things around a bit," she said, looking around the circle. "Corey? If you could come sit next to Faith . . . and Lincoln? If you could come sit next to Ally," she said, pointing at me.

A guy directly across from me unfolded his long legs and pushed himself to his feet. He had adorably mussed red hair and wore an old suit vest over a faded U.S. Navy T-shirt. He strolled across the circle with his backpack dangling from one hand and a white wax-paper bag clutched in the other. As he sat next to me, forcing the iPod girl to scoot away, he shot me a smile. It was a nice smile.

"Lincoln Carter," he said, his voice a surprisingly low

rumble. "Named after my parents' two favorite presidents."

"Really?"

"No." He opened the wax-paper bag and held it out to me. "Gummi bear?"

"Sure." I took a red one and popped it onto my tongue.

"Just don't call me 'Link,'" he said. "Makes me think of 'the missing link' and that's not something I want to be."

"Good," Mrs. Thompson said as Corey Hinds settled in between her and Faith. "The four of you play our two couples, so I think it makes sense for you to start getting used to being close to one another."

I looked at Lincoln and blushed. "You're playing Demetrius?"

"You're thinking about the kiss, aren't you?" he said with a grin. "Don't worry. I've been told by several people that I'm quite skilled."

I guffawed. "Really?"

His grin widened. "No."

He tossed three more gummi bears into his mouth and his elbow brushed mine. I had no instinct to move away and, in fact, suddenly found I couldn't stop smiling. Innocently flirting with this guy for the next month? Pretending to be in love with him onstage? That would definitely be a distraction.

jake

Ally hadn't looked up from her silverware in about ten minutes. Actually, the silverware at the country club is gold, but I've never heard anyone call it goldware. Whatever it's called, she kept flipping the pieces over, then flipping them back, like if she did it enough times she would open the gateway to the magical world of Narnia and be able to get the hell out of here. Not that I could blame her. For some reason I could think of exactly nothing to talk about. Well, nothing other than Chloe and the baby, which were probably not the best date topics. I wished I could ever think about anything else, but it was next to impossible.

"Are you okay?" I asked finally.

She stopped and forced a smile. "Yeah. I'm fine. This is . . . great."

Her eyes shifted to that spot across the room that I'd been glancing at all night—the table where my father, mother, and brother, Jonah, were sitting with a whole mess of my dad's colleagues, everyone dressed up for the occasion. Her mother and Dr. Nathanson were sitting a few tables away too. I guess Dr. Nathanson was invited because he and my dad worked at the same hospital or whatever, but having both sets of parents here just made it that much worse. When I'd asked Ally out for tonight, I'd completely spaced that my dad was getting some kind of philanthropy award and that I'd promised to come. I'd seen it on the kitchen calendar as soon as I'd gotten back from practice and was so pissed I'd practically put a hole in the wall with my head.

I just wanted to be alone with my girlfriend. Why was that so hard to do?

"I'm sorry," I told her. "I wanted to do something alone together, but with the Chloe crap about to hit the fan I figured it would be a bad idea to piss them off now."

Not that I had any idea when the Chloe crap was actually going to hit the fan. In the last week she had decided to tell our parents, then bailed on her plan five different times—once while I was in the middle of taking the SAT. I'd gotten a text from her when I'd turned on my phone during a pee break and I hadn't been able to concentrate for shit after that. Every time I got myself all psyched up to do it, she kept pulling the rug out from under me. But I, of course, hadn't said anything to her about it because I was a total frickin' wuss. Somewhere in the back of my mind, I think I was hoping that the whole thing would just miraculously go away.

"I get it," Ally said flatly. Her smile had completely died.

Alarm bells went off in my mind. Nice. The one thing I'd promised myself not to mention was the first thing out of my mouth. I was screwing this up royally.

Newsflash: When you're out on a date with your girlfriend, it's not a good idea to bring up the chick you impregnated.

"At least they let us get our own table," I said, feeling like a jackass.

"True." She tried even harder to smile. "And that salad *was* yummier than any salad should be. Plus it's not every day you get to hear a live string quartet, right?"

"Right." I couldn't tell if she was serious or not. As far as I was concerned, if she hadn't been sitting across from me, the music would have been putting me to sleep.

I had to figure out a way to save this night. Ally looked so pretty in this dark blue dress with teeny straps and her hair back in a ponytail, which always killed me. I wanted to reach over the table and kiss her, but she was giving off about as inviting a vibe as a barbed-wire fence.

Ally's mother got up to go talk to someone at another table and gave us a wave as she walked by. Suddenly I got an idea.

Someone had once told me that if you wanted to land a chick, you should make her talk about herself. Girls love to talk about themselves. I'd already kind of landed Ally, but maybe the tactic would get her to relax.

"So what's up with your mom's wedding?" I asked. "Everything cool?"

Ally shrugged. "Yeah. Except I have to make a speech and I have no idea what to say."

"You have to make a speech?" I said, my eyes wide.

"Maid of honor," she replied, raising her hand and faking a smile.

"Wow. That sucks." I took a bite of my food and chewed. "You nervous?"

"I just have no idea what to say," she told me, leaning closer over the table as her mom returned. She didn't stop at our table, though. Just went right back to Dr. Nathanson and laid a big kiss on him, like she'd been gone for weeks. "Ugh. I can't even look when they do that."

"Yeah. The speech could be a problem, then," I joked. "You should just keep it simple. Say something about how much you love her and you're happy to see her happy. You don't have to get, like, deep and mushy about it."

"You think?" Ally asked, sitting up straight.

"Dude, I have, like, a million cousins, so I've been to a million weddings." I leaned back as the busboy cleared our salad plates. "The best speeches are always the shortest ones. You ramble on, you lose the audience, and everyone starts to talk over you. . . . Keep it short and sweet and it's a win-win."

"Wow." Her smile brightened as she reached for her water. "Cool, thanks. That's good to know."

Just like that, I felt warm inside. I'd actually given helpful advice. And I'd actually put a smile on her face.

"Okay, I've got a plan. We sit here through my dad's award presentation, then grab one of those chocolate dessert things off the buffet and go eat by the pool," I suggested, leaning into the table and whispering. "Just you and me for real."

Her smile widened as she checked out the dessert table. "Okay. Deal."

The waiter delivered our pasta course and Ally sat up straighter. She even let him shred a whole mess of cheese on top of her penne, which was a good sign. When she's upset or annoyed, Ally doesn't eat. Which is weird, because I always thought girls binged when they were sad or angry.

"So how's the play going?" I asked her, figuring I should stick to what was working and make her talk about herself. I waved the waiter and his cheese grater away and concentrated on Ally. "You have a good part?"

Ally nodded. "Yep. It's even almost as big as Faith's!" she said with mock enthusiasm.

"Wow! Then it *must* be good," I joked back. I tore off a piece of bread from the loaf in the breadbasket and offered her some, which she took. Okay, this was better. This was normal. "I don't know how you do it, though. I can't understand Shakespeare to save my life. Do you even know what you're saying?"

"Most of the time. It's not one of his most complicated plays," she said with a shrug. "But the guy I'm supposed to be in love with in the play? Lincoln? He totally gets it. He explains it whenever anyone gets stuck."

I paused and my stomach sort of thumped the way your

heart is supposed to. She had a fake boyfriend in this thing?
"Lincoln? Who's Lincoln?"

Ally dipped the bread into the olive oil on her bread dish.
"Lincoln Carter?" she said, narrowing her eyes. "He's a junior.
Kind of tall . . . red hair?"

"You mean that dude who upchucked at the Woodmont car-
nival sophomore year?" I asked.

"Um . . . I don't know. I wasn't there," she replied, popping
the bit of bread into her mouth.

"Yeah. That guy. I know that guy," I said. "He ate, like,
twenty cotton candies on a dare then went on the Gravitron."

"Yeah. That sounds like him," Ally said with a laugh. For
some reason the laugh made my blood stop. It was like a private
laugh. Like an admiring laugh or something. Like maybe she
liked this guy. Suddenly I felt hot and prickly behind my ears.

"That dude's a total loser," I said. "You have to pretend to be
in love with him? Good luck."

Ally put her fork down. "Why's he a total loser? Because he
puked in public?"

"No. It's not just that. I mean, I just don't like him," I said.

She looked confused. "Have you ever actually talked to
him?"

"No. But who cares? I can tell if somebody's a tool without
talking to them." I shoved a huge forkful of pasta in my mouth,
feeling like a tool myself. Why was I getting so worked up? It
wasn't like that scrawny freak was a threat. But then again, why
was she defending him so much?

"Do you have to, like, kiss him?" I asked. My mouth was so
full that some tomato sauce shot out and landed on the white
tablecloth.

"Unbelievable," Ally said, sitting back in her chair. She crossed her arms over her chest. More alarm bells.

I wiped my mouth with my napkin and swallowed. The food felt like a baseball going down my throat. "What?"

"You're jealous," she whispered. "You're jealous and acting like I'm doing something wrong when all I'm doing is playing a part in a play. Meanwhile you got naked with Chloe and now you're walking around school acting like you two are a couple and I'm just supposed to sit back and be fine with it."

My neck got hot at the words "naked" and "Chloe." I tried to focus.

"I don't act like me and Chloe are a couple!" I hissed back.

"Yes, you do!" Ally said, leaning so far forward that her dress almost took on some tomato sauce. "The other day you two were—"

"Well, hello, Jake!"

Mrs. Corcoran, Connor Shale's grandmother, stopped next to our table on her way back from the bathroom, wearing a black sparkly dress that showed too much wrinkled, old-lady cleavage. Her white hair was piled up on top of her head like a pyramid and her teeth looked yellower than ever. I immediately tensed. Mrs. C was known for acting buddy-buddy with me and my friends, and even flirting sometimes. It was totally yack-worthy.

"Hi, Mrs. Corcoran," I said as Ally clamped her jaw shut.

"Well, don't you look handsome tonight?" she said, running her age-spotted hand down the arm of my suit jacket. "Where's Chloe?"

My eyes darted to Ally, who looked like she was about to either burst into tears or scream.

"Um, Chloe?" I said.

Mrs. Corcoran's eyes flicked to Ally dismissively. "Oh, I'm sorry. Did you two break up?"

Would it be wrong to strangle an old person?

"Chloe and I were never going out," I said quickly.

"Oh. Oh, my. How embarrassing." Her hand fluttered to her chest. "I'd heard that the two of you were . . . and then I saw you two the other day at the mall looking adorably cozy." She put her hand on my shoulder this time and squeezed. "I didn't stop to say hello because I didn't want to interrupt anything intimate, but I—"

I was going to kill her. Right here and now. I was going to commit murder.

"We're not intimate or cozy," I said, staring at Ally. "We're just friends."

"My mistake," Mrs. Corcoran said, fiddling with her earring. "Well. Congratulations to your father. I hope you and your friend here have a lovely time."

And then, mercifully, she was gone. But Ally had already pushed her chair back from the table.

"Al, come on. The woman's, like, senile," I said under my breath. "Last year she thought me and Hammond were a closeted couple."

"I need some air," she replied. "I think I'm gonna take that dessert by the pool early."

"Oh. Okay." I started to get up.

"Alone," she added pointedly.

I sat back down so quickly I bruised my ass. Ally walked across the room, dumped a huge slice of cake onto a china plate, and strode out the door. I sat for a second and tried to figure out what the hell had just happened. Clearly Ally was jealous I'd hooked up with Chloe, even though she'd said she wasn't. But what was I supposed to do about it? I couldn't take it back. And I couldn't ignore Chloe at school either. Ally was the one who had told me to be there for her, right? So what the fuck was the problem?

There was only one thing I knew for sure. This had just become the worst date ever.

ally

I was walking through the wings in the auditorium, on my way back from my first costume fitting, when I heard a noise that made me stop in my tracks. On the stage, my cast-mates were running through one of the Bottom-and-the-tinkers scenes, but I could have sworn the noise I'd heard had come from overhead.

"Psssssst!"

I looked up. The stage lights momentarily blinded me, but then I saw someone waving at me from the rafters. As the spots cleared from my vision, I could make out long legs dangling down, a striped vest, and a bright white candy bag.

"Lincoln?" I whispered. "What are you doing up there?"

"This is the best view in the house," he hissed back. "Come see."

I glanced out toward the seats in the auditorium, where Mrs. Thompson was growing increasingly frustrated with one of the tinkers' inability to pronounce the word "Pyramus." He kept saying "Paramus," which is a town near Orchard Hill that almost has more stores than people.

"How?" I asked, looking around for a ladder.

"It's over by the wall," he whispered, chucking his chin in that direction.

I turned around. The ladder in question was skinny, rickety, and seriously tall. Even if I could get to the top without slipping, I'd have to swing myself up onto the crisscrossing metal beams and crawl over to Lincoln without falling to my death.

"Come on. If I can do it, you can do it," he said.

I took a deep breath. My plan for the afternoon had been to go home, sit down at my desk, and crack open the book I'd taken out of the library about wedding etiquette and speeches. This, suddenly, seemed far more appealing. I brushed my sweaty palms off on the butt of my jeans and started to climb. The ladder made some ominous creaking noises but was surprisingly sturdy. When I got to the lowest rafter, the one Lincoln was sitting on like it was nothing but a big old log, I grasped the rails for dear life and crawled, realizing with a quiet laugh that I was more worried about looking inept in front of him than I was about actually falling. Finally, I managed to sit down next to him, letting my feet dangle over the heads of the actors below. From the bird's-eye position, I could see the parts in their hair and the top of one guy's butt crack above the waistband of his baggy jeans.

I wrinkled my nose. "I thought you said this was a good view."

Lincoln sighed and dug some caramel out of his tooth with his fingernail. "I know. I was hoping for real cleavage, not butt cleavage."

I snorted a laugh and he held out the candy bag for me. I took a caramel and tried to unwrap it silently. Didn't work. But no one seemed to notice.

"So what happens if we get caught up here?" I asked.

"Immediate expulsion," he replied.

"Really?" I almost choked on my caramel.

He smirked and tilted his head. "No."

I rolled my eyes, which threw me off. My stomach swooped and I grabbed on to Lincoln to keep from falling.

"Are you okay?" he asked, clinging to me.

"Fine. Fine." Except that my heart was pounding in my eyeballs.

He let out a nervous laugh, then put his arm around me and hooked his thumb through one of the belt loops on my jeans. I froze. That was kind of intimate, no?

"Um, what're you doing?" I asked.

"I don't want to lose you," he said.

Now my heart was pounding for a whole other reason. Lincoln was not unattractive. He was, in fact, pretty damn cute. But that didn't mean it was okay for him to have his arm around me.

"What? Are you afraid Jake Graydon's gonna come in here and pound me?" he asked.

I blinked. "So you do know I have a boyfriend."

"Everyone knows you have a boyfriend," he replied, glancing casually into the candy bag in his other hand. "But I'd like to think he'd thank me for keeping you from going splat."

I grinned. "You think?"

He turned and looked me directly in the eye. "If you were my girl, I'd thank anyone who kept you from going splat."

I couldn't breathe. Guys didn't look you in the eye like that unless they were going to kiss you. But if I moved, I was definitely going to fall. And also, there was this part of me—this teeny, tiny part—that didn't want to move. That tasted the danger of the moment and kind of liked it. Jake had had sex with Chloe. So what if I let this guy kiss me?

This was very not good. Very not me.

But then, suddenly, he looked away. "Anyway, I'm not worried."

"Why not?" I asked, my palms prickly. That was a near miss. Too near.

"Because, Jake Graydon has never graced this auditorium with his presence unless it was for a mandatory assembly," he said. "And I doubt he ever will."

A hundred different replies jammed up my brain space. That Jake *would* be here for our play, to see me. That Jake wasn't as big a Neanderthal as Lincoln made him out to be. That there was every possibility that Jake could walk in here right now to surprise me and take me out for pizza or coffee or something and when he saw Lincoln's arm around me, he *would* pound him.

But then I thought that would actually never happen. Because Jake was probably off with Chloe somewhere, shopping or eating or planning or just being. And just thinking about that made me feel like the decades of crud wedged between the floorboards on the stage below.

So I didn't move Lincoln's arm. And an hour later, we'd finished the entire bag of caramels. Together.

jake

When I turned onto Vista View Lane on Monday afternoon, I was singing as loud as I could. It was warm for October and I had the top down on the Jeep, but I wasn't in the best mood. Ally and I had made up on Sunday after the Saturday night date from hell, but I'd felt weird around her today. It was like I was so afraid to do the wrong thing or say the wrong thing that we'd barely talked. Then I'd had a pop quiz in Spanish, practice had sucked, and tonight Chloe and I were finally getting our parents together to tell them. So I wasn't singing out of joy or anything. I was singing out of terror.

Out of the corner of my eye I saw someone sitting on the curb and I slammed on the brakes. It was Chloe. She was doubled over with her head between her knees and it looked like she was heaving. I put the Jeep in park in the middle of the road—our houses were the only two on the street anyway, so who gave a shit—and ran over to her.

"Chloe! Are you okay?" I crouched down next to her.

She shook her head, keeping it down, the tip of her ponytail dragging through a pile of broken acorns near the curb.

"What happened? Is it the baby?" I asked. I went to put my hand on her back, but wasn't sure I should touch her.

"Do you . . . have any . . . water?" she said between gasps.

"Um, yeah! Hang on!" I ran back to the Jeep and grabbed the half-empty Vitamin Water I'd opened after practice. "Here," I said, sliding it between her legs under her hair.

She picked it up shakily and lifted her head very slowly. With her eyes closed she took a small sip. Then she took some more. She leaned into my side and soon she started to breathe normally again.

"What happened?" I repeated.

"I don't know," she replied. She breathed in and out slowly, like she was testing it out for the first time. "I went for a jog and I was totally fine, but then when I started up the hill I got dizzy."

"You went for a jog? Are you supposed to do that with the, I mean in your—"

Chloe let out a small laugh. "Charlotte did it in *Sex and the City*. Her doctor told her it was totally fine because she'd always been a runner, so I figured . . ."

Sex and the City? Seriously? That was where she was getting her medical advice?

"Did you ask *your* doctor?" I asked her, kneading my fingers together between my knees.

Chloe sat up straight. Her eyes flashed angrily. "I'm not gonna call her just because I want to go for a run. I felt fine. What's the big deal?"

"Okay, okay!" I said, raising my hands. "I was just asking." I licked my lips and looked down at her belly, which was starting to push out a little bit. "Maybe you're just nervous about tonight or something and it stressed you out."

"Maybe," she said, slumping. "I mean, I'm definitely scared out of my mind, so it's possible."

She drained the rest of the Vitamin Water and handed me back the empty bottle. "Thanks."

"No problem."

"So you and your parents are coming over at eight, right?" she asked hopefully.

I nodded, my heart pounding all over again. "We'll be there."

Chloe blew out a sigh. "I can't believe we're finally going to do this."

"Me neither," I said.

I turned my head to look into her eyes and she looked right back at me, completely determined. I hoped I looked the same way, but I had a feeling I looked how I felt.

Like I would do anything to be anywhere but here.

ally

"What do you think? Will people be comfortable buying coffee from a face like this?"

My dad turned to look at me. Faith had painted his face with all shades of gray, radiating black veins out from around his eyes and coloring his lips black as well. He was the perfect zombie.

"What? Is something different?" I joked.

He got up from his stool and made like he was going to give me a big smooch, and I shrieked and ducked away. A few of the Harvest Festival patrons saw us and laughed, probably thinking we were a carefree father and daughter, just having a good time at the school's annual autumn fund-raiser. Little did they know I was basically dying inside. Heck, my dad didn't even know that.

But tonight was the night. Chloe and Jake were finally going to tell their parents. Tomorrow, I could be planning my boyfriend's funeral. And I couldn't stop thinking about it, no matter how many pumpkins I painted onto little kids' cheeks, no matter how beautiful and sunny a fall day it was.

"Thanks, Faith," my father said, finally giving up on painting me with his face. He handed her a five-dollar bill and told her to keep the change. "I'll see you for dinner tonight, Ally?"

"I'll be there," I replied, retaking my seat at the face-painting booth.

My dad waved and disappeared into the crowd.

"Your dad is *so* sweet," Faith said, watching him go. She was standing next to my chair, wearing skinny jeans and a white turtleneck. As soon as we'd opened for business, she had painted a bunny face on herself, complete with a pink nose and whiskers. "I feel bad that I hated him for so long."

"Yeah. Thanks for that," I said, fiddling with the set of wax crayons in front of me.

It was nice that my dad had shown up to support the Drama Club's Harvest Fest booth, something my mother, who worked at the school that was two hundred yards away, hadn't bothered to do. She was, of course, out with Gray somewhere doing wedding stuff. Sometimes I felt as if Jake had replaced me with Chloe and my mom had replaced me with Gray. It was a good thing my dad didn't have a girlfriend or I might have started to feel like a seventh wheel.

"Does he know? About Jake and Chloe?" Faith asked.

My heart squeezed tightly in my chest. I felt like I'd been lying to both my parents for weeks. But was it really lying if you just weren't telling them something?

"Nope." I sighed.

"Okay, *what* is your deal?" Faith demanded, slamming the lockbox closed. "You just sighed three times in a row."

"Just wondering how, exactly, Mr. Appleby is going to execute my boyfriend," I said lightly, resting my chin on my hand. I had a ghost painted on one cheek, and made sure to keep my fingertips away from it so it wouldn't smudge. "Is he more of a gun person or a knife person?"

Faith clucked her tongue and reached back to check her braided bun, adjusting a bobby pin near the base. "And they call me a drama queen."

"Aren't you even a teeny bit worried?" I asked, raising my voice to be heard over some girl who was shrieking about her win at the dart booth. "I mean, that man is scary."

"Okay, yes." Faith sat down next to me and straightened our tools on the table. "I can't even imagine how they're dealing. But no one's actually going to strangle Jake, right? I mean, Mr. Appleby isn't certifiable. Just . . . intimidating. And besides, he forgave your father, right?"

Somehow her logic was not improving my mood. Part of the reason Mr. Appleby had been the first Crestie to forgive my dad for losing scads of money was because he was the only one smart enough not to invest with my dad, or so I assumed. My guess was Jake wasn't about to get the same kind of leniency. I was about to sigh again, but I caught myself just in time. Kids from school crowded the football field, gathering around the kettle corn booth and clamoring for the next shot at the strongman test. There were some younger moms there with their kids in strollers, most of whom had already dropped a buck for balloons, so colorful orbs bobbed around everywhere. It was festive in that quaint, autumnal Orchard Hill way.

I stared out at the happy faces surrounding me and couldn't help feeling the tiniest bit jealous. This was my senior year. My last Harvest Festival. Potentially my last fall in Orchard Hill. Shouldn't I be having fun instead of obsessing about my boyfriend and the girl he'd gotten preggers?

"This sucks," I muttered, picking at a piece of lint on my cords.

"Well, we're not making any money being depressing and pouty," Faith said. Then she stood up, plastered on a grin, and started shouting. "Face painting! Two dollars! Two dollars to be transformed into a totally original walking piece of art!"

Faith was just roping in a second grader and her mom when

Annie came bounding over to us wearing her black-and-white-striped tights, a black tulle skirt, a black long-sleeved T-shirt, and a witch's hat.

"Wow, you're in the spirit," I said flatly.

Annie's brow knit. "And you are *so* not. What gives, Little Miss Frown?"

"Tonight's the big reveal," Faith said, looking up from the spiderweb she was drawing on her little customer's face. "Jake and Chloe . . . you know."

She rolled her eyes up at the kid's mom, having enough sense, at least, not to mention what the big reveal was about.

"Ugh. I'm so sick of those two making you look suicidal," Annie said, earning an appalled look from the mom. She pursed her lips and studied me for a moment. "You know what you need? You need a random hook-up. A revenge hook-up. Square things up between you and Jake."

The little kid's mother gasped and tugged him off the chair before Faith could finish her masterpiece. They disappeared into the crowd, the mom shooting dirty looks back over her shoulder. Annie didn't even seem to notice.

"Great! You just lost us two dollars," Faith groused, throwing her hands up.

Annie ignored her and started to turn in a slow circle, tapping her index finger against her chin. "Now, let's see . . . who would be a good random hook-up for Ally Ryan . . . ?"

"Annie, stop. I don't want a random hook-up," I said, glancing nervously at Faith, who had one of the biggest mouths in Northern New Jersey. Neither of them knew I had already, briefly, psychotically considered a random hook-up with Lincoln. And neither of them would *ever* know that.

"Yes, you do. You just don't know it yet," Annie said. She tilted her head as a pack of jersey-sporting football players strolled by. "Hmmm . . . Will Halloran's kind of hot."

I gave Will the once-over and mentally agreed. Will had one of those compact, muscular, running-back bodies that made girls swoon whenever he happened to take his shirt off. Couple that with the warm brown eyes, the killer smile, and the genuine nice-guy attitude, and he'd be a good hook-up for anyone. Just not me.

"Not my type," I said, hoping she would drop it.

As the football team headed toward the popcorn booth, Lincoln himself sidled up behind Annie. He had an eye patch over one eye and a red bandana tied around his head. Wisps of his red hair stuck out over his eyes and around his ears.

"S'up?" he said, holding out his ever-present wax-paper bag. "Nonpareil?"

Annie turned and slowly ran her eyes over him. I blushed. Hard. Suddenly I recalled the feeling of his arm around me, his thumb hooked into my waistband, and I could hardly look him in the eye.

"How much sugar would you say you consume in one day?" I asked him, trying to be normal and pretend like I didn't know my BFF was sizing him up for potential sexual relations.

"It's less if you take one." He smirked and shook the bag in front of me. I rolled my eyes as I plucked a chocolate. Annie stepped behind him, checked out his butt, and gave me a thumbs-up over his shoulder.

"Stop it!" I said through clenched teeth.

"Stop what?" Lincoln looked confused.

"Nothing. Forget it."

I grabbed a handful of candy and stuffed it in my mouth. Annie stepped out from behind Lincoln.

"I'm gonna go check on the ice-cream stand," she said, narrowing her eyes. "Huge mistake assigning it to the jazz band. They're eating the profits and then some."

As she walked off, taking slow, sideways steps, she lifted a hand next to her cheek to block her lips from his sight, and mouthed to me, "He's cute! Do *him!*"

I almost choked. Luckily, Annie had had enough with the torture. She whirled away, tulle spinning, disappearing quickly into the crowd.

"So. Mrs. Thompson tells me I'm supposed to paint faces. Which is good because I rock at art," Lincoln said, using his tongue to dislodge some chocolate wedged between his teeth and his cheek.

"Really?" Faith said.

"No." He looked me up and down. "You don't look busy. Wanna give me a goatee and a scar? Make me look authentic?"

I swallowed the massive mound of melting chocolate and licked my lips. I felt hot from head to toe, and was glad to have something to distract me from thoughts of Lincoln's butt. Was Annie right about its thumbs-up-worthiness?

"Sure," I replied, gesturing to the chair at the end of the table. "Have a seat."

Lincoln complied, dropping the wax-paper bag on the table and dusting some white sprinkles from his fingers. I picked up a black crayon and hesitated, looking him in the eye.

Okay. No more butt-thoughts, but now I was looking right into his eyes. His intensely green, smiling eyes. And suddenly I realized there was no way to do this without touching his face. I'd been doing it all day. Holding the person's chin, tilting the cheek, tilting it back again. Was I going to touch Lincoln Carter's face right now? My pulse began to thrum in my ears. I could feel that I was blushing and I felt the sudden need to track down Annie and kick her in the shin.

"Just be gentle," he said seriously.

I laughed nervously and rolled my eyes. "I promise."

As I leaned in to start his goatee, Faith eyed me curiously. I hoped she wasn't putting two and two together—that she wasn't thinking I was considering Annie's suggestion. Because I wasn't. Not anymore. Lincoln just had a flirtatious personality. That was it.

Besides. I hadn't thought about Jake and Chloe in two whole minutes. That had to be some kind of record.

jake

I was sitting at the huge table in the Applebys' dining room, staring at this champagne pear salad thing that Mrs. Appleby could not shut up about, when Chloe's fork suddenly clattered against her china plate.

"Mom, Dad, there's something I have to tell you."

My legs stopped bouncing under the table. "What, *now?*"

We had decided to wait until after dinner. The plan had been hashed and rehashed fourteen thousand times. She couldn't just ditch the plan. Chloe gave me an apologetic look and shrugged. I glanced at her father, who was slowly finishing his last bite, and my life flashed before my eyes, right down to my goldfish, Beckham, who'd died in the third grade. But I guess I saw her point. Sitting here knowing what was coming was torture. Might as well get it over with. I pushed my chair back a little bit, in case I had to run.

"What is it, sweetie?" Chloe's mother asked.

She looked pale under her helmet of blond hair, and her hand fluttered up to fiddle with her pearls. For a split second I wondered if she already knew somehow. Woman's intuition or whatever.

"What's going on?" my mother asked, smiling at me. Like she was expecting good news. What that could be, I had no idea. Maybe she thought Chloe and I were going to tell them we were a couple, which was what my mom had wanted all summer. Suddenly I felt sorry for her.

Chloe laid her cloth napkin down flat on the table and pushed back too. I wondered if she was thinking the same thing I was— that we should have planned a strategic escape route. She'd told me she was going to be blunt, but what did that mean, exactly? I held my breath and prayed like I'd never prayed before.

"I'm pregnant," she said flatly. "Jake and I are . . ." She paused and shot me this pained look. Almost like she was apologizing. "We're going to have a baby."

Yep. That was blunt.

"*What?*"

That would be the four of them. At the same time. At roughly the same glass-cracking pitch. For a second there was silence, except for my heart beating in my ears, my eyes, my stomach, my toes. I glanced over my shoulder at the door.

"Young lady," Mr. Appleby said in a warning tone, gripping the edge of the table with both hands.

But he stopped there. His words just hung in the air over the table while the candles flickered. A pear slice slowly slipped from the top of my mound of spinach to the edge of the plate. It knocked a walnut onto the white tablecloth, and a brown stain of dressing spread all around. It looked like blood seeping from a gunshot wound.

"No," my mother said, standing suddenly. "No no no no no no no. You two aren't even . . . I mean, you haven't even . . . You're dating Ally!" she shouted at me accusingly.

"This happened before . . . that," I said.

"Are you absolutely sure it's yours, son?" my father said, his voice low.

Chloe was taking a sip of water—probably to fight off a panic attack—and choked on it.

"Excuse me?" Mrs. Appleby asked, lowering her hand from in front of her mouth for the first time in minutes.

"Just so we're clear, Graydon, are you calling my daughter a liar or a whore?" Mr. Appleby demanded, his face darkening quickly to a rank purple color.

"Daddy!" Chloe wailed. Her water goblet clanged against the side of her plate.

My father stood up from the table, his knees knocking against the edge, rattling every piece of crystal and silver. "I'm sorry, Charles, but this isn't the kind of thing a kid can leave to chance," he said, flattening the front of his wool dinner jacket. "I'm sure you'll understand if my wife and I request a DNA test."

Across the table Chloe started to shake. I got up to go over to her, but her father stood up too, and I knew there'd be no going around that end of the table.

"Get the hell out of my house," he thundered, his jowls trembling as he faced my father. "Get the hell out of my house *now!*"

Mrs. Appleby started to cry into her napkin.

"Clarice," my mother said imploringly.

For whatever reason, the sound of her own name made Mrs. Appleby wail even louder. She got up and fled the room. As soon as she was gone Chloe started crying too.

"Are you people going to go or am I going to have to make you go?" Mr. Appleby said. He took a menacing step toward us and I swear I almost peed my pants.

"No need. We're gone," my father replied, raising his hands. He turned around and strode out of the room.

I looked at Chloe. She looked so fragile and scared and sad. This had not gone anywhere close to what I'd hoped.

"Mom," I said. "Shouldn't we stay and, like, talk about this?" As much as I wanted to escape, I didn't want to leave Chloe behind. But I couldn't exactly take her with us either.

"There's no need for that, Jake," Mr. Appleby said. "I can take care of my own daughter just fine. In fact, as of this moment, you are no longer welcome in this house. Chloe, you are forbidden to see this boy, do you understand me?"

That got Chloe out of her chair too. She ran out the same way her mother had gone, her hair streaming behind her. I heard her footsteps pounding up the stairs, and a moment later, a door slammed.

So I guess our parents weren't going to help us figure out what to do.

"Let's get out of here," my mother said, her voice cracking. I didn't move. I couldn't. My shoes felt like they were encased in medicine balls. "Jake? Let's go."

She grabbed my arm and pulled, tripping me sideways toward the exit that led to the foyer and the front door. Toward freedom. Kind of, anyway. The worst part, I guessed, was over. Chloe's dad knew, and I was still alive.

I looked back over my shoulder one last time to see Mr. Appleby glaring down at the table, tugging his napkin between his two hands over and over again. I had no idea what kind of lecture waited for me at home, but I had a feeling that whatever was going to be said inside the Applebys' house was going to be a hell of a lot worse.

Did you guys see Chloe in gym this morning?

Uh, yeah. What is with the man sweats?

And did you notice her, um, gut?

Looked more like a bump to me, if you know what I'm sayin'.

No. What are you saying?

A bump. You know. Like a baby bump?

No!

YES!

Shut up! Are you serious?

Who do you think the father is?

Hammond Ross. It's gotta be.

I dunno. I've noticed Will Halloran watching her from afar with his mope on.

Please. Like Queen C would ever allow a Norm to enter her crystal palace.

What about Jake Graydon?

What? No.

You said it yourself. They have been spending a lot of time together.

OMG, poor Ally!

You mean poor Chloe.

Right. Her too.

ally

"It's official," Chloe said. "I'm going to have a baby."

Never had those words been uttered in such an unenthusiastic tone. Chloe sat down at the end of our lunch table, bringing with her a cloud of her rose-scented perfume, and placed a stack of lavender envelopes down in front of her. I closed my laptop, which was open to my mom's latest ten bridesmaids dress options, and looked at Jake. Shannen and Faith went silent. At the far end of the table, the Idiot Twins, Connor, and Josh were too distracted by their game of "can you squeeze juice out of an apple by wedging it in the crook of your arm and flexing superhard?" to overhear.

"Um, I thought we already knew that," Jake said.

Chloe hooked her bag strap around the back of the chair. "Yeah, but now it's definitely happening. My parents are one hundred percent against abortion, which I was dreading anyway, so . . . it looks like I'm about to get seriously fat."

She put her hand on her stomach under the table. She was wearing a cable knit tunic and leggings, which had become kind of her signature look lately, and she, of course, rocked it so well that some of the underclassmen were now mimicking it.

I stared at Jake, frozen. His right eye twitched, and from what I could tell he wasn't breathing. Did this mean . . . ? Was she saying she was going to keep the baby? I had this awful feeling I was about to see my boyfriend faint or explode.

"Wow. So . . . wow," Jake said, lowering his fork. He'd already wolfed down half of his cafeteria mac and cheese and looked to be regretting it.

"Don't worry. I'm giving it up for adoption," Chloe said. "My mom's interviewing agencies today, actually."

I blew out a breath and Jake did too. I saw Shannen and Faith exchange a relieved look. Talk about burying the lead.

"Oh, thank God." Jake exhaled, collapsing forward so fast his head almost hit the table.

"Wow. Tell me how you really feel," Chloe said with a touch of sarcasm.

"Oh." Jake blinked, sitting up straight. "Sorry. Are you . . . I mean, you're not upset, are you?" I saw him swallow when she didn't say anything, his Adam's apple bobbing over the collar of his rugby shirt. "Are you?"

"Yeah, I mean . . . this is a good thing, right?" I said, trying to help him out. "Some couple will get a baby they really want and it'll have a good home."

"Yeah, I guess. It's just so weird," Chloe said. Her eyes unfocused as she stared at a random point on the table. "The first baby I ever have . . . and it's not going to be mine."

Her hand was on her stomach again and I felt as if my own organs were turning to rock. I couldn't imagine what it must be like to be inside her brain, inside her body. Not even the tiniest bit. I looked over at Shannen, and Shannen looked from me to Faith. Clearly none of us had any clue what we were supposed to say.

This was one of those rare moments when I completely forgot she'd gone after the guy I liked and I just felt bad for her.

"But at least I get to stay in school," Chloe added. "My parents wanted me to drop out and get a tutor and try to keep the whole thing a secret, but I said no. I'm not ashamed," she said, her eyes shining. "And I'm not gonna miss my senior year."

I swallowed hard. I always knew Chloe was brave, but this was a level of strength I hadn't seen before.

"So. What're those?" Faith asked. She pointed at the envelopes, effectively changing the subject.

"Oh, invites to my birthday," Chloe said, slipping a few from the top of the pile. "I don't feel like having one, but Mom and Dad are all about keeping up appearances, so it looks like I've got a party to plan."

She placed an envelope down on the table near the top of my tray and I picked it up with both hands. She'd written our names out in swirly cursive with a pink glitter pen and stuck a rhinestone star in the corner. It seemed so wrong. So incongruently optimistic.

"Oooh! Pretty!" Faith cooed, tearing into her envelope and pulling out a sparkling pink card.

"Your dad's renting out the Hayden Planetarium?" Shannen asked, looking up from her own invite.

"Yep. The theme is 'Catch a Rising Star!'" Chloe said, spreading her fingers wide with a bright, fake smile. "Like I said, appearances."

"Do you need any help?" Jake asked, tucking his invite away without opening it. "I mean, I know how you guys plan parties. It's like a full-time job. And your doctor said you should be resting as much as possible. . . ."

I looked down at my congealing macaroni and cheese and my eyes blurred. Why? Why did I suddenly feel so sad? I should say something. Offer my help too. But I felt like Chloe's invitation had wedged itself inside my throat, preventing speech. From the corner of my eye, I saw Hammond approaching our table—something he hadn't done once this semester. His timing couldn't have been more awful.

"Thanks for the offer, but I had to beg on hands and knees just to be allowed to invite you," Chloe said.

"Aren't you grounded, anyway?" I said quietly. Jake hadn't been able to so much as go out for a run since they'd told his parents about the baby, so I wasn't sure how he was supposed to help out with the party of the century.

"Right," he said reluctantly. "Forgot about that."

"It's okay," Chloe assured him. "Honestly, I think the less my parents see of you right now, the better."

"Aw! Couple of the Year having trouble?" Hammond teased, pausing just off Jake's right shoulder. His blond hair had been cropped into a spiky 'do and he wore his varsity jacket over a white turtleneck sweater, which made him look twice his size—more shoulder, more chest, and more neck. Why did I get the feeling this was intentional?

Chloe rolled her eyes. "Hammond, please don't start."

"Sorry." And he actually did look sorry. For a second. "Do you need help with something?" he asked Chloe.

"No. I'm good. Jake was just offering to help plan my birthday party," Chloe replied. She tugged out Hammond's invitation and handed it to him. "But my parents . . ."

Jake shifted in his seat. He curled his fingers around the corners of his tray.

"Oh, well, if you need someone, I'm around," Hammond offered. "And last I checked, your parents still liked me."

He laughed in this obnoxious way and slapped Jake on the back. Jake shrugged him off violently, which just made Hammond smile wider.

"Yeah?" Chloe said, brightening slightly. "You'd do that?"

"Maybe not, like, picking out the flowers or whatever, but

if you've got any heavy lifting or driving or need me to pick something up . . ."

"Since when are you Mr. Helpful?" Shannen said suspiciously.

"Just trying to pick up the slack for my friend here," Hammond said, kneading Jake's shoulders now.

Actually, it was pretty clear he was just trying to get under Jake's skin. And even clearer, by the severe clench of my boyfriend's jaw, that it was working.

"Hammond, that'd be great," Chloe said. "Thanks."

"Sure. Of course. Just text me," Hammond said. "Whatever you need."

Jake's glare could have stopped a runaway train. Was he jealous or something? Mad that Chloe was choosing Hammond's help over his? Wasn't it enough that he went to every doctor's appointment with her now and carried her bag and made sure she always had a water bottle on her? What the hell?

Hammond turned sideways to slide behind Jake's chair, jostling it purposely with his knees so that Jake was shoved forward, and joined the guys at the other end of the table. Again, for the first time this semester.

"That was weird with a capital *W*," Faith said. "Has he even spoken to you since the big reveal?" she asked Chloe.

"Not at all," Chloe replied. "Maybe he's finally realizing what a jerk he's been."

"Like that's possible," Shannen muttered, pushing her fork around in her noodles.

Chloe lifted a shoulder as she stood. "Miracles do happen." It was amazing how she could still be all bright-side-focused with everything that was going on. "I'm gonna go get some food. Anyone want anything?"

"I'll get it." Jake jumped up like he'd been launched from a slingshot. "What do you need?"

Chloe laughed and touched his arm. I couldn't help staring at her dainty, manicured fingers on the sleeve of his blue sweater. "It's okay. I can handle a tray."

"I'll come with you," Jake said, turning up the aisle. "In case you need me to carry anything."

Chloe rolled her eyes but realized it was pointless to argue. "Okay, fine. We'll be right back," she said over her shoulder. It made me cringe, the way she said "we."

I watched as she walked away with my boyfriend, their heads bent toward each other in conversation. I watched as dozens of other people marked their progress toward the food line too. Some of them even looked back at me curiously, wondering what was going on. I caught Annie's eye across the aisle and she raised one eyebrow at me like, *Told you so.* I clenched my hands together under the table, telling myself not to care. Annie was wrong. Chloe didn't like Jake that way. They were just in this together. There was no getting around it.

Then Lincoln strolled past Annie, munching from a candy bag as always, and she very slowly licked her top lip. Suddenly I was both blushing and nauseous. When he saw me, he winked, and I was just grateful his back was to Annie when he did it.

"Don't let them get to you," Shannen said, knocking my arm with her elbow. Clearly she'd noticed the looks Chloe and Jake were grabbing. "People are morons."

"Yeah. I know," I replied, averting my eyes from Annie, who was now making kissy-faces. I watched as Jake's hip bumped

Chloe at the food line and neither one of them flinched away.

Shannen was right, of course. It didn't matter to me what anyone else thought. What mattered was what I thought. And I thought Jake Graydon and Chloe Appleby looked like a perfect couple.

ally

"You're nervous, aren't you?"

Lincoln stood so close to me I could smell the gummi bears on his breath.

"Me? No."

I took a deep, calming breath, but it caught on an itch in the back of my throat. My hand slapped over my mouth as I attempted to hold back the cough, my eyes burning with tears as the spotlights bore down on me.

"Well, I'm nervous," he said.

I held up a finger and turned around to cough my brains out. Nice. Very attractive. When I was done, I turned to him hopefully. "Really?"

He smirked. "No."

Yeah. Should have seen that one coming. I flicked a tear from the corner of my eye and sighed.

"Okay, people! Let's block this scene!" Mrs. Thompson clasped her hands together as she walked to the center of the auditorium. "I want Hermia and Lysander stage right. Demetrius and Helena right next to them. And the Duke should be center stage. Bottom, you stay where you are."

We glanced over at Kevin Parsely, who was playing the part of

Bottom. He'd been curled up on the stage floor for almost an hour.

"Are we gonna get some pillows, ever?" he whined, tucking his arm under his ear.

"I know. I know. I apologize," Mrs. Thompson said. "You'll have pillows to fall asleep on at the next rehearsal."

The cast cheered. I'd never realized how often the characters in *A Midsummer Night's Dream* passed out until I started rehearsing the play on the dusty hardwood floor. I guess that was why the word "dream" featured in the title.

"Okay, we're going to do Demetrius's big speech now," Mrs. Thompson said, gesturing up at Lincoln. "And from what I understand, Mr. Carter here has gone professional on us and memorized it."

"I have," Lincoln said, preening slightly.

"That's the spirit," Mrs. Thompson said, shaking one fist. "Now, as the speech draws to a close, you're going to share your first kiss with Helena."

A bunch of people in the wings hooted. I felt like I was going to melt from the humiliated heat my body was generating. Lincoln was clearly amused by my flesh-eating blush, so I glanced over my shoulder at Faith, who just grinned back merrily. I loved how everyone enjoyed seeing me uncomfortable. Too bad Annie was missing this. She wanted me to hook up with Lincoln? Well, I was about to finally grant her wish. With an audience.

"You truly believe you're in love with her, but more than that you want to sell it to the Duke," Mrs. Thompson said. "So sell it! And . . . begin."

Lincoln reached for one of my hands and began his speech to the Duke, who was played by Tyler Dross, a junior from the wrestling team who was about double the size of anyone else on the stage. I tried to watch Lincoln with loving eyes as he explained his shift of admiration from Hermia/Faith to my character/me, but I could think about only one thing.

Lincoln and I were about to kiss. Lincoln and I were about to *kiss*. The lights were burning a hole in the back of my neck and I felt sweat prickle my underarms. My hand was growing clammy in Lincoln's and I hoped he didn't notice. What if I had bad breath? What if our tongues touched? What if we bumped noses or I stepped on his foot or, God no, slipped and bit him in front of everyone? Before I knew it, Lincoln was coming to the end of his speech.

"'But, like in sickness, did I loathe this food,'" he said. Then he turned to me, and his eyes were so full of love, my heart actually skipped a beat. "'But, as in health, come to my natural taste.'"

He lifted his free hand and cupped my face. His fingers were soft and long and warm. I knew I should do something. Tilt my cheek into his touch, or at the very least smile, but I was frozen.

"Now I do wish it, love it, *long* for it," Lincoln said. He turned fully toward me, toe to toe, and released my hand, holding my face between both his hands now. "And will forever more," he said with a dramatic pause, "be true to it."

No one breathed. No one moved. No one spoke. Slowly, Lincoln lowered his face toward mine. Just before his eyes fluttered closed, he gave me the teeniest, tiniest smirk. And then, he parted his lips ever so slightly, and kissed me. I wasn't sure whether it lasted five seconds or ten or a hundred, but I do know he tasted like sugar, and his lips were perfectly moist, and by the time it was over I couldn't see straight.

"That was great, Lincoln!" Mrs. Thompson cheered. "Just great! Now let's do it again, and this time, Ally, try to *not* look as stiff as a corpse."

Everyone laughed. I felt like dying. "Sorry," I muttered.

"She was nervous," Lincoln explained, taking a step away from me. "Maybe I should slip her the tongue this time."

The laughter grew and there was more hooting and hollering. I hit Lincoln's arm with an open hand, but the embarrassed smile was stuck on my face.

"No slipping of the tongue will be necessary, Mr. Carter," Mrs. Thompson said in a warning tone. She looked up at me and curled her script into a tube. "Now, come on, Ally. You've been after this guy the entire four acts. This is the greatest moment of your life. You've finally snagged the guy you love! Show me that!"

Faith took a step toward me from behind. "Just think of Jake," she whispered.

A chill went down my back. The last thing I wanted to think about was Jake. Thinking about Jake would make me *seriously* tense. Like what if he walked in right now and saw me and Lincoln kissing? How would he react? Would he be pissed?

And then I thought, probably not. He'd be too busy wondering where Chloe was and whether she needed a foot rub or something.

Huh. Maybe I *should* let Lincoln kiss me with tongue.

"Okay, let's run the speech again!" Mrs. Thompson directed.

This time, I turned to look at Lincoln with stars in my eyes, and this time—with Jake and Chloe in the back of my mind—I kissed him back.

jake

"All righty, then! Just a few small adjustments and you'll get to see your baby!"

I looked at Chloe. She quickly looked away. Sometimes it seemed like all she did anymore was go to doctors. At least my dad had dropped the whole paternity-test idea once he'd heard the baby was being given up for adoption. That meant one less needle Chloe had to deal with.

The woman running the sonogram machine was so big I didn't know how she balanced on that little stool, but her personality was even bigger. She hadn't stopped grinning or humming since we'd been brought into this tiny room. Not while squirting that gross gel crap onto Chloe's stomach. Not while checking her chart. Not even when I stepped on her foot getting around the end of the table. She just kept smiling at me, but I was so tense I couldn't even fake-smile back. Chloe's mom had wanted to come to her first sonogram test thing, but Chloe had wanted me to be here, so both of us had lied to our parents about where we were going this afternoon. I kept waiting for her dad to burst in and throw me out on my face.

"Ya ready?" the woman asked finally.

"Um, I guess," I replied.

"Well, all righty, then! Here goes!"

The woman whipped out a wand with a ball thingie on the end and put it on Chloe's stomach. I didn't know what to expect to see on the screen, but it was nothing but a bunch of scraggly green lines. Chloe craned her neck to see and the woman tilted the screen in her direction.

"There you go, hon," she said, moving the wand around the whole time.

Suddenly a baby-shaped thing appeared on the screen and my heart flip-flopped like a dying fish. I saw a head. I saw a nose. I saw a belly. I even saw an arm and a hand.

"All righty, now! And there's your little one!" the woman announced happily.

"Oh my God," Chloe said shakily.

"That's really in there?" I said, glancing at Chloe's small stomach. "How does it fit?"

The woman laughed as she hit a few buttons on a keyboard. "Well, it's only about the size of a chicken nugget, hon, but it's in there!"

Chloe tugged her hand out of mine and tears seeped out the corners of her eyes. She put her head down again and turned away from the screen, but I couldn't tear my eyes off the baby. It lifted its arm and put it down again. It was moving around in there.

I leaned forward. The tech's free hand flew over the keyboard, making beeping noises and a sound like a picture being snapped. I stared at the baby's profile. That baby was part me. How freaky was that? Did it look like me? Was it going to be tall like me or short like Chloe? Would it have her green eyes, or blue ones like mine?

And then I realized I was never going to know. Because I was never going to meet this kid. My stomach suddenly felt like it was full of needles. For the first time I got it. I got what Chloe meant the other day at lunch. This was my kid. My *kid*. But it wasn't going to be mine. My eyes prickled and blurred. What the hell was wrong with me? Was I going to effing cry?

Suddenly the baby rolled over. The humming lady and I both jumped.

"Whoa!"

"What? What is it?" Chloe asked, her head popping up again. "Is something wrong?"

"No, no, hon," the humming lady said with a laugh. "Baby's just real active right now."

Suddenly my eyes were clear again and I couldn't stop staring at the screen. If it moved again I didn't want to miss anything.

"I didn't feel anything," Chloe said, blinking down at her stomach.

"You probably won't for a couple of weeks now, but baby's definitely awake in there. Have you eaten recently?" she asked.

"I had some ice cream about an hour ago," Chloe replied.

"All righty, then! That'll do it! Lot of sugar will always get 'em moving."

She went back to pushing the wand around, humming what sounded like "Joy to the World."

The baby kicked out a leg and I laughed. "Gonna be a soccer player like me."

Chloe stared at me. Her lip was kind of trembling and she looked pale.

"What?" I asked.

"I just . . ." she said, her voice wet.

"What?"

There was a long pause. A long, *long* pause filled with nothing but beeps and clicks and humming.

"Nothing." Then she looked away again, chewing on her thumbnail.

Oooookay. But I knew better than to press it. Chloe had been all over the place with her emotions lately.

"Can you tell if it's a boy or a girl?" I asked the tech.

"I don't want to know," Chloe exclaimed, so loud my heart stopped for a second.

The woman smiled and looked a little sad. "We can't tell that yet anyway, hon."

I cleared my throat. "Oh."

The baby lifted its hand to its mouth.

"This is so cool," I heard myself say under my breath.

Chloe gave me this look, like she didn't know who I was.

"Isn't it, though?" the humming lady said.

She gave me one of her huge smiles, and this time I couldn't help smiling back.

jake

The day I had been dreading was already here. SAT score day. I wished I was one of those kids whose parents were so busy they had no idea when these things were happening, but I wasn't. My mother'd had it circled on the calendar for weeks, even before our big baby announcement. Ever since I'd told my parents Chloe was giving the baby up for adoption, they'd chilled out on the safe sex and responsibility lectures and I'd been allowed to hang out with my friends again, but that just meant they were back to focusing on college and my probable failure. So I wasn't surprised that my mom was waiting for me the second I got home from our latest game (we'd pulled a win out of our asses and were now going to the district semifinals— no thanks to me and my two left feet). She was standing in the doorway between the foyer and the kitchen, the family computer screen glowing behind her.

"I've already got the website booted up," she said, clinging to her coffee mug.

Ironic, right? This was a perfect example of why I wanted to get the hell away from here and go to college—the fact that she was so effing obsessed with me getting into college that she wouldn't leave me alone about it. At least I *think* that's irony.

"Can I get something to eat first?" I asked, putting my duffel bag and backpack down on the floor. *We won, by the way, thanks for asking,* I wanted to add, but didn't. My mom had never been much for what she called "back talk" and these days it made her nuts.

I hoped whoever my baby's parents ended up being, they would be cooler than mine.

"It'll take thirty seconds, Jake," she said, turning sideways to let me through the doorway. "Let's just get it over with."

"Fine," I said with a huge sigh.

I tromped past her and over to the computer, flopping down into the chair, which was four inches too high for me. My knees hit the granite-topped desk, and I reached over to lower the seat. The chair let out a hiss as I dropped down. My mother put her cup down and pushed up the baggy sleeves of her even baggier gray sweater. Her diamond bracelets clicked together as she leaned over my shoulder and pressed her hand into the desk next to the mouse pad.

I so didn't want to do this with her here. This past summer

I'd had an SAT tutor, and my last couple of practice tests had been pretty good. My mom was so excited about those scores that she actually started looking at me differently. Like she was proud of me for something other than sports. I knew that I was about to let her down big-time.

Or maybe not. Maybe Chloe was right and miracles do happen. Maybe some of what I'd learned over the summer had made its way onto the test sheet without me realizing.

"What are you waiting for?" my mother said.

A time machine? I thought. Maybe my future self was about to come back to rescue me from this moment. Of course if he was gonna do that, I could think of some other big moments he could've saved me from first.

I slowly typed in my password and hit enter. Our state-of-the-art super Mac lived up to the high-speed hype. I hadn't even blinked before my numbers were right there on the screen.

My low numbers. My just-as-low-as-last-spring's-dismal-ass numbers. My heart dropped so fast I slumped a little. Fuck. Fuck, fuck, fuck. It was even worse than I'd thought.

Now I was hoping that whatever the baby got of mine, it didn't get my stupid-ass brain.

"Oh my God," my mother said. She stood up straight, put one hand over her mouth and the other on the kitchen island, and stared at the screen. "Oh my God, Jake."

"Mom, it's not that bad," I said lamely.

Her eyes got scary-big. "Not that bad? Are you seeing something here that I'm not seeing?"

"I could get into a state school," I hedged, spinning the seat only halfway around so I wouldn't have to face her completely. "Or I could maybe get a scholarship."

"A scholarship? You haven't scored a goal all season, Jake!" my mother said, raising her palms.

Oh, so she *was* paying attention. Joy.

"What about swimming? And lacrosse?" I said.

"Great! That's just great! Let's wait until May and just see what happens!" my mother ranted, pacing around to the other side of the island. "What happened to you, Jake? You were doing so well this summer!"

"I'm sorry, okay!?" I snapped, shoving myself out of the chair. "I kind of had a lot of things on my mind that day."

The color drained out of her face as she braced her hands on the countertop. "Things? Like Chloe?"

"Yes, like Chloe," I replied. "Like Chloe and the baby."

She hadn't said the word "baby" once since finding out. She just called it "it" the few times she talked about it.

"Well, that's just fantastic!" she shouted, throwing her hands up. "I hope you're proud of yourself, Jake, because you can forget about college now."

I opened my mouth to respond. Because lots of people went to school with scores like mine. They just didn't go to schools like Fordham, where my dad had gone. Where my parents wanted me to go. But I couldn't get a word in. My mother was on a tear.

"You can forget about playing college sports, you can forget about getting a good job. You threw away your entire future just because you couldn't keep it in your pants!"

My jaw dropped open. Even my mother looked stunned. I couldn't believe she'd just said that. My mother got uncomfortable when characters in movies started undressing.

She recovered herself quickly, though, and looked me in the

eye. "Go to your room!" she shouted. "You're grounded until further notice."

"But Mom—"

I'd just gotten *ungrounded.*

"Go!" she screeched, pointing toward the stairs behind me.

I rolled my eyes, but turned around and went. I didn't want to be anywhere near her anymore anyway. I snatched my bags off the floor of the foyer and took the stairs three at a time to my room, where I slammed the door as hard as I could. Then I flung both bags at the wall and let them drop with a thud. Standing in the center of my room, I tried to regulate my breathing. I tried to tell myself everything would be okay. That it would work itself out somehow. But one thought kept repeating itself in my mind.

Just because I couldn't keep it in my pants. Just because I couldn't keep it in my pants.

ally

I was beaming nonstop over the standing ovation and the third curtain call when I burst into the backstage area with the rest of the cast. Everyone was laughing and shouting—whooping it up, screaming out their relief, exhaling the last of their nerves. The performance had gone off without one hiccup. Well, unless you count the fact that Puck had his wings on backward for the first act and kept knocking trees and bushes over with them. But I couldn't believe I hadn't forgotten a single line—that I hadn't tripped over my gown once, or slid off that fake rock I had to sleep on—something I'd done way too many times in dress rehearsal.

"We did it!" Lincoln shouted, grabbing me up and spinning around. "You were amazing!"

"So were you!" I said, reaching back to keep my floral wreath from slipping off my hair. "But you almost made me laugh!" I hit his arm as someone jostled me from behind trying to get to their parents.

"I know, I know! I'm so sorry!" He put his hands over his eyes for a second. "My little brother came running down the aisle and started making faces at me. You couldn't see him from where you were standing, but I almost lost it and then *you* almost lost it and . . . yeah. That was no good." He looked around at the already packed backstage area, which was rapidly becoming more crowded with friends and family, boyfriends and girlfriends. "Where is that little bugger? I have to kick his scrawny ass."

I laughed, my face stretched tight from all the smiling. I felt like I was never going to stop smiling.

Over Lincoln's shoulder, I saw my mom, Gray, Quinn, and my dad elbow their way into the mayhem. My dad held a huge bouquet of colorful flowers. Behind them were Annie and David, who had a single rose. I stood on my toes, looking for Jake. Had he brought me flowers too? But the next person through the door was an elderly man, being helped along by a younger guy. Then a mom I'd seen lurking around during rehearsals some days. Then Faith's mom and her little brothers. But where the heck was Jake?

"So, where's the crown prince of Orchard Hill High?" Lincoln asked, apparently noticing his absence as well.

"He's here," I said confidently, but my brow knit. "Some-where."

"Ally!" my mom shouted, finally singling me out in the crowd.

"I better go," I told Lincoln. "I'll see you at the party!"

"I'll be there," he replied.

"Really?" I said.

He started to say "no," but caught himself and pointed at me as he backed away. "You almost got me!"

I giggled as I slipped past him, dodged Puck's wayward wings, ducked as Janine Cantor flung herself at her boyfriend, and found myself in my mom's arms.

"Ally! You were unbelievable! I'm so proud of you," she said, kissing the top of my head.

"Who knew we had *two* stellar actresses in the family?" Gray commented, referring to Quinn and her community theater experience. He reached out for a one-armed squeeze around my shoulders. I saw my dad's jaw clench at the contact and quickly slipped out of it.

"Awesome job," Quinn said. "I was surprised."

"Thanks!" I said, choosing to ignore the dig.

I turned to my father, who wrapped me up in a hug and presented me with the flowers. "You out-acted everyone else on the stage."

"Dad!" I said, blushing. "They can hear you."

Everyone laughed. David handed me the rose, and Annie held out her program to me.

"What?" I asked, looking at the wrinkled mess.

"Can I have your autograph?" she asked, breathless.

"Ha ha," I said drily. I tripped sideways as one of the moms shoved past me. "Have you guys seen Jake?" Annie bit her lip and David averted his eyes. Suddenly my smile wasn't quite so wide anymore. "What?"

"I'm not sure he ever showed," David said.

"Maybe he was in the back," Annie added as my face fell.

"Yeah. It's not like he would've sat with us anyway," David pointed out.

It was a nice try, but I knew he hadn't come. If he had, Annie would have seen him. She never missed anything. I felt like a black pit of tar was forming in my stomach area, expanding to engulf everything. Looked like Lincoln was right. Jake Graydon had no interest in gracing the auditorium with his presence. Not even for the girl he supposedly loved.

"Ally, get together with your friends. Your mother wants a picture," Gray said, holding his camera up with one hand and waving us together with the other.

I turned toward the lens and forced a smile, but I suddenly felt tired—exhausted. Jake was grounded. I knew this. I knew there had been a chance he wouldn't make it. But I couldn't help feeling like if he'd really wanted to be here, he would have found a way to be here.

"One more!" Gray said jovially.

"Can we please go?" I asked.

"What's wrong?" my mother asked me, slipping her arm around my shoulder.

"I'm starving," I lied. "I was so nervous I barely ate anything today."

"Okay, then. Let's eat!" my father said.

We walked up the steps, which let out onto the main hall. I was just slipping through into the hallway when Jake came bursting in, a smallish bouquet of red roses in his hand. For a split second my heart fluttered with relief. He hadn't forgotten about me. But then I realized his cheeks were red with cold, and he had his jacket on. He'd just come in from outside. He had missed the entire play.

"Hey!" he said with a huge smile. He walked forward and engulfed me in a frigid hug. "Congratulations!"

"Thanks," I said stiffly, stepping back. "You just got here?"

As soon as they heard my question, my family and friends decided it was a good idea to keep walking. They moved ahead a few paces and pretended to be fascinated by the posters advertising the names of Orchard Hill High's National Merit Scholars.

"Yeah. I'm sorry," Jake said, glancing back over his shoulder. "I went with Chloe to her appointment this afternoon and her parents found out about it—God knows how. But anyway there was this whole big drama and I couldn't get out of there. But the good news is, they decided to let me see Chloe. To, like, let me be involved. So now there'll be no more sneaking around."

"Great," I said, not managing to sound in the least bit happy.

Jake's face fell. "What's wrong?"

I knew I shouldn't say what I was about to say. I knew it was petty and that his problems were so much bigger than mine. But I had to stand up for myself too, right? He was supposed to be my boyfriend. How long was I supposed to just take the fact that I was coming in second to Chloe all the time?

"Okay, I know this is going to sound, like, beyond selfish and everything, but how could you not be here?" I asked. "This was the one night . . . the one night this whole year that was supposed to be about my thing, my play. But instead you spent the afternoon with Chloe and because you did that you had to spend the night with her too."

Jake licked his lips. "I'm sorry. I just . . . but it wasn't just about Chloe. It was about the baby."

The baby, right. And it wasn't like I could argue with the baby. I felt sick with guilt for even thinking about trying. I took a deep breath and told myself to chill. It was over. It wasn't like I could go back and make him be here for the performance. But he was here now. I tried to believe that was what mattered.

"Okay, well . . . you're meeting me later, right?" I asked.

We were having the cast party in Faith's basement and Jake had promised to sneak out and come with. I had a feeling I was going to need him after suffering through what was sure to be the most awkward dinner of all time, with my mom, my dad, my mom's fiancé, and his daughter.

Jake gritted his teeth and I took a step back.

"You're not coming?"

"You know I'm grounded," I said.

My face stung. "That didn't matter when you were going to the doctor with Chloe."

"I told my parents I had an emergency practice right after school," he said, sounding desperate. "I can't tell them I have another one tonight."

"Well, where do they think you are right now?" I asked.

"Getting pizza," he said. He glanced at his watch. "Actually, I should get over to Renato's if I'm going to get back without them getting suspicious. . . ."

"Okay, fine. Just go," I said, walking past him. I was so angry I was practically shaking. I held my dad's and David's flowers against my chest as tightly as I could, trying not to lose it completely.

"Ally, come on," he begged.

"No, no. You're late to get your pizza!" I stormed right past my family and started down the stairs.

"Don't you want your flowers?" he yelled after me.

Give them to Chloe.

"Not even a little bit," I replied.

Then I shoved my way out the front door of the school and into the cold night air. I couldn't believe that ten minutes ago I had felt so happy. So carefree. Now I felt bad about myself, I felt bad about my relationship. . . . I just felt bad in general. And I was about to have to put on a happy face for two hours of chowing down with my dysfunctional family. I had no idea whose car we were taking or where they were parked, but I made a beeline for the parking lot, just trying to get away, tears streaming hot across my already freezing-cold face.

ally

"Okay, this girl's basement is bigger than my entire house!"

Lincoln sidled up to me and handed me a clear plastic cup full of bright red punch. Around me people played on Faith's father's classic pinball games, traded memories of tonight's performance, and laughed as other cast members played Dance Dance Revolution on the TV, while I stood with my back against a pillar, wishing I could rewind the night and do something differently with Jake. Anything.

"That's where you're supposed to say 'really?' and then I say—"

"No?" I replied.

Lincoln leaned his hand against the pillar somewhere over my head. He wore an old brown-and-tan striped cardigan over a white T-shirt, and it fell open as he moved. "Normally, yes, I would say no, but this time I think I'd actually have to say yes."

"Okay, I just *barely* followed that," I said, standing up a bit straighter.

"Let me put it this way. Her game closet? About the same size as my bedroom," he said.

"Gotcha."

Lincoln took a long, long slug of his punch, looking me in the eye the entire time. Looking me in the eye until I had to blush and look away.

"So what's your deal?" he asked. "You don't seem to be getting the fact that this is a party."

"Oh?" I put my half-drunk punch on a nearby table, along with five other discarded half-drunk cups. "What does that mean, exactly?"

"It means you're supposed to be having fun."

Fun. Like I had any idea what that was anymore. This was my senior year and the most fun I'd had so far was probably the late-night rehearsals we'd had last week. Smuggling Burger King backstage on dinner breaks, swinging from the sets, making our voices echo in the deserted lobby. Actually, most of the play stuff had been fun. The play stuff. The one place where my boyfriend was not a factor. And tonight, the one night he *was* a factor, he'd just swooped in and killed my stage buzz.

My heart twisted painfully as I wondered, not for the first time, what I was doing going out with a guy who hadn't made me smile in months.

Yeah. I was definitely not in party mode.

Lincoln leaned over me and put his cup inside mine, where it forced some of the liquid up the sides. I expected him to go back to where he'd been standing, but he didn't. Instead he stood in front of me. One foot between my two feet, his chest mere inches from mine.

My heart began to pound as a million thoughts raced through my mind. He was going to kiss me. But no, he wouldn't kiss me. He knew I had a boyfriend. But maybe that didn't matter to him. What was I going to do if he kissed me? Where was Faith? Was she watching me right now? Would it be the biggest deal if I let him kiss me? I mean, I'd kissed him onstage a dozen times. What was so different if he kissed me now?

And also, Jake wasn't here. He was supposed to be here. And he wasn't. Maybe I *should* kiss someone else.

Suddenly, in the back of my mind, Annie's voice started chanting, *Do it! Do it! Do it!*

"Really?" I heard myself say. Stalling. I was stalling. I looked at his scuffed brown shoes, the worn knee of his jeans, the off-white rug where three pretzels had been mauled into dust.

Lincoln hovered closer. I looked up at him. He shook his head "no" but said, "Yes."

Then he leaned in toward me. His lips inched toward mine. I knew how they would taste, how they would feel, but I couldn't breathe. Jake's face flitted through my mind, clear and bright as day. And I saw exactly what he would look like if he found out I kissed another guy. I felt exactly the disappointment and betrayal and anger he would feel. Because I'd felt it myself the night I'd found out about Chloe.

I turned my face away. Lincoln's forehead collided with my temple.

"Ow!" he said.

"I'm sorry." I sidestepped away from him and backed up, tripping over someone's leg and falling sideways against the old jukebox in the corner. "I'm sorry, Lincoln. You know I . . . I have a boyfriend."

"Yeah, I know," he said, touching his forehead with his fingertips and wincing. "I just thought—"

"I have to go," I interrupted. Because I didn't want to hear what he thought. Did he think Jake and I were in trouble because he'd spotted us fighting tonight? Did he think Jake and Chloe were a couple now because Jake was *always with Chloe?*

God. Could my brain get any more screwed-up?

"I'm sorry."

I turned and headed for the door, needing to escape more than anything. I had to get out of here and think. I had to figure out how I felt, why I had almost just let that happen.

"You don't have to leave!" Lincoln called after me.

"Yeah, I kind of think I do," I replied. "I'll see you on Monday!"

I grabbed the banister on the stairs and hurled myself upward. As I shoved through the door to the first floor, cool air enveloped me and I finally felt like I could breathe. I could hear Faith's mom and dad chatting with some other parents in the kitchen and I dove for the coat closet, glad my mother had chosen not to come. Somehow I found my black coat shoved in among the other black coats, and I was outside within seconds.

I hurried down the front walk and across the crunchy frozen grass, relishing the fact that I could walk home from Faith's. At least *something* good had come out of moving to Gray's.

Suddenly, out in the frigid cold night air, everything seemed crisply clear. I was in love with Jake. Whatever he'd done, whatever was going on in his life, however mad at him I was, I was in love with him. I could never kiss another guy while we were together. I wouldn't do that to him.

Good. That was good to know about myself. But it didn't solve the other ten million problems with our relationship. One thing was for sure, though. Right then, I felt like the worst girl-friend of all time, and as I turned and headed toward "home," I decided that from now on, I was going to do everything I could to be better. I promised myself I was going to be the best girl-friend I could be. I was going to act like everything was okay even if it wasn't. Because maybe the more I acted like it was okay, it would actually start to be okay.

Or maybe I was just making no sense. Either way, I decided to walk slowly, even though it was freezing-cold out. If I walked slowly enough, maybe by the time I got back to the house, I'd have it figured out.

jake

"This is gonna sound weird, but I feel like I haven't seen you in, like, a month." Ally hooked her arms around my neck and we started to slow dance. Fake stars winked and streaked over our heads, as couples moved around us. I looked down into her brown eyes and she did, freakily, look different.

"Did you do something? Like, to your hair or something?" I asked.

"See what I mean?" she said with a laugh. "You don't even remember what I look like."

I blushed and rolled my eyes. "I remember. I see you every day."

"I know, but we're both always so busy," Ally said as we moved in a tight circle. "It's like 'hi' in the hall and 'what did you get on your quiz?' and then that's it."

I nodded even though I didn't get it. We ate lunch together no matter what, and I drove her to school every morning. I'd been seeing just as much of her as usual, except for being grounded until I finally got a good grade yesterday. What was she looking for? An apartment together downtown?

Near the edge of the dance floor, Chloe was slow-dancing with Hammond, but keeping a serious distance. Like a full arm's length. I guess with her trying to hide her stomach, she had to. She was wearing this black dress that was tight under her boobs and then seriously loose to her knees. You couldn't tell she was pregnant, but all the guys were staring at her boobs. They had never been that big before, and every dude in the room knew it.

"What're you looking at?" Ally said, glancing behind her.

I stepped on her foot to keep her from looking. I'm not proud of it, but a guy has to do what a guy has to do.

"Ow!" she said, pulling her toes up.

"Sorry." I gritted my teeth. "I know it sucks that I've been grounded, but at least it's over. Now we can do whatever."

Ally put her foot down again and gave me this insanely sexy smile. "What kind of whatever did you have in mind?" she asked, pulling me in a little closer.

Instantly every inch of my skin was on alert. Actually, come to think of it, it *had* been a long time since we'd been alone together. Like, *alone* alone. I hadn't done much more than peck her on the lips in days. Weeks maybe. I held her closer, and her breath caught, which just got me going even more.

"Think there's a private room around here somewhere?" I said.

She blushed purple. "I *know* my mom's around here somewhere."

I loosened my grip a little. "Talk about a buzz kill."

Ally laughed, but I wasn't exactly kidding. Then a fast song started up and the only semicrowded dance floor was suddenly claustrophobic. Ally started to bounce around to the music, so I tried to do the same. I'd never been very good at fast dancing. I just sort of stepped from side to side and counted the seconds until it was over.

There was a whoop and a shout and suddenly a circle was forming. Being taller than most people had its perks. I could see over everyone's heads that Faith and this junior girl, Ava Strathmore, were pulling Chloe out into the center. They started to do this dance together, like doing the same moves, and everyone clapped to the beat. Chloe was laughing and I had to smile. It had been a while since I'd seen her laugh.

"Did they actually choreograph something?" Ally said, standing on her toes so she could see. She was taller than most girls, too, just not most guys.

"They did this for the talent show sophomore year," Shannen said, coming up behind us. "It just ain't a party until Faith snags the spotlight."

In the center of the circle, Chloe leaned over and swung her hair around and around like she was a propeller . . . or maybe a stripper. I swear I thought one of her boobs was gonna pop out of her dress, and I think everyone else did too. Every guy in the room was holding his breath. Then her mother broke through the crowd and went pale, hanging on to her pearls for dear life.

"Um, should she be doing this?" Ally asked.

"She's fine!" Shannen shouted, raising her arms over her head. "God, let the girl have a little fun."

Then Chloe flung her head up and stood straight and suddenly her eyes sort of crossed. Just like that I remembered that day on the side of the road. The day she almost fainted. Someone in the crowd gasped. Chloe staggered sideways. Her dad jumped out of the crowd behind her with his arms outstretched, and she went down.

"Omigod!" Ally cried, hand over her mouth.

My heart completely stopped beating.

The baby. Just don't let the baby be hurt.

I shoved through the circle and was on my knees next to Chloe. Hammond did the same on the other side. Luckily her dad had caught her before she hit the floor, but she was completely out.

"Chloe! Chloe, can you hear me?" her father asked.

"Charles?" Chloe's mother wailed.

"Get Gray!" he growled. She disappeared into the crowd just as Dr. Nathanson came into the circle from the other side. Ally's mom went straight to Ally's side.

"What happened?" Dr. Nathanson asked, kneeling next to me.

"She just fainted and went down," I said.

Mr. Nathanson looked Chloe over. "Charles, I hate to have to ask this, but is your daughter . . . pregnant?"

I looked down. On her back, with her dress flopped to the floor, it was obvious. Chloe's belly was like a mountain. Mr. Appleby nodded and Gray looked, well, gray.

Everyone was dead silent, but the music was pumping. Kids started snapping pictures with their phones, sending texts or tweets. I wanted to pummel every one of them.

"Boys, I'm going to need a little room," Dr. Nathanson said to me and Hammond.

"Yeah, dude," Hammond said, glaring at me.

"Me? You're the one that should back off," I spat.

Hammond's eyes went wide. "I was with her for two years!"

"Yeah, and she broke up with you, like, six months ago, jackass!" I shot back.

"Boys! Both of you! Get out of the doctor's way!" Mr. Appleby shouted. "This is not about your egos right now!"

Hammond and I both stood up. I turned away, turned toward Ally, but her expression kind of killed me. She looked sad, helpless, jealous, and mad all at once. I put my hand on the back of my head and looked at the floor. I could feel everyone watching me. Wondering why *I* had gone to Chloe's side. Maybe even realizing the truth. Thumbs flew over keyboards, everyone here telling everyone I knew what they thought they now understood. Finally the music was cut dead.

"Chloe? Are you okay?" I heard Mrs. Appleby say, after what seemed like forever.

I whirled around. Chloe was sitting up. Blinking.

"Where are we?" she asked, staring up at the fake sky. Then her face filled with terror. "Oh my God. The baby! Is the baby okay?"

Now there were gasps. As if they hadn't seen the belly bump, hadn't heard the doctor's question.

"Let's get her out of here," her father said. "She needs some fresh air."

Dr. Nathanson and Mr. Appleby helped Chloe to her feet, supporting her on the way out the door.

"Wait, but the party," I heard Chloe say. And then she was gone.

Mrs. Appleby stood there in the center of the dance floor by herself, sort of wavering back and forth on her heels. Shannen's mother came out of the crowd and went over to her, and the two of them clasped hands for a second. Then Mrs. Appleby looked up and focused. It was like she finally saw the audience. Saw everyone staring at her.

"Yes, my daughter is pregnant, okay?" she half-cried, half-screeched. "And this party is officially over."

Then she yanked her hand away from Mrs. Moore, turned, and stormed out. The whole room was consumed by whispers and questions and some laughter. I walked over to Ally and her mom. Ally kind of robotically took my hand. I squeezed her fingers, but she didn't squeeze back.

"Well, I guess we should—"

"Jake?" Mrs. Appleby's voice stopped me cold. She had her coat over her arm and she snapped her fingers at me from across the room. "Chloe's asking for you. Let's go."

My mouth fell open. Every single pair of eyes in the room was on me. I felt like someone had jammed a dirty sneaker into my throat, making it impossible to speak or breathe.

"Let's *go*," she ordered me.

I turned to Ally. Her eyes were shining. She dropped my hand, crossed her arms over her stomach, and looked at the floor.

"Um, you have a ride, right?" I said.

"Of course she does," her mother said, putting her arms around Ally's shoulders. Her mouth was this ugly thin line, and she looked like she wanted to put me in a chokehold. Guess someone had figured out for sure what was going on around here.

"Okay. Thanks. I'll call you later?" I said to Ally.

She barely nodded. I turned around and strode across the room, trying to keep my head up. When I passed Hammond he shot me a death glare. I paused and looked him in the eye.

"Well," I said. "There you go."

I couldn't help it. Then I followed Chloe's mother out to the car. Her dad was in the front seat. Dr. Nathanson was in the back with Chloe. I got in next to her and she fell sideways into me, resting her head on my lap.

"Do you think the baby's okay?" I asked Ally's almost-stepfather.

"It wasn't that bad of a fall," he said, his face stiff. I was sure he was judging me. Realizing his fiancée's daughter was going out with someone else's baby daddy. "But we won't know anything for sure until we get her to the hospital."

The hospital. My throat felt dry and coarse. *Please just let the baby be okay. Please just let the baby be okay.* Chloe was crying, but totally silent. I had no idea what to do with my hands. Then I noticed her hair was over her face, so I brushed it back behind her ear. It took a few swipes, but she stopped crying. So I just kept doing that, all the way to the emergency room.

ally

The garage door scrolled open in front of us. My mother and I sat there in silence. Just like we had the entire drive from the city. My mother put the car in park and I held my breath.

Here we go.

"So, are you going to tell me what's going on?" she asked.

"As if you haven't figured it out already," I replied acerbically, toying with the strap on my black evening bag.

She shifted in her seat, angling her back against the door and her knees toward me.

"Why don't you try me?" she asked. "Because I'm hoping that what I'm imagining is actually worse than the truth. That's often the case with parents, fyi. Our imaginations are hugely overactive."

I scoffed and shook my head. My eyes stung like they'd been branded. The moment I'd been dreading for so long was finally here, but I somehow couldn't believe it was happening. I couldn't believe I was going to have to talk to my mother about this. I decided for the Band-Aid approach. Quick and painless. Well, quick, anyway.

"Okay, here it is. Over the summer when Jake and I were broken up, he and Chloe had sex. Apparently they made a baby. So now, here we are."

My mother stared. "How long have you known about this?"

"Since the night before school started," I said, then braced myself.

"That long? Ally!" My mother dropped her hand into her lap and raised her eyes to the heavens. "How could you have kept this a secret?"

"It's not like it was easy, okay?" I said, my voice breaking as I turned my palms to the sky, my hands in my lap. "But it wasn't my secret to tell! Chloe's parents didn't even know about it." My mother had this incredulous look on her face. Like our relationship should have trumped everything else.

I looked down at my lap again. "Besides, you've kind of had other things on your mind."

"Oh, don't do that. Don't act as if the wedding prevented you from confiding in me," she snapped, annoyed. "I knew something was up with you. I *tried* to talk to you. You wouldn't tell me."

I gazed out the windshield, frozen. She was right, of course. She'd asked and I'd lied. But I just didn't feel like talking about this right now. This wasn't my fault. None of it was. And all I cared about right then was finding out where Jake was. And, maybe a little bit, finding out if Chloe was okay. I couldn't believe the way she'd just gone down. I'd never seen anything so scary in my life. For the first time in a long time, I remembered that she wasn't just a villain. She was someone who needed taking care of.

I just wished, for the millionth time, that it wasn't my boyfriend taking care of her.

"I'm sorry, okay? I am. I wish I'd told you, believe me. But now you know," I said with a shrug. "Can we just go inside and see if Gray is back yet?"

"I need to ask you something," she said.

I sighed, my shoulders slumping. So much for this conversation being over.

"Okay."

"Have you . . . I mean, you haven't . . . slept with Jake, have you?"

I never knew my body could get that hot that fast. "What? Mom! No! What do you think he's doing? Running around school knocking everybody up?"

"I'm sorry!" she said, raising her hands. "It's just when you find out your daughter's boyfriend has been sexually active, you start to wonder if—"

"Oh, God, Mom!" I groaned, gagging. "Please never say that again?"

"What? Sexually active? Well, it's pretty clear he is, kiddo!" she replied indignantly.

"Okay, okay!" I was so uncomfortable I could have clawed my way out of the car. "Look, I'm not an idiot. I'm not Chloe."

My fingers clenched into fists. I just wanted to end this awful night.

"I know you're not, Ally. I know." She reached over and patted my hand. She blew out a sigh, and I imagined it was pure relief. Until she said: "But we're clear on everything, right? Condoms can prevent diseases, but they don't always prevent pregnancy—"

I scoffed, my face prickling. "Yeah. Apparently not."

She paused. "They used a condom?"

"I can*not* believe I'm talking about this with you," I said, looking out the side window.

"But they—"

"Yes, okay!? They used a condom. Jake's not an idiot either."

Just kind of a slut.

Suddenly I wanted to punch someone. Maybe myself. Maybe Jake. I wasn't sure.

"Okay, well, that's good. That's . . . good to know. So are you okay?" she asked, tilting her head. "I can't imagine it's easy, the guy you love having a baby with someone else."

A tear unexpectedly plopped onto my lap. I felt more coming and bit them back. "No, it's not," I said, my voice full. "But, Mom? Can we talk about this tomorrow? I'm tired. I just want to go inside and go to bed."

She pressed her lips together and I could tell there were ten million more things she wanted to say, ten million more questions to ask. I was grateful beyond imagination when she faced forward, put the car in gear, and nodded.

"Sure, hon." She sighed again and pulled the car into the garage. "Whatever you say."

ally

Everyone was watching me. At least that's how it felt. Two hundred people, a dozen scantily clad cheerleaders, and a huge, face-melting bonfire, and they were watching me. I stood on the baseball field with Annie, David, Marshall Moss, and Marshall's girlfriend, Celia Linklater—all five-foot-one, ninety-five pounds of her—a safe enough distance from the fire to not catch a spark, but close enough to stay warm, and tried to be inconspicuous. Marshall had been my prom date last year and was still a good friend, but I barely saw him because he was always with Celia. Still, I was glad they were both here tonight for extra support. Somehow I'd thought that the night-before-Thanksgiving football pep rally—a traditionally Norm-only event—would be a respite from the rumor mill. Apparently I was wrong.

"Oh, man. I forgot my flask! Did you guys bring a flask?" Annie joked, clucking her tongue.

I glanced in the direction she was looking and, sure enough, saw three members of the JV football team passing around a leather bottle. They couldn't have looked more suspicious if they tried, their eyes darting around, their feet so close their toes were touching.

"Nope. Forgot the pot, too," David said, sniffing the air, his hands jammed into the pockets of his varsity soccer jacket. "How does anyone get away with this stuff when there are cops and firemen everywhere?"

"Because half the cops went to our school and don't give a crap," Marshall said, wrapping his arms around Celia from behind. He had to bend down to rest his chin atop her curly brown hair. "Jason Krantz will probably confiscate all of it and have a party in his parents' pool house."

Celia laughed as the officer in question, who didn't look a day over eighteen even though he'd graduated three years ago, strolled by with his shoulders rolled back, his head swiveling from side to side like he was auditioning for a new *Terminator* movie.

"Uh-oh, Ally," Celia said suddenly. "Incoming."

The little hairs on the back of my neck stood on end. I didn't know Celia that well—only from the few times we'd hung out together—but being a peripheral friend, she knew all about the Jake/Chloe/Ally triangle situation. I looked over my shoulder. Lincoln Carter was strolling toward us, his hands in the pockets of his brown corduroy jacket.

I didn't know what I had been expecting, but it wasn't Lincoln. Celia and Lincoln were friendly, so I wondered if he'd maybe told her what had happened at the cast party and I suddenly felt betrayed. Prickles filled my stomach and I went hot around the collar, more in the spotlight than ever.

"Hey," he said, pausing in front of me.

"Hey."

I glanced over at my friends, then moved a few feet away. Lincoln followed. Luckily, the others took the hint and didn't.

My throat was dry and tasted like ash from the fire. I licked my lips nervously and looked up at him.

"What's up?"

He lifted his shoulders, keeping his hands in his pockets. "Not much. I guess I'm just wondering . . . how you are." His expression was somewhere between concerned and hopeful. I didn't get it.

"How I am?" I said dumbly.

He pressed his lips together, like he was maybe regretting coming over here. "Yeah, I mean. I heard about . . . you know, Jake and Chloe and I just wondered . . . if you're okay."

My stomach dropped. This felt completely wrong, talking about this with him. Lincoln had been my escape from the reality of my life. And now here he was, stepping right into the thick of it. It wasn't his fault, I knew, but I didn't like having him in my reality. I wished he'd stayed separate. I wished he'd stayed clean.

"Yeah, I'm okay," I said. "I've known about it for a while, actually."

"Oh. Really? So you guys are still . . . ?"

My face burned. "Yeah. We're still together. We're fine. Better than ever."

The hope died off his face and I felt the prickles in my stomach harden into a rock-hard ball. That was maybe overkill, but what was I supposed to do? I didn't want him to go on thinking that he had a chance with me just because everyone now knew my boyfriend was gonna be a father.

"Oh. Okay." His expression darkened. Like maybe he was seeing me in a different way suddenly. Like maybe he was judging me for staying with a guy who was obviously a slut player.

He could join the club.

"Anything else?" I said, feeling defensive. I lifted my chin.

"Nope. I guess I'll just . . . see you around."

"Yeah. See ya," I said softly.

He turned and was gone, walking back to his friends a lot quicker than he'd come. Guess if I ever *was* looking for a random hook-up in my future, it wasn't going to be with him. Annie appeared at my side, watching him go.

"It's too bad you two never smooched for reals," she said. "Because *damn.*"

"Why don't you go out with him, then?" I asked, annoyed. That conversation had left behind an icky, sticky feeling in my gut. I liked Lincoln. And I didn't like the idea that he might think less of me now.

On the far side of the bonfire, the cheerleaders launched into some elaborate pyramid and the team began to gather together near the dugouts. I saw their coach looking over some notes and realized the show was about to start—the speeches and cheering and actual rallying. I'd never come to a football pep rally when I'd lived in Orchard Hill the first time, and I was kind of curious to see what went on.

"Welcome, everyone, to this year's Orchard Hill High football pep rally!" the football coach suddenly shouted into the microphone.

As the baseball field filled with cheers, I glimpsed one maroon-and-gold jacket set apart from the rest. It was Will Halloran, running back and cocaptain of the team. He was about twenty yards off from his teammates, at the end of the dugout—an area that was mostly in shadow. He was talking to someone, but I couldn't see who.

"What's Will doing over there?" I said, mostly just to change the subject. "Isn't this his big night?"

As everyone turned to look, he shifted position and we saw that he was in a deep one-on-one with none other than Chloe Appleby. Her baby belly, which I guess she was no longer hiding, stuck out between the open flaps of her camel, leather coat.

My skin sizzled with intrigue. What the hell were Will and Chloe talking about? I'd never seen them speak to each other in my life. I'd noticed him looking at her longingly a couple of times this year, but I figured he was just suffering an unrequited crush. As we stared, Chloe gave a desperate gesture with her hand and Will touched her arm in a way that's usually reserved for boyfriendly types.

"That's . . . interesting," Celia said.

"Ho. Lee. Crap." Annie brought her hand to her forehead and turned around. Her eyes were so wide they were like doughnuts.

"What?" I said, my pulse starting to race. If there was one thing I knew about my best friend, it was when she had good gossip to spill.

"Oh my God," she said, covering her face with both hands now. "Oh my god oh my God oh my God. She couldn't. She . . . she wouldn't."

"Who couldn't what?" David said, looking around at the rest of us. "What the hell is she talking about?"

"Oh my God, she can't possibly be that evil," Annie said,

dragging her fingers down her face and smudging her eyeliner. "Can she possibly be that evil?"

My stomach started to slowly clench into a marble-size ball, and I wasn't even sure why. I glanced over at the spot where Will and Chloe had disappeared, as if they'd signal the answer to me via flash card.

"Who?" Marshall asked, baffled.

"Annie, what's going on?" I asked. "What do you know about Chloe and Will?"

"Are they, like, together or something?" Celia asked.

And suddenly, just like that, this snatch of conversation from last summer came back to hit me in the face. I had asked Annie if she knew anything about Jake and Chloe and she'd told me they *had* been hanging out a lot, but then she added, "The weird thing is, Chloe's also been hanging out a lot with—"

And then she'd been interrupted when David and Marshall had come bounding through the door like two puppy dogs.

Suddenly my brain went fuzzy. The wind shifted and my senses filled with the acrid, smoky scent of the fire. I reached out and clutched Annie's forearm, like she was going to anchor me to a sane reality. Because right now, my brain was going to some seriously *in*sane places.

"You don't think Chloe and Will . . . over the summer . . . the other guy . . ." I couldn't even form a real thought, let alone a sentence. Had Chloe and Will hooked up? Had Chloe and Will had sex?

Annie nodded, her dark eyes bright with suspicion. "He was the other guy," she confirmed. "I kept spotting them together everywhere—at the movies, the farm, at Stanzione's. . . . But

143

you don't think she would . . . I mean, she wouldn't actually *lie* about who her baby daddy is, would she?"

I just stared at Annie. Chloe would never. She couldn't ever. Why? Why would she do something like that? I couldn't believe it, even though a huge, huge part of me was dying to believe it.

"I mean, after I heard about Jake and Chloe I just figured I was wrong about *Will* and Chloe, but, I mean . . ." She gazed off toward the dugout. "Son of a—"

"Wait a minute. Will and Chloe hooked up?" David blurted.

"And now, like, two seconds after everyone finds out she's pregnant, they're having emotional tête-à-têtes?" Celia put in.

"Oooh, I love it when you talk French," Marshall said, nuzzling her from behind. Then, suddenly, his head popped up. "I bet he thinks he might be the father! I bet that's what they're talking about!"

My mind was reeling. It was like the entire bonfire was trying to swallow me whole. The light, the heat, the ash, the laughter, the screaming, the music, the drums. I couldn't think straight. Couldn't see.

"Okay, everyone, just calm down," I said, splaying my fingers. "We just jumped to about a million conclusions." I turned and walked toward the chain link fence around the field. Moving away from the fire helped, and leaning my weight on the fence helped even more. "What do we actually know? Do we *actually know* Chloe and Will were a thing?"

Annie bit her lip. "We're ninety-nine point nine percent sure. At least I was then. And I am now."

I swallowed hard. "Then we don't actually *know* anything," I said, looking at each of them. "Maybe they were just hanging out. Maybe they were just friends. Maybe she came here to, like, talk about a bio project or something."

"But what if—" Annie began.

I shook my head, clutching the cold links of the fence behind me. "I can't believe Chloe would do that. I mean, why would she do that?"

"I believe it," Annie muttered, crossing her arms over her chest. "If you were queen of the Cresties, who would you rather get knocked up by? Jake or Will?"

I tasted bile in the back of my throat. Because she was right. If Chloe had to be in this awful situation, it would be a lot more livable with a fellow Crestie and Country Club member like Jake by her side than with a blue-collar worker like Will. It was disgusting, but it was just how Orchard Hill had always functioned. But Chloe was a good person. I'd known her my whole life. Compared with the rest of the Cresties, she'd always been the most human, the most kind, the most down-to-earth. I couldn't imagine her screwing with people's lives this way. But if there was even a chance . . .

"We gotta find out," David said, his jaw set. "I mean, if the baby isn't Jake's—"

"He needs to know," I finished. I cleared my throat and took a deep breath. "Okay, okay. Here's what we're going to do," I said, pacing away from them, then back again. "I'll tell him about Chloe and Will, and then he can ask her about it. Because technically, this is between them, right?" There was a prolonged moment of stoic silence. "Everyone good with that plan?"

My friends just stared at me. My throat filled with nervous desperation.

"You guys can't tell anyone," I said. "You *can't*. I swear, if I hear this around school before I get a chance to deal with it, I will disown each and every one of you."

We looked around the circle solemnly, each of us meeting everyone else's gaze. My friends looked so sure that our hastily woven story was true, my heart pounded an excited beat. Because for a split second I let myself believe it too. I let myself imagine what life might be like if Jake wasn't actually the baby's father.

Everything would go back to normal for us. All the strain and jealousy and tension? Gone.

"Do we have a deal?" I asked pointedly. I put my hand in the middle of the circle, like I was one of the Three Musketeers or something.

"Deal," Marshall said, putting his hand atop mine.

Celia groaned reluctantly. I knew that sharing gossip this huge about two of the most popular Cresties would totally improve her status. Right now she was seeing that possibility slip away. But she put her hand on top of Marshall's.

"Deal."

"Deal," David said, adding his hand.

Annie took a deep breath. She looked up at the sky, blew out a cloud of steam, and shuddered in her Doc Martens. Then, finally, she slapped her hand down so hard on top of David's that he winced.

"I just want you people to know this is the hardest thing I've ever had to do in my life. And you're looking at a girl whose appendix burst on the same night her pet hamster died," she said. Then she looked me in the eye and I just knew that whatever happened next, she was with me. "Deal."

december

Can you even believe that Ally Ryan and Jake Graydon
are still together?

I know! Shouldn't he, like, be going out with
the mother of his baby?

Do you think he and Chloe did the deed while he
was with Ally?

No way. She definitely would have broken up
with him if he cheated on her.

Not necessarily. He's Jake Graydon.

So?

So? With that face? Everything's forgivable.

Nah. Ally Ryan isn't like that. She has, like,
integrity and stuff.

If she has integrity, shouldn't she break up with him
so he can be with the girl he impregnated?

Okay. This is making my head hurt.

Tell me about it. When did other people's
relationships get so complex?

ally

"Where have you been?"

I scurried to the end of the counter at Jump, Java, and Wail! on Sunday night, grabbed Jake by the apron with both hands, and kissed him. Someone nearby went "Aw!" One of Jake's coworkers muttered, "Get a room."

Jake leaned back, blushing. "Philadelphia, remember? I just got back a couple of hours ago. Also, your dad's in the office, so maybe chill with the PDA."

"Noted," I said. I lowered my voice as I slid onto the last stool. "So? Did you lose your phone? Fry your laptop? Forget how to work a landline? I left you, like, a million messages."

Jake's blush deepened. He wiped his hands on a clean towel and looked around, as if any of the middle-aged couples huddled around tables were interested in us. Sunday night was not usually a big night for our age group at Jump. Which was probably why it was always packed with adults.

"I know," he whispered. "I'm sorry. It was just a crazy weekend."

I made a surprised, choked sound. "Crazy enough to not respond to a text that said 'You might not be the father'?" I whispered.

I saw Jake's jaw working as he stood up straight. He glanced over at his coworker as he untied his apron. "Chase, I'm taking my fifteen."

"Got it, bro," the guy replied, not looking up from his iPhone. So much for my dad's strict rule about not texting while on shift.

Jake came around the end of the counter and tugged me

toward the back of the shop, where we sat down at the most secluded table there was—the one cornered by the door to my dad's office and the emergency exit. The one no one from school ever came near. Jake sat down and blew out a sigh. He was acting beyond weird. Shouldn't he be excited? Angry? At least moderately annoyed or intrigued? I tugged off my scarf and hat and sat across from him.

"I already know about Will Halloran," he said. "I know he and Chloe went out this summer."

Someone had left a glass canister of cinnamon on the table and he started to fiddle with it, sliding it back and forth from hand to hand across the pebbled marble. I felt like he'd just whipped my chair out from under me.

"What?" I whispered, leaning into the table. "And you didn't tell me?"

He shrugged. "It doesn't matter."

I felt like reality had just reversed itself. "How could it not matter? How do you know Will's not the father?"

"Because. Chloe never slept with Will," Jake replied, holding the canister with both hands now. He scratched at some crust on the side with his thumbnail.

"How do you know that?" I asked.

"Because she told me," he replied.

My jaw dropped. "And you believed her? Just like that?"

From the corner of my eye, I saw my dad emerge from the back room. He looked like he was about to say hi, then noticed how serious we looked and thought better of it. He moved to the other side of the shop.

"Do you really think Chloe would lie about something like that?" Jake snapped defensively.

149

I sat back. For a long moment I couldn't locate my voice. Was he seriously defending Chloe's honor to me right now? When I was trying to help him? When I was trying to throw him a lifeline? I couldn't believe that he didn't grasp the seriousness of the situation.

"Well, let's see, I never thought she was the kind of person who'd fool around with two guys at one time, but apparently I was wrong about that," I said finally. "And I didn't think *you* were the kind of person who'd have sex with someone else when you were supposed to be in love with me, either."

"We were broken up!" Jake snapped angrily. "God! I thought we were done with this."

"Yeah, well, I guess not," I said, pushing my chair back. I wanted to storm out, but I couldn't. I needed more from him. I needed him to say that he'd talk to Chloe. That he cared enough about knowing the truth. That he cared more about being with me than hurting her feelings. "Don't you think you should just ask her again?" I said. "See what she says? This is a huge deal, Jake. For you and for Will."

"I know it's a huge deal, Ally!" he whisper-shouted angrily. "Do you think you know better than me what a huge fucking deal this is? I've *seen* the baby. I've seen it roll over and kick and suck its thumb. There's a baby out there that's mine and sometimes all I can think about is that I never even get to name him or talk to him or see him play soccer. I'm dealing with that. Maybe *you're* the one who's not."

Suddenly I saw something in his eyes that stopped me cold. It was fear. Just the tiniest flicker, but it was there. He was scared of asking about Will again. He was scared he might find out he wasn't the father.

Jake wanted the baby to be his.

And I was going to be sick.

"I have to go," I said, standing, trying not to cry in front of him.

"Ally, wait. I'm sorry," Jake said.

"Forget it," I said.

I shoved through the door and onto the wintry sidewalk, the bell jangling jauntily above my head. I'd gotten about five steps along the salted sidewalk when my dad came after me.

"Ally! Wait up!"

I whirled around, took one look at my father in his brown apron and T-shirt, his breath making fog clouds in the frigid air, his eyes concerned, and I burst into tears.

"What is it?" he asked, hugging me to him. "What just happened?"

For the splittest of seconds I considered not telling him. He loved Jake. And he was Jake's boss. I didn't want to take their good relationship away from them. But then, screw that. He was my dad first.

"Chloe's pregnant," I sputtered into his chest. "And Jake might be the father."

"What?" my father croaked, stepping back so I could look at him. "I'll kill him. I'll kill the little—"

"We were broken up when it happened, Dad," I said, sniffling. Always protecting Jake. Even when my heart was breaking. "You don't have to kill anyone."

My father shifted and brought his fist to his mouth for a second. It looked like it was taking all his self-control to keep from running back inside and flinging himself at Jake, Ultimate Fighter style.

"Are you okay?" he asked finally.

"No," I replied, a fresh wave of tears choking me.

My dad looked at the light traffic on Orchard Avenue. The sky was pitch-black in the way only a winter sky could be, and only a few crazy people had braved the cold. He hooked his arm around my neck. "Come on."

"Where're we going?" I asked.

"To my place."

My dad lived in an apartment across the street from Jump, right above the town apothecary where the rich moms bought all their magic youth-making potions.

"But aren't you working?" I asked as we crossed the street.

"I don't think I should be anywhere near Jake Graydon right now, and you are in desperate need of a warm blanket and a junk fest." He hugged me a bit closer to his side and I tilted my head against his shoulder. One thing I had always loved about my dad? He always knew exactly what I needed.

I wished, not for the first time, that we were both going home to my mom, instead of home to his place. That we could all curl up on the couch together, eat crap, and watch bad movies like we used to. That we could be a family again. But I had to take what I could get.

And now, at least, everyone knew. Mom, Dad, friends. At least that awfulness was over. I just wished I knew where I stood with Jake. I glanced over my shoulder at the window-walls of Jump, Java, and Wail! but I couldn't see him at the counter or anywhere, and for this one weird, out-of-body moment, I felt like he was just gone. Like I was never going to see him again.

ally

Monday afternoon I was the first person dressed and on the court for basketball practice. I stood at the free throw line with the ball rack next to me, shooting one after the other after the other. Every time, the ball slammed against the backboard and ricocheted off in another direction. And every time, I saw someone else's face.

Jake.

Chloe.

Will.

Hammond.

Lincoln.

Apparently I was pissed at the world.

But mostly, I was pissed at Jake. And myself. And I was tired. Tired of feeling like second-runner-up to Chloe. Tired of trying to convince myself it was okay. And after that conversation I'd had with Jake, after finding out that he basically didn't care about a way out, didn't care about getting us back to being us, I was starting to think that breaking up with him was the only option. It was the only way to save my self-esteem.

I took a shot, and the ball sailed clear over the net, the backboard, everything.

"Ugh!"

I let another ball fly. It hit the backboard hard and boomeranged right toward my face. Luckily I got my arms up in time. Shannen came jogging over, plucking up a few of my errant basketballs. Her dark hair was slicked into a ponytail, her bangs held back by a two-strand headband, and she wore a white Orchard Hill basketball T-shirt with the sleeves rolled up to expose her cut shoulders. She unloaded the balls onto the rack and smirked.

"If you need someone to rearrange your face, your boyfriend's father's a plastic surgeon. I'm sure he'll give you a reduced rate," she said wryly.

I grabbed a ball and set up for the shot. "Yeah, well, I'm not sure how much longer he's going to be my boyfriend." Somehow, saying it out loud made me feel both nauseous and free at the same time. I let the ball fly over her head. She reached up and blocked it down into her other hand.

"*What?*"

I tipped my head back and trudged over to the bleachers. The rest of the team was trickling out from the locker room and starting to warm up. I dropped down onto the bottom bench and Shannen perched next to me, draping her arms over the basketball in her lap, her wrists crossed over each other.

"If I tell you this, you can*not* tell anyone," I said. "Swear on your mother's life."

"I swear," Shannen said, wide-eyed. "I mean, I know I don't have the best track record with secrets, but I'm working on it with my therapist," she added with a smirk.

I took in a sharp breath. She was referencing the very public way in which she'd spilled my father's big secret last spring. But that was different and we'd both been trying to put it behind us ever since. Besides, there was no video of this particular secret in action.

God, I hoped there wasn't.

"Look, I get it if you don't want to tell me," Shannen said, starting to get up. "But if you want someone to talk to—"

"Wait."

I did want someone to talk to. Someone with a new perspective. Annie and I had spent half the weekend talking it over and over and over, and her solution was to tweet about the whole mess with thinly veiled pseudonyms (her suggestions: Carly, Bill, and Jack) and see how Chloe reacted. Not exactly subtle. My mother was an option, of course, but I just couldn't break it to her that this whole thing had gotten even more nasty and sordid than it already was. Shannen and Chloe had been friends forever. Maybe she'd have something useful to say.

Shannen sat her butt down again and waited. I took a deep breath and held it.

"Chloe and Will Halloran had a thing this summer. Like, a serious thing," I whispered, turning my face toward hers so far I touched my chin to my shoulder.

"Oh my God." Shannen looked out across the gym, where sneakers squeaked and balls pounded the boards. "Huh. He's hot."

"Okay, kind of missing the point here," I said.

Shannen's head snapped around. "Wait. You don't think he's the father?"

"I don't know what to think," I told her, pulling my knees up under my chin. I fiddled with the laces on one of my sneakers. "She told Jake that she never had sex with Will, and he believes her, but . . ."

"Ally. You have to do something," Shannen said loudly.

"Shhhh!"

I looked up at the court, but no one was paying any attention to us. Most of our teammates were either gossiping or drilling layups. Coach walked in from the lobby and flipped through her clipboard, her silver whistle dangling low around her neck. Practice was about to start.

"It's not up to me," I whispered, my pulse racing. "Jake doesn't want to hear it and I don't know. . . . I have to believe that if Chloe thought Will might be the father, she would have said something. She couldn't do this to Jake."

"You think Chloe's going to admit to her parents that their pristine little girl isn't only a nonvirgin, but she's also had sex with more than one guy?" Shannen whispered incredulously. "Are you kidding me? She'd kill herself first. Someone has to talk to her."

"Well, I can't do it," I said. "Jake would freak."

"Then I'll do it," Shannen said, getting up.

I jumped from my seat. "No! You just promised me you wouldn't say anything."

Shannen's jaw set. "Well then, I'll *do* something."

There was another objection on the tip of my tongue, but I hesitated. "Like what?"

Slowly, wickedly, Shannen's lips twisted into a smirk. She began dribbling the ball at a very even, deliberate rhythm. Her eyes went a bit blank, distant, like she was already imagining the possibilities. Finally she focused on me and smiled.

"Oh, you know me," she said. "I always think of something."

Coach blew the whistle to call us to attention, and Shannen turned her back to me. I reached out a hand to stop her but quickly snatched it back.

I'd already awakened Shannen's inner beast, and it wasn't like I could change that. Now Shannen was going to do what Shannen was going to do. This whole mess was out of my control. And I was kind of curious to see what might happen next.

jake

Ally was amazing on the basketball court. She was so focused. And she was so . . . graceful. That's the only word I can think of for it. Even when she was slamming into defenders, sweating everywhere, and shouting at her teammates, she was just graceful. It was like she was born to be out there.

I sat near the top of the bleachers with Connor, Josh, and the Idiot Twins at her Wednesday night game, and I couldn't take my eyes off of her. Even though the Idiot Twins were wearing huge, curly maroon wigs and had their faces painted and kept trying to start the wave, all I could see was Ally.

I had texted her that I was coming tonight. She hadn't replied. She hadn't talked to me since the fight we'd had on Sunday. Shannen had told me to give her space, but I couldn't do it anymore. We'd had enough space. That was the problem. She'd even said it herself. I just hadn't heard her.

Over the past few days I'd realized what she'd meant that night at Chloe's party. How she felt like she hadn't really seen me in a while. Over the summer, when I was with her, some part of my body was always touching some part of hers. Either I was holding her hand on the street or had my leg hooked over hers on the couch or had her head resting on my shoulder. We were always talking about all kinds of stuff—our crazy families, how school could be totally lame and kind of fun at the same time, how weird it was that in a year we would be living somewhere else. Everything. And we laughed. A lot. We were always laughing about something.

I couldn't remember what that felt like anymore. And I think I'd realized that too late.

As I watched her score a three, and the Idiot Twins went berserk, I suddenly felt heart-numbingly sad. Because she was going to break up with me. I could feel it. I knew that when I found her tonight, she was going to say something to end it. Unless I said something to stop her first.

As the final buzzer sounded, I stood up, determined. I'd already lost everything else. I couldn't lose Ally, too.

Ally and the rest of the team slapped hands with the other players. Then everyone gathered around the coach. I made my way along the wall under the backboard and toward the exit that went right to the girls' locker room. I was standing there when the team started to go through, my heart pounding a mile a minute. Shannen shot me a weird look but kept moving. Then Ally was there. Right in front of me. I couldn't breathe.

"Nice game," I said.

She tucked a stray hair behind her ear and looked away. "Thanks."

"I need to talk to you," I said.

"Can this wait? Until I've, like, showered?" she asked quietly. My heart sunk. She was definitely, definitely going to break up with me.

"No. It can't," I said.

She crossed her arms over her chest. Behind her the gym was emptying out. Her coach gave me this scolding look as she went by, but at least she went by.

"Jake—"

"I have something I have to say," I told her. I wiped my sweaty hands on my jeans.

"Okay, fine," she said, lifting her chin. "What?"

I licked my lips. My pulse pounded in my ears. My mind

was a total blank. The guys were hovering by the door to the lobby, waiting for me. My collar itched. The lights in the gym had never been so bright.

"What is it, Jake?"

Then I did the only thing I could think to do. I grabbed her by the waistband of her maroon-and-gold shorts, pulled her to me, and kissed her like I'd never kissed anyone before. I held her sweaty ponytail against the back of her neck and just kissed her and kissed her and kissed her. When she finally pulled back, I didn't let her pull too far. I held on to her as hard as I could.

"I know I suck," I whispered, looking her in the eye, feeling desperate. "I know I don't deserve you. Just don't leave me. Please? I'll be better, okay? Just don't leave me."

Part of me couldn't believe I'd just said anything that pathetic. Now she knew how much she mattered. And I looked like some kind of whipped asshole with no life.

But honestly? I didn't care. I was just kind of glad no one else had heard me.

There was a long, long, long pause. Then Ally buried her face in my sweater and put her arms around me.

"I won't," she said. The fist around my heart finally released. "I won't."

jake

"Dudes. This is *not* a good idea."

I stood in the middle of Dr. Nathanson's study, watching my friends be their usual jackass selves. It was the holiday Sunday night dinner, and Ally's mom was hosting. For whatever reason, the Idiot Twins had decided it would be cool to build one of those wineglass pyramid things on top of the glass coffee table so they could make a champagne waterfall. Of course, we had no wineglasses *or* champagne, since our parents were right down the hall, so they'd spent the last half hour smuggling glasses in from wherever they were kept, two at a time, under their dinner jackets. Ally had no idea what was going on, because she'd disappeared a while ago too—probably helping her mom with something. But I knew she was going to freak when she got back, so I figured it was my duty to stop them. I'd spent the last three weeks being the perfect boyfriend, but if I stood by and watched my friends destroy thousands of dollars of crystal and furniture, I'd be toast.

"Dude. Stop being such a buzz kill," Todd said. He misplaced a glass and it tumbled sideways. I made a grab for it, but it fell right back into his hands.

"Oh. Oops," he said. Then he and his brother doubled over laughing.

"If you guys break anything, you're so dead," I said through my teeth.

"What? Mini-Nate is right there. If she had a problem, she'd say something."

Trevor used the stem end of a glass to point at Quinn. She was standing by the fireplace, which was decorated with about two tons of evergreen branches, flirting with Hammond. The girl looked completely gone over the deep end as she blinked away at the assface I used to call my best friend. I don't think she knew there was anyone else in the room. Chloe and Faith stood a few feet away, shooting them obnoxious looks, which

I didn't get. Chloe didn't like Hammond anymore, right? So what was the big deal if he went after some sophomore?

Girls. Sometimes they made zero sense.

"What are you guys doing?!"

I froze. Ally had just walked up behind me. The Idiot Twins froze too. I turned around, grabbed Ally's hand, and pulled her toward the door at the other end of the room. She was wearing a dark red strapless dress and strappy shoes with a red flower on them and had never looked hotter.

"You saw nothing," I said. "Come with me."

"But they—I—" She pointed back over her shoulder as I dragged her into the next room, which was a smallish, leather-covered TV room—and closed the door behind us.

"If you didn't know about it, there was nothing you could do to stop it," I told her, raising my palms. "I use that excuse every time my brother tries to jump his skateboard off some planter in the backyard. Works every time."

"Good plan." Ally smiled as I slipped my arms around her waist. "I'm not supposed to be in here, you know. This is, like, Gray's man-cave or something," she said, though she made no move to go.

"We were never here," I promised.

Then I kissed her, holding her as close to me as I possibly could without tearing both our clothes off. She clung to my neck and kissed me back, her lips pressed hard against mine. Over the past couple of weeks I had totally noticed a change in the way Ally kissed me. When we first made up, she wasn't that into it, but now she was back to her old self. I guess calling every day, leaving her random presents in her locker, and taking her out on weekends was working. The lucky thing was,

Chloe hadn't been around much this month. She'd stopped calling me and she was never around at lunch. I had no idea who she was hanging out with or where, but except for one doctor's appointment, I hadn't seen her. Which was good for me and Ally.

But Chloe *was* still texting me stuff that was going on with the baby, like that she'd felt it kick, and that she'd set up an appointment for her next sonogram. Ever since the first time I'd seen the baby move, I couldn't stop thinking about it, or the fact that I was never going to get to know it. I mean him. Or her. Whenever I thought about that, I felt this kind of weird, awful tug in the center of my chest. Like I didn't want to miss anything, but I knew I was going to miss everything. So I wanted to be as much a part of its life as I could, even if the baby wasn't born yet. And I also wanted Chloe to know she wasn't alone. Now it was like we'd found the perfect balance. Ally didn't have to have Chloe shoved in her face anymore, but I knew what was up with my spawn.

Spawn. Funny word. Todd had used it one day to describe the baby and it had been stuck in my head ever since.

"What's that?" Ally asked, pulling back suddenly.

I blinked, confused and already missing her lips. "What?"

She pointed at my jacket and I realized. "Oh, right. I almost forgot. Merry Christmas."

I tugged out the long, skinny box and handed it to her.

"Jake! I haven't even wrapped yours yet," she said, smiling.

"I know. It's kind of early. But I thought maybe you could use it tonight," I said. I plopped down on the leather couch and it hissed, the cushion deflating under my butt. "Open it."

She sat next to me and pried open the box. Her jaw dropped when she saw what was inside—a platinum watch in a diamond setting. It wasn't too big or gaudy, because Ally didn't like that stuff, but it was still bling. The saleswoman had called it "tastefully understated." Which sounded like Ally to me.

"Jake! I love it!"

"You always wear a watch, every day, but I noticed you never wear one when we go somewhere fancy, so I figured you needed a fancy watch."

"Fancy? Did you just use the word 'fancy' twice?" she joked. She made to get up from the couch. "I have to go tell the guys."

I grabbed her wrist and pulled her back down again. "Do and die."

Then I pulled her onto my lap—her silky dress made it easy to slide her right on there—and kissed her again. My hands went around her waist, and then I slowly, slowly, slowly moved them upward, holding my breath while I waited for her to stop me. But she didn't. I hadn't even gotten within inches of her boobs in a month, so just feeling them from over her dress was, like, the hottest thing ever right then. I thought she'd pull away, but she only deepened the kiss, pressing herself closer to me, like she wanted more.

Shit. This was the best Sunday night dinner ever.

I shifted a little, giving her a hint I wasn't sure she would take, but she did. She straddled my legs, putting her knees on either side of my thighs, and just like that I was ready to go. I could have had sex with her through our clothes I was so ready. I was just contemplating my next move when—

Crash.

"Oh, fuck," I said under my breath.

Ally jumped up and ran for the door. I couldn't move, thanks to my below-the-waist situation. I closed my eyes and tried to calm my breathing. Tried to think very un-hot thoughts. I wished I had a bucket of ice.

"What are you doing here?"

I blinked. That didn't make any sense as a response to two dozen shattered glasses. And also? Ally hadn't said it. It was Chloe.

Clearing my throat, I got up from the couch. I adjusted myself and buttoned my jacket, hoping to cover up my situation. I stood behind Ally at the door to hide it, but then forgot all about it.

Shannen had just arrived, looking almost hooker-level slutty in a low-cut, shorter-than-short black dress. And she had Will Halloran with her.

ally

Will and Shannen stood in the double-wide doorway, her hand resting lightly on his shoulder. Chloe stood on the other side of the room in her silvery-white maternity dress, her face red with confusion. Between them, on the floor, was about two tons of shattered glass.

"Omigod! Is that my mother's good crystal?!" Quinn cried, tears already streaming from her eyes. "What's the matter with you guys?"

The Idiot Twins backed themselves into a corner fretfully, Todd clutching an unbroken glass.

"It's okay. It's not," I told Quinn, stepping forward, being careful to avoid the destruction. "Your mom's stuff is packed away for you. Those were the new ones my mom just bought."

"Are you sure?" Quinn asked, her bottom lip quivering.

For the first time since I'd known her, I felt protective of her. Maybe I *was* becoming a big sister.

"I'm sure." I looked around at the couple dozen frozen classmates around the room. Half the girls were wearing skimpy high heels. With all the glass, this place could turn into a bloodbath pretty quickly. "I think the party's over in here. Quinn, you want to take everyone into the theater until dinner?"

"Okay. Yeah," she said, sniffling.

She shot the Idiot Twins an uncharacteristically evil look before grabbing Hammond's hand and leading everyone out, skirting the destruction. The only people who didn't move were me, Jake, Chloe, Shannen, and Will. So I guess this was Shannen's plan. Shove everyone in a room together and see what happened. For the past couple of weeks the whole Will situation had seemed less urgent to me—probably because Jake had been back to his old self and had barely mentioned the baby, and Chloe had gone kind of MIA. But apparently Shannen had spent that entire time coming up with and executing this scheme. I only wished that she had warned me, because about two seconds ago I had been seriously considering letting Jake get to second base—maybe even letting him round third. This was like getting shoved into a cold shower.

"Hey, Chloe," Will said.

He slid his hands into the pockets of his gray suit. His light brown, longish hair fell low over his forehead and he looked seriously handsome in a crisp white shirt and red tie. He smiled at Chloe, but she didn't smile back. She was too busy nervously darting her eyes around at the rest of us.

"Hey," she said offhandedly. "What's up?"

He took a step forward, then paused, thinking the better of getting near the glass. "I . . . Shannen told me you had something for me. A Christmas present or something?"

I felt Jake stiffen next to me. The blood drained out of Chloe's face.

"Shannen? Can I talk to you for a second?" Chloe's voice was shrill.

"Sure." Shannen opened her arms at her sides, holding her clutch purse out. "What's up?"

"Not here," Chloe said through her teeth.

She carefully stepped around the outer rim of the crash zone, took Shannen's hand, and dragged her out of the room toward the foyer. Okay. There was no way I was letting this conversation happen without me.

"I'll be right back."

Jake and Will were like roman statues as I chased the other two down. I found them in the hallway between the foyer and the living room. Chloe had practically pinned Shannen against a gilt-framed painting with her baby belly.

"What do you know?" she demanded as I came around the corner.

"I don't know anything," Shannen said innocently. "What do *you* know?"

"Can we just drop the whole wordplay thing?" I said, walking up to them. "We're supposed to be friends here."

They broke eye contact with each other. Chloe turned around, chewing on her thumbnail as she paced to the opposite wall. Shannen stood up straight and waited. Looked like I was going to have to be the one to start.

"Chloe, we know you and Will were going out last summer,"

I whispered as a round of laughter sounded from the garden room, where the adults were indulging in music, cocktails, and hors d'oeuvres.

"And it's obvious he still likes you," Shannen said.

Chloe looked over her shoulder at us. I recognized the look in her eyes as hope. "You think so?"

"Dude. He refused to come here with me until I told him you wanted to see him. Guys don't turn *this* down unless they're jonesing for something else," Shannen said, gesturing at her tight-ass dress.

Chloe bit her lip and looked at the floor.

"Chloe," I said, stepping closer to her. "Is there any possible way that Will could be the father? Because if there is, you *have* to tell him."

When Chloe looked up at me, her eyes were swimming. And I knew. I just knew. My heart felt like it was suspended on a tightrope, hanging on for dear life.

"Jake has been nothing but good to you," I whispered hoarsely. "If the baby's not his, he deserves to know too."

Tears spilled out onto Chloe's cheeks and she sniffled, her nose sounding completely clogged. "Do you have any idea what my parents will do to me?" she whimpered. "Do you have any idea . . . the guy they hired . . . to work on our house. The electrician's son? Do you have *any* idea—?"

"Is he the father?" I demanded, my blood starting to boil. "That's what matters, Chloe. Is Will the father?"

Chloe covered her entire face with her hands and let out a very tortured, very wet "yes."

My mind went weightless. Not "I don't know." Not "maybe." Just "yes." She was that certain.

Then she buckled at the waist and just cried, pressing one hand against the wall to steady her off-kilter body. Shannen shot me a *holy crap* kind of look before putting her arms around Chloe and letting her sob on her shoulder. I took a couple of steps backward and sat down on the skinny bench near the top of the hall. My legs felt numb. My hands felt numb. All the blood rushed to my head and it suddenly weighed ten thousand pounds.

Jake is not the father. Jake is not the father. Jake is not the father.

"Are you sure?" Shannen asked, rubbing Chloe's back.

Chloe nodded into her shoulder. "I didn't know for sure at first. I thought it was Jake's when I first told him because of the timing, but then the doctor told me . . . a while ago . . . when the baby was conceived. I was with Will then. It was, like, a month before Jake and I—"

"How could you do this?" I said quietly, my voice shaking with rage. "How could you do this to him?"

"Ally, I'm so sorry," Chloe said, her face streaked with mascara and eyeliner. "I didn't know what else to do."

"You didn't know what to do other than fuck up Jake's entire life?" I whisper-shouted.

Shannen and Chloe both stared at me. I never cursed. Almost never. So they knew I was serious.

"I just . . . I just . . . I just . . ."

"Just what? You wanted it to be him, right?" I said, thinking of what Annie had said the night of the bonfire, of what Shannen had said when I'd told her. "You couldn't stand the idea that some Norm knocked you up, so you just started lying your ass off."

"Ally," Shannen said. "You know what her parents are like."

"And now you're defending her?" I cried.

"No, I'm just—I'm just saying, I get what she was thinking," Shannen said as she rubbed between Chloe's shoulders. "And it's not like Jake didn't do the deed. He just as easily could have been—"

"Yeah, but he's *not.*"

I turned my back on both of them and tried to catch my breath. I breathed in and out, in and out, listening to Chloe's muted crying. Listening to the sound of my own heart.

Shannen was right about one thing. Nothing mattered more to the Applebys than being the cream of the crop, the A-number-one most revered family on the crest. Chloe would have known that just learning their daughter was pregnant was going to destroy them. It would tarnish their image, it would make them doubt who they were, and it would make everyone look at them differently. But finding out that she was pregnant by some electrician's kid from the other side of town? Yeah, that would probably kill them.

But so what? She couldn't screw with Jake—not to mention Will—just to save face. How could she not see how wrong that was?

"You have to tell him. You have to tell both of them," I said. "Jake has a right to know he's free, and Will deserves a chance to be there for you."

"She's right, Chloe. You've gotta fess up," Shannen said, pushing some of Chloe's hair away from her tears and back from her face.

"I've tried, okay?" Chloe said. "I almost told Jake a million times. And Will, he cornered me at the bonfire as soon as he heard I was pregnant and asked if it was his. I wanted to tell him the truth, but I just couldn't. It physically wouldn't come out of me."

"Well, you have to make it come out," I said firmly.

Chloe shook her head at the floor. "Everyone's going to hate me."

That's what she was worried about? I wanted to scream so badly my throat hurt.

"Chloe, I swear . . . if you don't tell them, I will," I said.

"No," Chloe responded. She took in a deep breath. "I'll tell them. I promise." She turned toward me and made a move to touch me, but thought better of it at the last second. Which was a good thing. Because I wasn't sure what I would have done if she had. "Just let me do it, okay? I don't want them hearing it from someone else."

I glanced at Shannen. She gave me a slight nod.

"Fine," I said with some effort.

"Promise me you won't tell Jake," Chloe said.

Honestly, I wanted to pound her for saying that—for thinking that she had any right to tell me what to do when it came to me and Jake. But my heart hurt just thinking about what his reaction would be. I had an awful feeling he'd be crushed. And I didn't want to be the one to crush him. I shouldn't *have* to be the one to crush him. "I promise I won't tell Jake," I told her flatly. "I'll let you do it. But I swear, Chloe, if you don't do it before New Year's, I will."

Did you guys hear? Will Halloran went to the holiday Sunday dinner.

What? I thought that was Cresties only!

Apparently not anymore. Guess who brought him?

Who?

Shannen Moore.

Oh, well she is a Norm now, I guess.

Then she shouldn't be invited either. This is so unfair.

I cannot believe Shannen's slumming it with a Norm.

Slumming it? Will's totally hot.

Not as hot as Jake Graydon or Hammond Ross. Or even Connor Shale.

Granted. But if he were my boyfriend, I wouldn't care what kind of slums he hung out in.

ally

January seventh. It was January seventh. It had been almost three weeks since Chloe had confessed. We'd been back in school for five days. My deadline had come and gone. She couldn't use holiday break and the fact that the major players had been scattered on various vacations as an excuse anymore. She saw Jake every day. She saw Will every day. And she still hadn't told.

Of course I hadn't told either, but I kept telling myself it wasn't my responsibility. I kept hoping she'd live up to her end of the bargain and do the right thing. But I kept being disappointed.

I couldn't take it anymore. My body was filled from head to toe with white-hot, indignant fury. Every second of every minute of every hour of every day. If I didn't do something soon, I was going to explode. Or punch Chloe in the face. Which probably wouldn't do much for my karma—flattening a pregnant girl.

As soon as the bell rang on Friday afternoon I practically sprinted to Chloe's locker. Jake was already on a bus to an away swim meet, so there was nothing she would be able to do right now, but she lived across the street from him. She could practically spit on his bedroom window from her own. If I had anything to say about it, today was the day Jake would be set free.

Chloe was slowly placing books inside her backpack. The moment she saw me coming she started to work a hell of a lot faster.

"Hey, Ally," she said, closing her locker door as I arrived. "I'm just on my way to—"

"You're telling him today," I said through my teeth. My fingers curled into fists and I had this awful feeling that if she said anything other than "okay," I was going to hurt her.

"I . . . I can't," she said, glancing nervously past me down the hall.

I cupped one fist with the other hand. "Yes, you can. You promised me, Chloe. You promised me you'd do it by New Year's."

"I know, but . . . we're meeting the parents tomorrow," Chloe said, adjusting her backpack straps over her shoulders. "The adoptive parents? They want to meet both of us. Apparently it's important to them to talk to both the baby's parents and—"

"Then maybe you should invite Will," I said through my teeth.

Chloe took a deep breath, as if for patience. Was she kidding me? She was going to stand there and act as if I was making an unreasonable request? Buttoning her coat over her boat-size belly, she started to walk slowly down the center of the hall. I fell right into step with her.

"But Jake's excited about it too," Chloe said, averting her eyes every time someone turned to stare at her stomach. "If I tell him now . . . he's going to be devastated."

"And telling him after he meets these people will be so much better?" I said.

We reached the end of the hallway. A right turn led to the lobby. A left to the gym. Down the hall behind her I could see a bunch of guys from the basketball team messing around, downing Gatorades before hitting the weight room. Will was one of them, his maroon-and-gold b-ball shorts hanging low.

"Ally, this is hard enough," Chloe said, taking an almost condescending tone. "Just let me get through this weekend, and then I promise I will tell him."

Will glanced over at us, checking Chloe out in a longing sort of way. I blinked, and it was as if I was being cooled by a calming breeze. Just like that, my anger was washed away. Just like that, I saw everything with perfect crystal clarity. I knew what I had to do.

"Fine," I said.

Chloe pulled back, surprised. "Fine?"

"Yes. Fine. Whatever you say," I told her, pressing my lips into a thin line. "It's your baby."

"Thank you," she said, relief crossing her face, flattening the worry lines on her brow. She started past me, headed for the lobby. "I'll see you at Annie's party tomorrow night!" she said brightly, like we were just two friends chatting.

"You're going to Annie's party?" I asked, shocked.

Annie hated Chloe. She hated all Cresties. Except Jake. But especially Chloe. What was this about? And why hadn't Annie told me?

"I know. I was surprised too," Chloe said, lifting her hands and shoulders. "Later."

Then she traipsed off toward the lobby. Well, more like trudged. I suppose it's hard to traipse when you're carrying an extra thirty pounds or so.

Slowly I turned around to face the gym again. The guys were busy being guylike, laughing and shoving one another like they always seem to do. I took a breath, squared my shoulders, and steeled myself. My heart pounded with uncertainty, but my mind was completely made up. Chloe was clearly never going to

come clean. She'd made a promise and was continually breaking it. The girl may have been pregnant, but that didn't mean
she could do whatever she wanted. That didn't mean she could
lie to everyone. I was doing the right thing.

Besides, I'd promised her I wouldn't tell Jake, but I'd never
said a thing about Will.

I stepped up next to the pack of guys. They stopped talking
to look me up and down in my hugely sexy baggy jeans and
long-sleeved T-shirt.

"Will?" I said.

He dragged the back of his hand across his mouth, clearing
away the red Gatorade mustache he was sporting.

"Hey, Ally," he said. "What's up?"

I clenched my jaw. "We need to talk."

ally

"I can't believe I never realized that Will was the real father,"
Annie said as she stood on her tiptoes on the top platform of a
rickety step stool in her basement. The whole thing leaned to
the left and David and I both lunged to steady it, but she didn't
even notice. She just tacked the end of the colorfully striped
streamer into the corner near the ceiling, then jumped down.

"Yeah, well, maybe that's because you're not evil like some
people," I said, tossing the streamer wrapper into the trash.

"Um, yes she is," David said.

Annie picked up a stuffed jelly bean and threw it at his head.
It was Saturday afternoon, and the three of us were decorating
for her birthday party that night. Annie had decided on a candy

theme, so we'd spent the last hour in her basement stringing rainbow-colored streamers, sticking huge paper M&M's, lollipops, and peppermints to the walls, and filling up a zillion colorful balloons. She'd blown her entire paycheck on employee-discounted lollipops, Hershey's kisses, peanut M&M's, Jolly Ranchers, jelly beans, and caramels, which overflowed from bowls crammed onto the bookshelves and tables. It was only five o'clock and I was already so hopped up on mindlessly consumed sugar I felt like I was having a heart attack.

"*I* can't believe you actually invited Chloe to your party," I said, filling another balloon with helium from the rented tank. "What's *that* about?"

Annie shrugged, turning away from me with a paper M&M and some tacks. "Nothing."

My eyes met David's across the room. Uh-oh. "That was not a *nothing* nothing," he said. "That was a *something* nothing."

"Annie, please don't tell me you've got, like, a bucket of green slime set up for her or something like that," I said. As much as I hated Chloe right now, she didn't need any more public humiliation. She just needed to tell the truth already.

"What, like she doesn't deserve it?" Annie countered, shoving the tack through the paper and into the wall.

"Annie!" David and I said in unison.

"Oh my God, no. I don't have a bucket of slime, okay?" Annie said, raising her hands in surrender. "The truth is I sent out the invites in the five minutes between everyone finding out about her quote-unquote *shameful situation*, and us figuring out the Will thing. I kind of felt . . . bad for her."

My jaw dropped. "You felt bad for Chloe Appleby?"

Annie hung her head. "I know, I know. I could flog myself."

"Whatever," David said, taking the filled balloon from my hand and tying it off. "She's just one person. She's not gonna make or break the party."

"True dat," Annie replied.

They bumped fists and got back to work on the streamers as I busied myself with balloons, wondering if Will had talked to Chloe yet. He'd been stunned when I told him the news yesterday in the hall. He'd said he asked Chloe about it himself the night of the bonfire and she'd sworn the baby wasn't his. Big shock there. I couldn't believe how casually she was going around lying to people she was supposed to care about. And now, tonight, Will, Jake, Chloe, and I were going to be in the same place. Together. Like four pieces of a social time bomb that, if assembled just the right way, could take out the whole party.

David and Annie laughed over something and I chewed on my lip. It was a good thing Annie lived for Crestie scandal. Because I had a feeling that I'd already set up the best birthday present the girl could ever wish for. Big-Time Drama.

ally

"The mom makes movie soundtracks for a living," Jake said that night as David's band, Controlled Chaos, screeched into a heavy-metal version of happy birthday. "Who knew you could even do something that cool as a job? And the guy coaches soccer. It was, like, meant to be."

"Yeah. I guess," I muttered.

On the other side of the room, Will stood with a few of his friends, his body rigid as he watched the band. Now and then I caught him glancing over his shoulder at us, and every time he did I tensed. Had he talked to Chloe yet? What if he said something to Jake before Chloe had a chance to?

Why, why, why had I gotten myself even deeper into this mess?

"I wonder where Chloe is," Jake said, checking his watch, his knee bending and straightening awkwardly to the beat. Well, roughly to the beat, anyway. He checked the stairs, which were partially obscured by a million strands of plastic M&M's beads. "I thought she'd be here by now."

"I just can't believe Annie invited her," I said, reaching for another handful of chocolate-covered pretzels.

Jake plucked one from my hand and popped it into his mouth. It made me think of Lincoln, and I suddenly wondered what he was doing right now. What life would be like if I'd kissed him that night at Faith's. It was so weird how I could be seriously considering kissing someone one day, and then a few weeks later have zero contact with him. Just thinking about it made me blush. Luckily Jake didn't notice. Or if he did, he didn't ask about it.

"Why not?" he asked.

"Why not what?"

"Why can't you believe Annie invited Chloe?"

I blinked. Was it possible that he was that clueless to what went on around him? Guys and oblivion. They seemed to go hand in hand.

"Because they've always hated each other," I said with a serious "duh" tone.

"Really? Why?" Jake said, his brow knit.

I just rolled my eyes and ate another pretzel.

Just then the door to the basement slammed closed and a few people flinched. Minutes later, Chloe came teetering down the stairs, clinging to the railing as if for dear life. Even hugely pregnant, she was more stylishly dressed than half the girls in the room. She wore a black bias-cut skirt and a hot pink sweater with a boat neck and fluttery sleeves. Her skin was dewy with makeup and her light brown hair had been curled and pulled back from her face, just a few tendrils scooping around her cheeks. Jake stepped away from the wall at her arrival and she brightened at the sight of him, fluttering a wave in our direction. Looking for an open pathway through the crowded basement, she turned sideways to try to slide over, but she'd barely taken a step when Will was right in front of her.

My heart hit my throat and choked off my air supply. The music was loud enough that I couldn't hear every word, but not so loud that a few didn't make it through. Words like:

"Tell me?"

"Lying?"

and

"Loved you."

Suddenly Chloe's skin wasn't quite so dewy anymore.

"What's his deal?" Jake asked me, his nostrils kind of flaring.

Chloe shot us a helpless look, then reached for Will's hand. He yanked it away and, at that moment, David's rendition of "Happy Birthday" finally came to a wailing, pounding end.

"Just tell me! Am I the father or not?!" Will shouted.

"What?" Jake blurted.

The basement was so silent you could have heard a jelly

179

bean drop. Will looked around, clearly embarrassed, and Chloe started shaking.

"Chloe?" Jake said, walking toward her. Everyone got out of his way. "What's going on?"

Chloe put one hand on her stomach and reached for Jake with the other. He automatically supported her arm, which it looked like she very much needed. Annie watched the action hungrily from the corner, and . . . was that a video camera in her hand? I felt so hot I thought I might faint.

"I can't," Chloe said. "I can't—"

"Just tell me, Chloe," Will said quietly, gently. "If I'm the father . . . you have to tell me."

"Dude. Back the fuck off," Jake said.

"Maybe you're the one who should back off, *dude*," Will said sarcastically, his face reddening. "I was with her for three months. I was in love with her. Who the hell are you?"

"I'm the father, asshole," Jake shot back.

And Chloe just stood there. Shaking. She looked like she was about to faint. Some people might have enjoyed this—might have enjoyed watching Chloe squirm after everything she'd done. Some people might have even relished it. But apparently that just wasn't me, because all I could think about was that this was my fault. At least this part of it. I'd brought this awful scene—the whispers, the staring, the suspense—to life. And now I had to do something to make it stop before it got any worse.

"Chloe," I said loudly. *"Say something."*

Everyone turned to stare at me. Everyone but Chloe. Chloe was looking at the floor. The questions, the fear, in Jake's eyes nearly killed me. Slowly Chloe drew her arm away from Jake.

"No, Jake," she said finally. "You're not the father."

"What?" Jake breathed.

Will brought his hand to his forehead.

"It was Will. It's Will's baby," Chloe whispered, her voice catching.

"Holy shit." Will sat down on the nearest chair, bringing both hands to his mouth. "Holy, holy, holy shit."

"But you said . . ." Jake looked around at the practically drooling audience, then lowered his voice, leaning toward Chloe's ear. "You said you two never—"

Will snorted. "You said that?" he asked Chloe. "And you believed that?" he said to Jake.

Jake went white. Almost gray.

"I'm not the father?" he said, stepping away from her.

"Jake, I am *so* sorry," Chloe said, tears streaming down her cheeks. "I wanted to tell you so many times. At that first sonogram, I almost did, but I—"

Jake backed away farther, his heel knocking into an old CD rack and rattling everything on the shelves. "I don't believe this."

"I'm sorry," Chloe said again, quietly, looking at the floor. "I don't know what to say."

But it didn't matter that she didn't know what to say. Because Jake was already gone. He took the basement steps in two leaps and slammed the door so hard a dozen strands of beads slapped to the floor, bursting from their strings and rolling over the tile.

That was when I knew for sure I was right. Jake had wanted to be the father. His heart was broken. And there was nothing I could do to unbreak it.

jake

I found my mother and father sitting in the kitchen with HGTV on the mini flat-screen, eating Thai takeout. My legs felt stiff as I walked in and tossed my keys onto the counter. My fingertips tingled. Everything looked dull, from the marble counters to the wooden cabinets to the glare of the lights reflected in the sliding glass doors.

I was not the father. It was over. I was free.

"Jake." My dad drew my name out slowly, his fork suspended over his noodles. He looked at me like he thought I might crack. "You're home early."

"Everything okay?" my mother asked.

I pressed my fingertips into the top of the island. Pressed down as hard as I could. Gritted my teeth. My eyes felt like they were about to pop. I actually thought I might cry.

My mother and father exchanged a concerned look. She got up and came over to me. Her hand was on my hand.

"Jake, honey? What's wrong?"

I just stared. I felt like I couldn't breathe. What was wrong with me? This was not what freedom was supposed to feel like. In my pocket, my phone vibrated for the hundredth time since I'd left the party.

"I'm not the father," I said. My eyes flicked to hers. I watched them flood with hope, and I wanted to hit something.

"What?" my father said, standing.

My mother's hands fluttered to cover her mouth.

"I'm not the father," I said again, the words like sour milk in my mouth. I backed up from the island. "I'm not the father. Some other guy is."

"Oh my God! Jake! Thank God!" my mother exclaimed.

"I knew it. I knew we should have forced that paternity test," my father said, standing next to her now. "We could have known this so much sooner."

Suddenly *he* was what I wanted to hit. Didn't he get it? Didn't he get that none of that mattered? I was not the father. The baby was *not* mine. That was all that mattered. I turned around and started out the door of the kitchen.

"Jake? What's wrong? This is fantastic news!" my mother shouted after me.

I had a zillion comebacks on the tip of my tongue. Of course they thought it was good news. Of course they did. They never understood why I cared. Why I wanted to go to the doctor with her. Why it mattered. They never got it. They never fucking got it.

I tore up the stairs and into my room, slamming my door as hard as I could. Staring at me from the center of my classic sports car calendar was the date of Chloe's next doctor's appointment. I ripped the calendar down from the wall and hurled it across the room. I whipped my coat off and threw that, too. What I wanted to do more than anything was go back to Annie's house and find Chloe. I wanted to find her and shake her and ask her why she'd done this to me. How long had she known? Why had she made me be there for her, made me care about this? What the hell was she thinking?

I covered my face with both hands and tried to think. I tried to see this how my parents saw it. I tried to focus on what was supposed to be positive.

The baby wasn't mine. So what? It was never going to be mine anyway. It wasn't like I'd been planning on taking it and raising it and being its dad. The second it was born, those people we'd met this afternoon were going to take it away and I was never going to see it again anyway. So who the fuck cared?

And now . . . now I wasn't even going to have to be there. I wouldn't have to be at the hospital, I wouldn't have to hold Chloe's hand, I wouldn't have to see her cry. I was off the hook. That was Will Halloran's problem now. That baby in the sonograms, the one I'd seen roll over that day, the one I'd wondered about being a soccer player like me . . .

It wasn't going to be. Because it had nothing to do with me.

My phone vibrated again. I took it out of my pocket and threw that across the room too. Then I flung myself down on my bed face-first, covered my head with my pillow, and tried to breathe.

Tried as hard as I could not to be the pussy who cried at being let off the hook.

ally

On Sunday afternoon, Chloe was curled up in her bed, half under the covers with graham cracker crumbs scattered across her chest, watching *The Vampire Diaries* on DVD with the drapes closed. She looked over at me and squinted as I opened the door.

"Can you please close that?" she said, her voice whiny. "It's too bright."

This was very not good.

I closed the door behind me. She lifted a remote from the bed, paused the picture on a highly flattering half-naked shot of Damon Salvatore, and let her hand drop again. Crumbs bounced off her pink flowered comforter and onto the hardwood floor.

"So are you in training to *be* a vampire?" I joked lamely.

Chloe sighed and brushed more crumbs off her belly. "I think I shouldn't go to parties anymore. Parties and me don't mesh well." Pressing her hands down at her sides, she shimmied her way up into a sort of half-seated position.

I swallowed hard, my guilt trying to choke off my air supply. "It's my fault, Chloe. I told Will."

"I know. He told me," she said, averting her eyes.

"I'm so sorry—" we both said at the same time.

I stopped talking. She laughed ruefully. "Me first?" she suggested, raising her eyebrows.

"Okay."

I sat down at the end of her bed. A small amount of light peeked in from a crack between two curtains and emanated from the TV screen behind me. I felt tense. Like I shouldn't get comfortable. I was so shocked she had let me in that it was like I was afraid to make any sudden movements—like I might startle her into recalling that I was the enemy. So I just sat there, half-turned toward her, my legs dangling awkwardly toward the floor.

"I'm sorry for what I did to Jake . . . and to you," she began, picking up a crumb and crushing it between her thumb and forefinger. She kept her eyes on the bedspread. "It was wrong. I know it was. I just . . . didn't know what else to do. Will and I had broken up already when I found out about the baby, and Jake . . . he's a good guy. He's a friend. He's . . . I don't know . . . safe? It felt safer than . . . the alternative."

The alternative being the truth.

But I didn't want to get angry again. I was tired of being angry. I wanted to give her a chance to explain. I did. Because I wanted a chance too.

"And then, all of a sudden, the whole thing was out of control," Chloe continued, her eyes filling rapidly. "And everyone was talking about me. Everyone had an opinion. Everyone had something to say—most of it horrible. And meanwhile my back hurts and my ass is, like, huge, and I've got gas *all the time*, and my boobs? My boobs started leaking last week! Right in the middle of French class!"

My jaw dropped. Leaking boobs? What the hell was that about?

"I know!" Chloe said off my expression. "This whole thing is disgusting and I just want it to be over." She covered her eyes and sniffled. "But at the same time, I keep catching myself talking to it—to the baby—like it's in the room with me. And sometimes I think . . . I can't wait to meet him or her. And then I realize I can't. Because everyone says if I do, I'll want to keep it and I can't . . . I can't . . . keep it."

Chloe hiccupped and then started crying in earnest. My heart felt like it was tearing to pieces, and not in some neat, ordered way. More like some animal was going at it with its claws.

"It was so much . . . I just couldn't deal," she said through her tears. "I couldn't deal with Jake and Will and the truth. I just couldn't."

"God, Chloe, I had no idea," I said. "I mean, I knew it had to be hard, but I had *no* idea how bad it was."

She started to say something but couldn't get it out past the crying. Her nose was swollen and her eyes were like slits, but I found myself staring at her belly. That big mound where her flat abs used to be. It must have weighed a ton, or at least felt like it did. As guilty as I'd felt when I walked into the room, that feeling was suddenly compounded eighty times over. I had never considered how Chloe was feeling. I'd had fleeting thoughts about it, sure, but most of my focus had been on Jake. How unfair this was to him, how it was affecting his life. But clearly it was affecting Chloe's a hell of a lot more. Just because she couldn't resist a hot guy one summer night.

I was never having sex. I decided right then and there. Fit me for a chastity belt, stat.

"Can you . . . I need a tissue. . . ." Chloe said, catching her breath.

She was reaching toward her side table but couldn't quite grasp the box. I jumped up, grabbed it, and handed it to her. She blew her nose spectacularly and let her hands drop again.

"I'm sorry. Crying is, like, my number one pastime lately," she said, attempting a sad smile.

"I think you have the world's greatest excuse," I replied.

She toyed with the crumpled-up tissue and sniffled loudly. "Do you hate me?"

"No," I said truthfully. "I don't hate you."

"Does Jake hate me?"

She looked up through her lashes hopefully. I took a steadying breath.

"Honestly? I don't know. He hasn't answered my texts or calls since last night. I was thinking about going over there next, but—"

"Well, if you see him, just tell him I'm so sorry, okay? I didn't mean for it to go this far," Chloe said.

I looked down at the floor and nodded. For some reason I suddenly didn't want to go over to Jake's. All I wanted to do was go back to Gray's, curl up in a ball, and not uncurl till morning.

"Okay," I said.

There was a knock on her door and it opened a crack. Will Halloran stuck his head in, blinking in the darkness.

"Hey," he said, looking between the two of us warily. "Can I come in?"

"Um, sure." Chloe suddenly sat up straight, swiped under her eyes with her fingertips, and brushed the crumbs off her shirt. I handed her another tissue and made a wiping motion at my nose. She blew again and gave me a grateful look. Gross as it was, I swiped her snotty tissues and shoved them in the pocket of my peacoat, which I'd never taken off.

"Hey, Ally," Will said as he awkwardly stepped toward me. He had a box of Entenmann's chocolate chip cookies with him—Chloe's favorite. "Hey, Chlo."

"Hi," she replied.

"I guess I should go," I said. As I turned around I saw Damon's chest glistening on the screen. I grabbed the remote and hit the power button, then opened one of the curtains a bit so Will and Chloe could see each other. "I'll see you guys at school."

"Hey, Ally?" Chloe said.

I paused with my hand on the doorknob.

"Thanks," she said. "For being so cool."

I blushed, embarrassed. I felt anything but cool. I felt like an immature jerk who really needed to stop being so self-involved.

But Will and Chloe were looking into each other's eyes now and this was clearly not the time to bare my soul.

"You're welcome," I said.

But I don't think either one of them heard me. They had already started whispering to each other when I closed the door.

jake

Monday morning I faked a stomachache. Then I stayed in bed until noon. Around two thirty I went over to my dad's home office, which had the only window that looked out at Chloe's front door. I could see her driveway from my room, but once a car got behind the hedge, nada. And I wanted to make sure I saw Chloe come home. I had to make sure I didn't miss her.

So I sat there in his ergonomic chair and waited. And waited. I squeezed on his stress-ball thing. And waited. I crumpled about a hundred pieces of paper and launched them at his trash can. And waited. Then it was three thirty and it was clear Chloe hadn't gone to school either. Or if she had, she wasn't coming back at a normal time.

"Fuckin A," I said under my breath. I ran downstairs, grabbed my ski jacket on the way out, and sprinted across to Chloe's. Instead of climbing to her room this time, I just walked in the front door. The place was deserted and quiet like a graveyard. I went up to her bedroom. She wasn't there. I went back down to the media room. She wasn't there. I finally found her in the library, lying on a couch, reading. She almost had a heart attack when I walked in.

"Jake!" She sat up straight. "Hi!"

She looked good. Neat. Happy. Her hair was in a ponytail and she had on a tight white T-shirt and a loose gray sweater. The sight of her looking so relaxed and happy made me want to slam that heavy book on her fingers.

"What the fuck, Chloe?" I said, striding around the couch. "What the fuck were you thinking?"

She went white, which was at least a little satisfying, and pushed herself up straight. Or as straight as she could get in her condition.

"Did Ally not talk to you?"

I blinked. "What? No. I haven't been up for talking."

And what would Ally say to me that would make Chloe look better, anyway? Ally was on my side.

"Oh." She cleared her throat. "I'm really sorry, Jake," she said, looking down at her hands. "I don't know what else to say, but I'm—"

"You don't know what else to say?" I shouted, hovering over her. "Do you even realize what you did to me? Ally and I almost broke up over this! I tanked the first semester! I tanked the frickin' SAT! I might not get into college now, and for what? Because you felt like fucking with my head."

Chloe struggled her way up from the couch. Her stomach sort of hovered between us like a planet. I used to think it was kind of mesmerizing, but now the sight of it made me want to hurl.

"I didn't do this to mess with you," she said. "I was confused, okay? I didn't know what to do."

"Well, here's a newsflash, Chloe," I spat back. "Next time you want to slut it up with more than one guy and get yourself knocked up, make sure you saddle the right one with all the crap."

I never even saw the slap coming. She wailed me across the face so hard my dry bottom lip split.

"Fuck you," I said, my cheek on fire.

"Right back at you," she replied, shaking.

I turned around and stormed out of the house, slamming the heavy door behind me as hard as I could. My fingers clenched into fists as I booked it down the driveway, the frigid air stinging my face where she'd slapped me.

I couldn't believe she'd slapped me. She had ruined my life and she thinks I deserve a smack? How self-centered and completely insane could one bitch be? I couldn't believe I had ever thought Chloe Appleby was cool. Clearly she was pure, unadulterated evil.

I came around the bend in my driveway and slowed down. Ally was sitting on the front step. She scrambled to her feet when she saw me.

"Hey! No one answered the door so—" She paused and narrowed her eyes at me. "Are you all right?"

I touched my fingertips to my lip and they came back bloody.

"No, okay? I'm not all right," I said, striding toward her.

"What happened?" she asked, her breath making steam clouds in the air. "Your face is red." Then her eyes widened. "Did you just get in a fight?"

"What?" I scoffed, pausing next to her. "No."

She went to touch my cheek, but I flinched away.

"Well, good," she said, shoving her hands under her arms. "Because Hammond already pounded on Will after school today, so—"

"Yeah?" I said, imagining Will Halloran's smug face purple and swollen and gross. "Good for him."

191

Maybe Hammond wasn't such a dick after all.

"Good for him?" Ally said, her face screwing up. "What did Will do?"

"Will exists, okay?" I shot back, even though it sounded completely stupid. "Will is the reason I'm in this mess."

"No. He's not," Ally said. "At least, he's not the only reason."

Great. Now she was going to get on my case about how if I'd never had sex with Chloe in the first place, none of this ever would have happened. Which was true, of course. Which was why I'd been saying it to myself over and over and over again all weekend. All month. All frickin' year. I didn't need her rubbing my face in it like a holier-than-thou priss right now.

"I have to go," I said, shoving past her.

I opened the door and went inside.

"Jake—"

"I'll call you later," I lied.

Then I closed the door on her half-pissed, half-disappointed face.

jake

WAY 2 BAIL LOSER. U BETTER B SPITTING UP BLOOD.

I turned off my phone after the tenth angry text from my swim teammates and tossed it onto the coffee table. They were pissed that I'd missed today's meet, but if I had my way, I'd be missing a lot more. When I'd talked my mother into letting me stay home again she'd said fine, but I was going on Wednesday no matter what. Yeah. We'd see about that.

What was the point, anyway? College applications were due,

like, now. I'd scored myself a solid low-C average for the first
half of the year, and those were the grades they were going to
see. Who cared if I flunked the rest of the year? I saw no point
in sitting in class for the next six months. It was over. I was
going to community college. If I was lucky.

The doorbell rang and I stayed where I was, on the couch
in front of the Duke-Clemson basketball game. Then I heard
footsteps behind me.

"Hey."

I turned around, stunned. "Ally."

She was the only person I hadn't gotten a text from today, so
I figured she was mad about me blowing her off yesterday. Her
being here now was a surprise.

"Feeling any better?" she asked.

She came around the side of the sectional couch and sat
down next to me, but kept a safe distance.

"Um, yeah," I muted the TV and sat up straight. "Sorry
about yesterday. I got into it with Chloe and—"

"Yeah. She told me."

My face felt hot. "She *told* you? I can't believe you're even
speaking to—"

Ally held up a hand. "I don't want to talk about Chloe.
Actually I think we should talk about anything other than
Chloe."

I motorboated my lips and slumped back again. "Sounds
good to me."

"So . . . I talked to the coach at Rutgers today," she said, putting on a bright smile as she shimmied out of her coat.

"Yeah?" I said.

"Looks like I'm going to be a Lady Knight," Ally said.

I felt this ridiculous surge of excitement, followed by complete jealousy. "Yeah? That's great!" I reached over and hugged her.

"I know, right?" Ally said. "She said to send my application through her and it would be taken care of."

I crossed my arms over my chest as I sat back again. "You sure you want to stay so close to home? I thought UNC was calling your name."

Ally lifted one shoulder. "I don't know. Rutgers has a great program and they need forwards right now, so I might actually get playing time next year. Plus it feels far enough away that I can live there, but close enough that if I get homesick I *can* come home. I think it'll be good."

"Good," I said. *And if I'm at Bergen Community next year, I'll get to see you whenever you do get homesick.*

"So what about you? How're the applications coming?" Ally asked, bouncing back on the couch, and a little closer to me.

"They're nonexistent," I replied.

"What?" she asked.

I shrugged, picked up the remote again, and turned up the sound. The Duke fans were chanting while the timer ticked down. "What's the point? I'm not getting in anywhere, so . . ."

"They don't just look at your grades, you know," Ally said, sounding very cheerleader-y. "There's your sports and your job . . . and you aced a college course last summer. That has to count for something."

I scoffed. When I thought about that class, I thought about Chloe, who'd taken it with me. And thinking about Chloe was dangerous at the moment.

"Right, so how am I supposed to explain my two-point-oh average after acing a college class?" I said, turning my palms up. "'Sorry, admissions board, I got lazy'?"

Ally chewed on the inside of her cheek for a second. She rested the side of her head on her hand, her elbow on the back of the couch. Then she sat up straight.

"I've got it! The essay!" she said, grinning.

"What do you mean?"

"You explain the first two semesters' grades with your essay! You tell the truth!" she exclaimed.

I laughed so hard I thought my ribs might crack. "Are you serious?"

"I'm totally serious!" Ally pulled her school-issued laptop out of her bag and powered it up. "Everyone wants a personal statement, right? So we write an essay about the pregnancy scare, how much it affected you, how much it *changed* you . . . but most important, how it matured you and made you see what's important in life."

I blinked. "What's that?"

She rolled her eyes at me. "Hard work. Getting good grades. Planning a future. The admissions people live for a good life lesson learned. They'll be eating out of your hands!"

I muted the TV again and sat up straight. I did dimly recall one of the lecturers at one of our many college-planning assemblies saying something about admitting faults to the interviewers. Something about how no one was perfect and admissions boards hated it when people pretended they were.

"Dude. This could actually work," I said.

"See? Something good could come out of all of this," she replied happily.

Out of nowhere, I felt mushy and choked up. I stared at Ally as she opened up Word and started a new document. What had I done to deserve a girlfriend like her? I'll tell you what: nothing. Zippo. Nada. She'd stuck by me through the miles and miles of crap with Chloe. I'd slammed a door in her face just yesterday and now here she was, helping me. Either she was completely deranged, or she honestly did love me.

"Ally?" I said.

"Yeah?"

"You're kind of awesome, you know that, right?" I said.

Ally grinned. "I do feel rather awesome right now."

I cracked up. "Good. Because you are."

Then I leaned in to kiss her and she kissed me back.

"Okay. Now that that's out of the way, let's start writing," she said.

As we got down to business, I made my first New Year's resolution. From here on out I was going to be the best boyfriend ever. Now that Chloe and the baby were out of the picture, I could focus my energy on Ally. And I was going to do whatever it took to deserve her.

ally

When the doorbell rang on Wednesday afternoon, my mom and I both went to get it at the same time. She glanced outside and paused.

"Who is it?" I asked.

"It's your father," she replied, her tone unreadable.

My heart skipped a nervous beat. I hadn't been alone with both my parents since last summer, and none of those meetings had gone very well. At least if he was going to show up at our doorstep, he'd picked a moment when Gray was at work and Quinn was at musical rehearsal. My mother took a deep breath and opened the door. Dad stood on the flagstone porch wearing his coat and hat and clinging to about a dozen red, black, and white balloons.

"Hello, Christopher," my mother said coolly.

"Melanie," he replied with a nod. Then he turned his attention my way. "Congratulations, kiddo!" he shouted, shoving a huge gift bag at me. He pulled me into a hug, and the balloon ribbons tangled around our arms.

"Um, thanks!" I said as my mother closed the door behind him. "What's with the gift?"

"Open it up!" he said happily, shoving his hands under his arms.

His wool hat was pulled low over his brow, and his nose was red from the cold. He made no move to take off his coat, and my mom didn't ask him to. Feeling a little awkward standing in the middle of Gray's marble foyer with my estranged parents, I put the bag on the floor and tugged out the tissue paper. Inside was a huge black teddy bear wearing a red Rutgers sweatshirt.

"This is so cute!" I said, turning it around to show my mom.

"Aw, Chris. You didn't have to do that," my mother said, smiling nonetheless. Well, at least she was thawing.

"Are you kidding? It's not every day your only daughter decides on a college," my father said. "There's more in there, you know."

I pawed through the bag and found a black Rutgers hoodie, a set of Rutgers pencils, a laptop cover, a pair of flannel pj pants, a coffee mug, and a Scarlet Knight bobble head.

"Where did you get this stuff?" I asked, gathering the swag up in my arms.

"I had the day off, so I drove down there and pretty much cleaned out the bookstore," my dad told us. "I'm so proud of you, kiddo."

"Thanks, Dad." I piled the many gifts back into the bag and gave him a hug.

"And I was thinking . . . maybe I could take you out to dinner?" he asked, looking at the both of us. "To celebrate?"

"Both of us?" my mom squeaked.

"Yes, it would be the three of us," my father said, his voice just the slightest bit sarcastic. "Mel, I know you've moved on, and I've accepted that. At least, I'm working on accepting it. But something tells me that Ally might like it if the three of us could be alone together without a fight breaking out. I'm willing to give it a shot if you are."

My pulse raced as I waited for my mom to answer, and I knew my face looked like a hopeful puppy's. My dad was right. I would pretty much kill to spend some regular family-time with my parents, and with the wedding planning and Gray always being around, I was starting to think it might never be a possibility.

"Please, Mom?" I said. "Gray's not getting home till late anyway, right?"

"And Quinn's going over to Lauren's after rehearsal . . . ," my mom said, thinking aloud. I bit my lip. My dad seemed to be holding his breath. "All right. Why not?"

She went to the closet to grab our coats, and my dad and I exchanged a grin. For the first time in a long time I wasn't thinking about Jake or Chloe or the baby or anything else. I mean, I knew one dinner wasn't going to change anything big—my mom was still getting married, of course—but it felt like, in some small way, I had my family back. And at the moment, that was all that mattered.

ally

At school, things got bad for Chloe fast. Everyone was texting crap about her, giggling behind her back in the halls, whispering and snickering whenever she walked by. She tried to ignore it, but it seemed like there were unshed tears in her eyes every minute of the day. It had been bad enough when she was just pregnant, but now that she was onto her second baby daddy, the whole school was buzzing with amused disgust. Someone wrote the word SLUT on her locker in indelible marker. Her Facebook page got so bad she had to block almost everyone. And next to her picture in the hallway—the one announcing that she'd won most likely to succeed—the words had been taped over with a sign that read MOST LIKELY TO GET VD.

If I didn't hate my school before, I did now.

The deluge of crap she was dealing with made it that much harder to hold on to any residual anger and resentment I had toward her. Instead I felt sorry for her and indignant on her behalf. And now my rage was focused on everyone else.

One afternoon, Jake and I were hanging out by his locker, making plans to get me to his away swim meet, when Chloe and Will came walking down the center of the hall together. Will was the only bright spot I could see in the pregnancy fog. The two of them had been inseparable since that day he'd come to visit her at her house with the cookies, and nothing seemed to faze him. Not name-calling, not graffiti, not the fight with Hammond, nothing.

"Hey, Chloe. Are you *sure* it's Will's this time? 'Cause, you know, maybe it's mine!" some jackass from the football team shouted after them as they neared Jake's locker. "I know you were a little drunk that night, baby, but don't you remember me?"

Will's jaw clenched as his teammates cackled. So much for being unfazeable. I had a feeling he was about five seconds away from another throwdown.

"Just ignore them," I said under my breath, but loud enough for Will and Chloe to hear. "Their heads are so far up their asses they can't see daylight."

Will managed a smirk, but Chloe was too busy staring at the floor. Or she would have been if her massive belly hadn't been in the way. She lifted her eyes slowly and looked at Jake, who was busy shoving things in and out of his locker. Things he'd already shoved in and out.

"Hey, Jake," she greeted him hopefully.

"I gotta get to the bus," Jake said, slamming his locker door closed and tugging on my arm. "Let's go."

I felt prickly and sick as I shot an apologetic look at Chloe. As far as I knew, Jake hadn't spoken a word to her since their fight, and it didn't look like he was about to start today.

"I'll call you later," I said as I was tripped off down the hall. I let Jake have his way for about two yards before I wrenched my arm out of his grasp and stopped walking. "God! What's the matter with you? I'd like to keep that attached to my body, please."

Jake turned to me, an exasperated look on his face. "Why are you being nice to her? Did you space on what she did to me? Shouldn't you hate her as much as I do?"

I took a deep breath for patience. Jake had been through a lot and I knew it was going to take him a while to get over it. But he'd been acting nonstop pissed off for, like, two weeks now, and being the person who spent more time with him than anyone, I was so beyond over it. My fantasy about things going back to normal in our relationship if he wasn't the father? That was definitely not coming true.

In some ways, yes, he'd been the model boyfriend, sending me flowers for no reason, leaving little notes in my locker, texting to say I looked pretty or that he loved me or that he was thinking about me. But in other ways he was completely distant. He shut down whenever Chloe was in the room, and even after she left it was like he couldn't get comfortable. Like something was eating him raw from the inside out.

"Jake, I know what Chloe did was huge, but she was terrified and . . . and hormonal," I said under my breath, deciding not to feed him the gory details of her bodily functions and discomforts—details *I* was having nightmares over. "It's over now. She told the truth. Your applications are in, you're doing better in school. . . . Can't you at least just be human to her?"

Jake looked at me as if he didn't even know me. "No," he said. "I can't."

"Jake," I implored.

A few of his swimming buddies walked past toward the gym, and one of them reached out to slap his hand. He gave the guy a tight smile and our conversation was momentarily suspended.

"You know what? I don't want to talk about this with you anymore," he said finally. He sounded more resigned than

201

angry. "I don't want to talk about Chloe at all. Can't we just . . . pretend she doesn't exist?"

I wasn't entirely sure how that was possible, but right then, I was sick of thinking and talking about it too. So, just to end the conversation, I said, "Sure. Fine. We'll pretend she doesn't exist."

Jake smiled. "Thank you."

He was just leaning in to kiss me when Hammond appeared from behind.

"Hey, hey, hey! You ready for the big meet?" He lifted his hand to slap Jake's, and Jake's grin widened.

"You know it!"

The two of them clasped hands and bumped shoulders. Crazy. Guys in general were certifiably crazy. Two months ago these two wanted nothing more than to beat the crap out of each other. Now they were suddenly best friends again, united in their anti–Will and Chloe front. The weirdest thing about it was, when Hammond found out about Chloe's fling with Jake, he'd entirely blamed Jake and forgiven Chloe. But now that he knew she'd also flung with Will, he was pissed at Chloe and Jake was somehow forgiven. It was almost as if the fact that both Jake and Hammond now thought Chloe was a slut had somehow brought them together.

Just trying to figure it out gave me a headache.

"You going?" Jake asked. "'Cause Ally needs a ride."

My jaw dropped. Like I wanted to spend half an hour alone in a car with Hammond?

"Oh, yeah? I can drive you, Ryan. Let's go."

"Cool. I better go before I miss the bus." Jake gave me a kiss and a wave and was gone. Just like that, the boy passed me off to his former number one enemy—the guy he used to be so jealous of he hated picturing the two of us together. I looked at Hammond and wondered what *he* was thinking. Was he remembering how he'd kissed me over the summer at the old condo? How he'd confessed that he liked me? How I'd completely refused him?

"So." Hammond twirled his keys once and caught them, a big-ass grin on his face. "Ready to roll?"

Guys. I just could not figure them out.

february

Who do you think would win in a fight, Will Halloran or Jake Graydon?

Oh, please. Jake, no contest.

I don't know. Will's on the football team.

He's always slamming into people and getting back up again.

True, but Jake's just bigger. Plus he's Jake Graydon.

So? What does that mean?

He's, like, the golden boy around here. Can you even imagine him losing anything?

But Will's a Norm. He's probably been in a ton of fights. Jake's never been in any.

True. Experience has gotta count for something.

jake

"I can't believe we're out of here in, like, four months," Trevor said. He was bouncing up and down on his toes, trying to stay warm. Why we were not allowed inside in the morning until the bell rang was a mystery to me. Only special cases were allowed past security. Like if you had a meeting with a teacher or needed to see the nurse or had before-school detention. But if your nuts were freezing off in subzero weather? Sorry. Grin and bear it, my friend.

"Four months and then we're basically adults," Todd added, slurping on his hot chocolate. It dribbled down his chin and seeped into his light blue scarf, but he didn't notice.

"Yeah. Adults," Hammond said. "And then we won't have to take shit from anyone."

I rubbed my knees together, my hands shoved so far down in the pockets of my varsity jacket, I think I was shrinking. Four months and we would be graduates. And I had no idea if I had even the smallest shot at going to college. This was not the way it was supposed to be. By now I was supposed to have five offers for soccer scholarships and be making my own damn choices. Instead I was waiting to be approved by someone—anyone— like every other mediocre zero in my class.

God, I fucking hated Chloe.

"Dude. Check this out." Connor lifted his chin toward the driveway. Speak of the she-devil. Chloe had just pushed her massive self out of the passenger seat of her mom's car and was now waddling slowly up the stairs, holding on to the railing. A few girls giggled as she went past, and most people turned to stare. Without even looking over at us, Chloe headed straight for the front door. Guess she was one of those special cases.

She had just opened the door when someone on the other side of the steps let out a "Moooooo!" Chloe froze. Then Hammond made this elephant noise that was so on-the-money perfect, the rest of us cracked up laughing. Chloe ducked her head and rushed inside. Someone slammed me in the back of the shoulder and I whipped around. Weirdly, it was Ally.

"Hey," I said, my breath making a steam cloud in her face. "What?"

"What the hell was that?" she demanded, backhanding Hammond in the chest.

He just laughed.

"What's the matter with you guys?" she hissed. "Are you in kindergarten or something?"

"Actually, we're almost adults," Todd said proudly, grinning over the top of his chocolate-stained scarf.

"Then start freaking acting like it!"

"God. Calm down. It was just a joke," I said, embarrassed. I didn't like my girlfriend getting mom-ly in front of my friends. What was up her ass anyway? Since when had she named herself Chloe's personal protector? "She brought it on herself anyway," I said, rubbing my bare hands together. "You're gonna sleep around, you gotta be ready to suffer the consequences."

"Truth," Connor said, slapping my hand.

"Oh my God! You're such a hypocrite!" Ally said, almost laughing. "Are you forgetting that *you* slept around too? You could have just as easily been the father."

"Yeah, but I'm not," I snapped. "At least I'm smart enough to use protection, unlike that stupid Norm."

"Good thing, too," Connor said. "Girl like that? Who knows what kinds of diseases she could be passing around?"

"You guys make me sick," Ally said. "*That girl* is your friend. She's *your* ex-girlfriend!" she said to Hammond.

"Thank God for the 'ex,'" Hammond said with a cackle.

Ally was so pissed, she looked about to cry. Suddenly I sobered up and started to feel just the tiniest bit guilty. But for what? Didn't Chloe deserve to have people talking about her? Look at what she'd done to me. To Will, even. To her parents and Hammond and Ally. She'd spent half the last year lying and cheating and ruining lives.

"What?" Ally said to me. "What are you thinking right now?"

The guys stared at me. My face stung from the cold. I looked down at her and blew out a breath. "Nothing you want to hear."

She groaned and stormed away as I turned my back on her. My insides felt twisted and torn, knowing she was mad at me again, but I tried to ignore it. I was mad at her, too. She was my girlfriend. She was supposed to be on my side. Why couldn't she figure that out?

ally

This was déjà vu–ish. Walking into Chloe's house with Shannen and Faith. Toting gifts and movies and snacks. Giggling as we tiptoed past the living room, where her dad was passed out and snoring in front of Fox News. I'd done this with the two of them a million times in my life, but not once in the past three years. As I stared down at my feet, making sure not to kick a table leg or trip on the edge of the antique rug, it was like I'd entered a time warp and landed right back in freshman year. Except now I had better shoes.

"I don't know about this, you guys," Faith whispered as we reached the bottom of the wide, carpeted staircase. Her hair was back in a ponytail and she wore a pink hoodie, gray fleece sweats, and Puma sneakers, like a comfy little fashion plate. "She's been so depressed lately. What if she's up there crying?"

The three of us looked up warily. Over our heads, the thousand-pound crystal chandelier tossed its light against the cream walls. When I was a kid, I'd always been terrified that thing was going to come crashing down and crush me, but Chloe had just laughed and said, "At least you'd have a sparkly death!" Girl had always been positive to a fault.

I pushed my hesitation aside. "That's why we're here, remember? To cheer her up."

I'd come up with the idea after witnessing the guys' immature antics before school earlier this week. It had been bad enough when random people were discreetly whispering about her, but now the people who were supposed to be her friends had gotten in on the action, and it was like they'd made it okay for the whole school to be as vocal as possible. Every day the teasing seemed to be getting worse, and I wasn't proud of the fact that my boyfriend was one of the ringleaders. Organizing a night of pampering for the girl was the least I could do to make up for his ass-ish-ness.

"We can't wuss out now," Shannen said, adjusting the gift basket full of chocolate, chips, nuts, and candy in her arms. "And this thing's getting heavy. Let's just go."

I followed Shannen's lead, and after a moment, Faith steeled herself and trailed behind us. At the top of the steps we nearly slammed right into Mrs. Appleby. She brought her hand to her chest and closed her eyes like she was praying for patience. Her blond hair was back in a perfect chignon and she wore stiff gray slacks, a soft turtleneck sweater, and full makeup. Even though it was Saturday night and she was clearly not going out. Right now my mom was in sweats and a blue pore-cleansing mask, watching TV with Gray and chowing on Chinese food. Things were definitely done differently at the Appleby house.

"Girls! You must learn how to use the doorbell!" Mrs. Appleby whispered.

She'd been saying this pretty much every time we'd come over here since the age of seven. And as always I thought to myself, *Why don't you just start locking your door?*

"Sorry," Shannen said offhandedly.

Mrs. Appleby shook her head and stepped aside to let us pass. "She's in her room."

We thanked her and crept over to Chloe's door. She still had the white placard with the painted ballet toe-shoe on it and the words "Chloe's Room" written in pink script. Shannen quietly turned the knob and we peeked inside. Chloe wasn't crying. She was sitting in her armchair with a blanket over her belly, reading aloud from *Peter Rabbit*.

For a second, we just froze. I looked at Faith. She looked at Shannen. None of us knew what to do. Chloe was reading to the baby. And suddenly I wanted to burst into tears. I knew we should back away. We should just go. We shouldn't interrupt such a private moment. But then Chloe started to look up, and I did the only thing I could think to do. I grabbed Shannen and yanked her through the door with me.

"Surprise!"

Chloe dropped the book. "You guys! What are you doing here?"

"We brought snacks!" Faith announced with a big, forced grin. She held up her gift bags and nail kit. "And presents!"

"And movies!" Shannen added brightly, unbuttoning her varsity jacket. "And pedicure stuff!"

Chloe pushed herself up from her chair with both hands, the book forgotten. "I can't believe this!" she said, eyeing the booty we'd splayed across her bed. When she looked at us, her eyes were shining. "It's just like old times."

"That's kind of the point," Faith told her, rolling her eyes in an amused way. She walked around to Chloe's side of the four-poster bed. "Now get up there so I can start your toes. I bet your feet are gnarly."

"I'm not sure, actually. I haven't seen them in a while," Chloe said, struggling her way onto her bed.

Shannen popped a movie into the DVD player. I opened a bag of Baked Lays and busted out the Snapple. The two of us crawled into bed next to Chloe and propped ourselves up against her many, many throw pillows just as the FBI warning glowed blue on the screen.

"Pink or red?" Faith asked, settling herself in at Chloe's feet and opening her nail kit. Inside, a dozen shades of polish were lined up neatly on tiny shelves, while the bottom well was filled with cotton balls, swabs, tweezers, cuticle pushers, clippers, and files.

"Got anything with glitter?" Chloe asked, craning her neck to see. "This baby's gonna pop out soon, and when it does I want to be glam."

"Got it." Faith lifted a bottle of hot pink polish with glitter. "But first, we work on these heels. Because ew."

Chloe blushed and I tried to refrain from smacking Faith upside the head.

"Want a present?" Shannen asked.

"What do you think?" Chloe asked, reaching into the chip bag.

Shannen grabbed a small one from the pile and tossed it at Chloe, who deftly caught it. She tore it open and grinned. "Cashmere socks?"

"Perfect after a pedicure," I said, handing her a lemonade.

"You got *17 Again*?" Chloe asked, her mouth dropping as Zac Efron appeared on the menu screen.

"A classic," I conceded.

"It's my favorite," Chloe said.

Shannen squirmed around, trying to find the perfect comfortable position against the pillows. "Again. Kind of the point. Is she not getting the theme here?" she said to me facetiously, making me laugh.

The movie started up and Chloe looked down at her belly, where she'd laid out her new socks, and at the bottle of lemonade in her hand, while Faith rubbed peppermint lotion on her feet.

"You guys?" Chloe said, her voice cracking.

My heart froze. *Please don't let her cry.* The whole point of this night was to cheer her up, not to make her cry.

"Yeah?" Shannen said warily, holding her iced-tea bottle an inch from her lips.

"Is it lame that this is the best night I've had in months?" Chloe asked.

The rest of us laughed. "Don't get ahead of yourself," I said. "We could still disappoint you."

Chloe leaned back into her pillows and let out a contented sigh. "Yeah, I just don't think that's possible."

ally

"I'm so bummed. This is the second year in a row I'm going to be dateless for Valentine's Day," Faith lamented, spearing a bright red tomato in the center of her salad, her head held up by her free hand.

"Remember when we used to do Guys Suck Day?" Annie asked, not looking up from her laptop, where she was typing away.

"Omigod, yeah. That was so much fun," Faith said.

I looked back and forth between the two of them and held my breath. Annie had been psyched to sit at our table with us, the better to spy on the Cresties, but I hadn't actually expected her to interact with anyone, and now this? Were Annie and Faith actually talking to each other and not sniping? Unprecedented. At least in the last two years.

"What's Guys Suck Day?" Shannen asked.

Annie's head suddenly shot up. Then Faith's did the same. They looked at each other across the cafeteria table like they'd just realized where they were.

"Oh, nothing," Faith said, grabbing for her soda.

"It was stupid," Annie added. Both of them were blushing.

"Does it involve hating on guys on Valentine's Day?" Shannen asked. She glanced toward the far end of the table

212

where Hammond, the Idiot Twins, Connor, and Josh scarfed their double burgers. "Because I'm in."

Faith cleared her throat and looked down, rubbing her hands together under the table as she glanced around for a change of topic. Her eyes finally fell on Jake, who sat at the end of the table, catty-corner from her and me, scarfing his own double burger.

"What about you, Jake? What are you guys doing for V-Day this weekend?" she asked.

Jake didn't answer. He was too busy glaring toward the food line, his latest bite of burger bulging inside his right cheek. I tilted my head and leaned out into the aisle to see what he was looking at and spotted Chloe and Will. My heart sunk. Of course.

"I haven't even thought about Valentine's Day," I said, filling the awkward silence. "I just want to get through the game tonight."

"Nervous 'cause your new coach is coming?" Shannen said in an overly teasing voice. The Rutgers coach had sent me an e-mail letting me know she was going to be attending the game tonight with a couple of members of the team, kind of a cool way to support the new recruit. Of course the added pressure felt anything but supportive, but if I wanted to play at RU, I was going to have to get used to it. There were some pretty high expectations surrounding that team.

I glanced sideways at Jake. He was still glaring.

"Well, that and it *is* the Valley game," I replied. "We *must* beat them down."

"I heard that," Shannen said, slapping my hand.

"Great. Basketball. Rah, rah, rah," Faith said facetiously.

"But no one has answered my question." Everyone looked at Jake. There was no indication that he even knew any of us were there, let alone talking.

"Ja-ake!" Faith sang. She reached out and snapped her thin fingers in front of his face.

"What?" A couple of sesame seeds flew out of his mouth and she grimaced.

"I *said*, what are you guys doing for Valentine's Day?" Faith asked again.

I held my breath, curious to hear his answer. Chloe and Will started to make their way down the aisle. He held their shared tray with one hand and clutched her fingers with the other.

"Oh, um—"

Just that one second of hesitation made my stomach flip.

"We don't have a plan," I interjected, feeling embarrassed.

"No. We do," he said, putting his burger down on his tray. He dusted his fingers and reached for his soda cup. "We have plans, you just don't know what they are."

"Really?" I said, shocked. Jake hadn't mentioned Valentine's Day once, and I'd started to think that he was too wrapped up in his anti-Chloe obsession to plan anything. Plus things hadn't been great between us lately, with his moodiness and my irritation over the way he'd been treating Chloe. I figured maybe he wasn't interested. "You planned something?"

"Of course I did," he said, leaning in to give me a kiss. "It's Valentine's Day."

A smile twitched its way to my lips, and I reached for his hand. It was the first time since he'd found out about Chloe's lie that I felt even remotely close to him. But just when my fingers were about to brush his under the table, Chloe and Will were passing by.

"Nice lunch, Chloe," he said, his back to her. "I thought you were eating for two, not ten."

The guys at the far end of the table cackled. Faith and Annie froze. My hand fell back into my lap.

"Jake . . . ," Shannen said in a disappointed, warning tone.

Will put the tray down on the end of the next table and turned toward Jake. "Do you have a problem, man?"

Jake wiped his fingertips on his napkin and shook his head, avoiding eye contact. "Not anymore, dude. It's your problem now."

Chloe shook her head. "I'm going to the bathroom."

"You don't have to go," I said. But it was too late. She was already waddling away. Faith got up to follow her, and Jake shot her this evil look, like he felt betrayed. In that moment his face looked entirely different. Sharper. Uglier, somehow. I barely even recognized him.

I was going to be sick. I really was.

"Why don't you try saying that to my face?" Will said, taking a step closer to Jake.

Instantly, the guys at the far end of the table stood up, their chairs scraping against the linoleum. Will's face got blotchy red, but he didn't look away from Jake. In fact, I couldn't understand why the heat of his glare wasn't boring a hole in Jake's skull.

"Okay."

Jake got up as well. He was taller than Will, but only by a couple of inches. The two of them stared at each other, and I swear I could taste the flying testosterone.

"You guys, come on," I said nervously. People were starting

to take notice, getting up from their chairs, straining to see what was about to go down. "You don't have to fight."

"Oh, I actually think it's long overdue," Will said.

"Don't talk to her," Jake spat.

Will laughed under his breath. "Now you're telling me who I can and can't talk to? Who the hell do you think you are?"

From the corner of my eye I saw one of the history teachers, Mr. Bucolli, making his way toward us. He was short, neckless, and seriously stocky, and people had been calling him Mr. Troll-ie for years. The door to the teacher's lounge opened and the vice principal, Dr. Giles, walked out as well. It was like he had a sixth sense for when a student was out for blood.

"I'm the guy who's about to pummel your ass," Jake said.

He grabbed the front of Will's sweater and I yelped. At that moment, Mr. Bucolli's beefy hands met Jake and Will's chests and pried them apart. Man was definitely a wrestler in his earlier life.

"No one will be pummeling anyone's anything," he growled.

Jake and Will were both panting like bulls about to be released into a fighting ring. If Mr. Bucolli lowered his arms, they would have cracked skulls. Instead, the VP arrived and cleared his throat.

"Mr. Graydon, Mr. Halloran," he said, tugging on the cuffs of his shirtsleeves beneath his jacket. "My office. Now."

Neither one of them moved.

"Jake," I pleaded.

He glanced at me then, but his eyes were blank. Then he reached down, grabbed his backpack, and stormed off, shoving open the cafeteria door with the heel of his hand.

"You too, Mr. Halloran," Dr. Giles said.

Mr. Bucolli released him, and Will seemed to deflate. "Would you guys make sure Chloe eats something?" he said, glancing over at their forgotten tray.

"We're on it," Shannen said.

"Thanks."

Then he turned around and trudged out with Dr. Giles at his heels. The guys slowly lowered themselves back into their chairs, and gradually the noise level in the cafeteria returned to normal, maybe even louder than normal, as everyone started blabbing about what had just happened. I stared down at my untouched pasta, feeling somehow hot and frigid at the same time.

"You okay?" Annie asked me.

"Sure." I picked up my water bottle. My hand was shaking. I managed to take a sip, then cleared my throat. "Know how you guys were talking about Guys Suck Day?" I said weakly.

"Yeah," Shannen and Annie said in unison.

"Well, I think I'm in for that," I said grimly. "I think I'm most definitely in."

jake

"It's not like I don't know what's going on around this school," Dr. Giles said.

The dude was seriously tall with dark skin and graying hair, but not intimidating. When he sat on the edge of his desk and crossed his arms over his thin chest I couldn't help thinking I could take him. If they needed a disciplinarian around here, they should've given Mr. Troll-ie the job. His hand had felt like a brick against my chest. For a second there I thought he was going to snap me in half. Plus you don't fuck with a guy who has that much hair growing out of his ears. There's definitely something wrong there.

"I know what's going on," Dr. Giles continued. "The Internet age has been most enlightening." He tugged a Droid phone out of his pocket and lit up the screen. "Thanks to this I can find out who's doing what around here at any given moment of any day just by logging on to Twitter."

I swallowed, but my throat was dry, which made me cough. Dr. Giles was reading our tweets? Okay. Maybe he *was* intimidating. My leg started to bounce up and down. At the far end of the couch, Will was frozen.

"I understand that the two of you are in a trying situation," he continued, slipping the phone back into his pocket. "And I sympathize. I do."

He got up and walked around his desk, then leaned both fists into it.

"But let's get one thing clear right here and now," he said, looking us each in the eye. "The animosity between you two will *not* manifest itself within these walls. Is that clear?"

"Yes, sir," Will barked, like a soldier.

Kiss-ass. I couldn't even remember what "animosity" meant. Let alone "manifest."

"Good. Because if it does, you'll both be suspended. This is your warning." Dr. Giles stood up straight. "If I hear about one punch, one kick, one shove, you're both out for a week. Understood?"

Right. That was clearer.

"Yes, sir," Will said again.

"Yeah," I muttered.

"Good. I'm glad we're all on the same page." He crossed over to the door, stepping over my backpack to get there, and yanked it open. "You can go now."

I snatched my bag off the floor and walked out into the deserted hallway. Will was right behind me, but he speed-walked past me toward the caf, probably running back to Chloe.

"Watch your back, man," I said under my breath.

He stopped in his tracks. I was surprised but kept walking. When I came up even with him, he turned to face me.

"What the hell is your problem?" he hissed.

"Seriously?" I blurted.

"Yes. Seriously. If anything *I* should hate *you*," he shot back. My jaw dropped, but he kept right on talking. "I was going out with Chloe all summer and she cheated on me with you! Then you get to be there for her for months while she's going through this stuff and I—"

"I *get* to be there with her?" I blurted, my face screwing up in disbelief. "Are you shitting me? You think that was fun?"

Will just stared at me. The silence, even five seconds of it, made me squirm.

"Because it wasn't."

My face was on fire. Because I was lying. I realized it just like that and it killed me. Dealing with Chloe and the baby, it hadn't exactly been fun, but it had been kind of nice. Being there for her. Feeling like she needed me. Knowing there was going to be a kid who was a part of me. I'd felt . . . important. And now I was just the idiot who'd fallen for the biggest lie of all time. I was the jackass. I was the punch line.

And this guy, Will, was the father.

"Whatever, dude," I said, shaking my head and turning away. "Like I said, she's your problem now. Have fun."

ally

"I can't decide whether I want the centerpieces to be colorful and eclectic or sleek and sophisticated."

My mom had been making figure eights around the four round tables of floral arrangements for at least half an hour. She paused in front of a spherical silver pot filled with white roses, and a tall, clear vase bursting with wildflowers. We'd left school together as soon as the last bell rang to squeeze in this shopping trip before my basketball game tonight. The biggest game of the year in more ways than one. I should have been hyped up and nervous. Instead I was tired and dreading it. In fact, I was dreading everything.

"Colorful and eclectic," I replied, leaning my hip against the table.

"You think?" she asked.

"Mom, this is you we're talking about. Look at you."

She glanced down at her outfit—floral peasant top in deep purples, paired with jeans and mustard suede boots—and laughed. "You make an excellent point."

"I know."

I shrugged and glanced around the greenhouse. Up front, the florist was behind the counter, working the phones feverishly as he fielded his last-minute Valentine's Day orders. He'd run off ten minutes ago to deal, promising to be right back, but we hadn't seen him since. Now, just hearing him repeat people's loving messages back to them made my heart hurt. After the way Jake had acted at school today, I wasn't even sure I wanted to be around him, let alone go out with him on the mushiest day of the year.

"Oh, and you can wear these gardenias in your hair!" my mother said, placing a pair of yellow flowers just behind my ear. "They'd be just the right pop of color with your black dress. And Jake could wear a matching tie!"

She shoved the gardenias into my hand, whipped out her notebook, and started making notes. I looked down at the blooms, twirling the stems between my thumb and forefinger until the color blurred. I wasn't even sure that Jake was going to be coming to the wedding at this point. I mean, the thing was in May. Right now May seemed very far away.

"Ally?" my mom asked suddenly. "Are you okay?"

I blinked back my tears and tried to smile. "Yeah! I'm fine!"

"Sweetie, are you sure?" She put her hand on my shoulder. "You look like you're about to cry."

My heart welled up into my throat. I wanted to tell her what was going on. I so did. But she was so happy and excited. And this was the first time we'd gotten to do anything wedding related together without Quinn. I didn't want to ruin it for her. If Jake and I broke up tomorrow . . . then I'd tell her about it tomorrow.

"I'm just happy for you," I said, my voice thick.

You'd think I'd just told her I was going to be valedictorian, that's how happy she looked. "Aw, Ally!"

She pulled me in for a hug, and I pressed my face into her shoulder, letting myself squeeze out a few tears. When she pulled back again, I was smiling. The remainder of my inevitable breakdown was going to have to wait for a better time.

"I love you, kiddo," she said as the florist finally appeared at the open doorway.

I tossed the gardenias onto the table and stood motionless while one of them tumbled to the dirt-covered floor. "I love you, too."

ally

Thirty seconds left in the first half. Sweat dripped down the back of my neck. My pulse pounded in my ears, muting the sounds of the crowd. The ball was in my hands. I looked left. I looked right. The Valley players were everywhere, blocking out my teammates, practically tackling them to the floor. I dribbled twice for good measure, stalling. What should I do? What the hell should I do? Take the shot from here? Take the ball to the net? Make the pass? What, what, what?

Twenty seconds left. My eyes darted around the gym. Coach screaming to make the play. The players from Rutgers on their feet. My mom, dad, and Gray, sitting together, cheering like crazy. Jake shouting his head off. It was too much. I had to focus. We needed a score to go into halftime up. We needed a score now.

Suddenly Shannen slipped away from her defender. I saw her long arm reach out toward the sideline. I looked away from her to the left, trying to fake out the girl guarding me, and tossed it to Shannen. The girl cursed under her breath as she lost her balance and her fingertips grazed the shiny wood floor. Shannen turned. Set up the shot. Let it fly.

"Go, Shannen!" I heard Chloe scream.

I hadn't even realized she was here.

The buzzer sounded, and the ball swished through the net.

"Three points at the buzzer!" the announcer called out. "And the score at halftime: Orchard Hill, twenty-three; Valley, twenty-one."

I ran over and gave Shannen a half hug as we joined the rest of the team by the bench. The Rutgers coach was on her feet along with my two soon-to-be-teammates, cheering for me. Our ball girl handed out Gatorade. I tried to catch my breath. Tried not to grin too hugely. The hordes emptied out down the bleachers and toward the door, going for the snack bar while the cheerleaders launched into their halftime routine. Chloe and Will were on the bottom bench. He whispered something to her and got up. Right then, just as Coach was saying something about stepping up the offense in the second half, Jake trudged down the bleachers and slammed Will's shoulder from behind with the full force of his body.

No. No, no, no. Not now. Please not now.

And suddenly the entire world zipped into focus. Will whirled around and slammed his fist into Jake's jaw. Chloe and I both screamed. Everyone scattered away from them like ripples from a tossed rock, moving up the bleachers, across, toward the door. Jake recovered and threw himself on top of Will, and then they were both on the floor, wailing on each other like rabid animals.

"Jake! Stop it!" I shouted, starting across the gym floor.

Blood, I wasn't sure whose, splurted across the boards.

"Ally, don't."

Coach Prescott's hand was on my shoulder.

"What?" I looked over at her, confused and terrified.

"They're watching," Coach said, giving a surreptitious nod toward the stands.

My throat went dry. I didn't completely understand why it mattered that my college coach and teammates were eyeing me—what that had to do with the fact that my boyfriend was staging an impromptu wrestling meet as a halftime show—but I decided to trust Coach and didn't move. Seconds later, I completely understood. Two uniformed cops descended on the mess of flailing arms and legs and fists and feet and tore Will and Jake apart. Blood seeped from a gash across the bridge of Jake's nose. Will's eye was already turning purple. I glanced up at the Rutgers coach and held my breath. If she'd seen me go over there, she would have drawn so many conclusions. Conclusions about who I was, whom I chose to spend my time with. Right now, Jake looked like a psychotic loser with a violent streak, ready to go postal at any moment. If I'd run to his side, she would have forever associated me with him.

Coach Prescott had just saved my ass.

"Thanks, Coach," I said, my eyes filling with tears as the police hauled both Jake and Will outside through one of the side doors.

Shannen put her arm around my waist as we turned back toward the huddle.

"Holy shit," Shannen said under her breath.

"Tell me about it." I glanced back again. I couldn't help it. "Do you think he's okay?"

"Who cares?" Shannen said. "Screw him. This is the biggest game of your life and he pulls that crap? Don't let it distract you."

"As much as I don't appreciate the language, Shannen's

right," Coach Prescott said. She looked around the circle, meeting everyone's eyes solemnly. "As far as I'm concerned, that didn't just happen. Everyone needs to stay focused. We can win this thing if we get them on their heels, but I need everyone's heads in the game." She looked me dead in the eye. "Nowhere else."

The rest of the team turned to look at me, and my fingers curled into fists. In that moment, I hated Jake. I couldn't help it. Shannen was right. He should have known this was a huge night for me. He should have thought about that for five seconds before making a spectacle of himself and distracting me. But no. It was far more important for him to mess with Will and Chloe yet again. And now I had my teammates doubting me, doubting my focus.

"Are you with us, Ryan?" Coach asked.

"I'm with you, Coach," I said, clenching my jaw. "Let's beat these losers."

The team cheered and clapped, several of them slapping me on the back, and we got down to our game plan. From that moment on, Jake was no longer an issue. He wasn't even on my radar.

jake

When the doorbell rang that night, I half expected it to be Will, stopping by for round two. I trudged over to the door in my sweats and glanced out. It was Ally, freshly showered after the game. For the first time ever, I just wanted her to go away. Because just seeing her standing there made me feel like an asshole.

I opened the door. A light, freezing drizzle was coming down from the sky.

"Hey," she said quietly. I'd never seen anyone look at me with that much hurt, pity, and anger.

"Hey."

I released the door handle and started back across the foyer, turning my back to her. Not wanting to look in her eyes any longer than I had to. Figuring she'd follow.

"I don't know if I'm coming in."

I stopped. My heart shriveled. What the hell did that mean? Whatever it was, it couldn't be good. I set my jaw, resolving not to let her see me sweat. If she was going to end it, just let her end it.

"What does that mean?" I asked her.

She blinked and shuddered in the cold, pulling her jacket tighter. "Aren't you even going to ask me if we won?"

"Did you win?" I asked, placing one hand on the doorknob and the other on the far side of the doorjamb, as if I was blocking her way.

"Yeah." Her voice broke. "I scored the game-winner."

"That's great," I said, my voice sour. "Aren't you even gonna ask me if I'm okay? Because that jackass almost broke my arm."

Ally titled her head. "Oh, did he?" she said sarcastically. "I'm so sorry for you. Poor, poor Jake. Almost got hurt in the fight *he* started."

"Why are you being such a bitch?" I blurted.

Her jaw dropped, but I kept going. My defenses were up, and I was keeping them there.

"I'm the one who got hauled off by the police tonight," I said, bringing a hand to my chest. "I'm the one who got suspended for a week. I'm the one who almost had to get stitches thanks to that asshole."

Ally scoffed and shook her head. "God! Do you even hear yourself? I may be a bitch sometimes, but at least I'm not a big, whining baby."

She turned around and started to walk away, headed for her mom's car, which she'd parked near the end of the driveway.

"I'm not a baby!" I shouted after her.

"Whatever, Jake," she said, lifting a hand but not turning. "I'll see you around."

"What the hell is that supposed to mean?"

She paused at the driver's side door. For a long second, she just stared at the window, the icy raindrops sticking to her hair. Then she popped the handle and looked up at me. All of a sudden I remembered what she'd looked like the first day I met her, right here in this driveway on a hot, sunny day. So fearless. So beautiful. So perfect.

"It means I'm done," she said. "We're over. I can't take it anymore."

"Take what?" I shouted, my voice harsh. I felt like she was yanking my heart out through my mouth. "What can't you take anymore?"

"You! This! All the negativity and the cruelty and the violence!" she shouted back. "I keep waiting for you to get past it, for you to go back to being you . . . the sweet, thoughtful, and yeah, maybe sometimes dense, but also cool guy I fell in love with! But clearly that's not going to happen."

I clenched my jaw. "Yeah, well, maybe this *is* me," I said, even though I knew it wasn't. Even though I hated me right then almost as much as she did. But it wasn't my fault. I couldn't stop feeling like this no matter what I did. I'd tried to stop feeling sad and angry every second of every day, but I just couldn't.

"I hope not, Jake," Ally said, shaking her head. "That would just be sad."

Then she got in her car and drove away.

ally

"Welcome to Guys Suck Day!"

Standing in the open doorway at the front of her house, Annie wore a red, satin, strapless dress with a poofy skirt that I couldn't believe she owned, and a four-strand rhinestone necklace that covered half her chest. Two minutes ago, I'd felt droopy, tired, and heartbroken, wondering what Jake had had planned for us tonight—if he actually had planned anything. Now I was simply stunned. Annie looked me up and down and her grin went south.

"You didn't dress up!" she whined, closing the door as I stepped inside.

"I thought you were kidding," I replied. I shook off my coat and hung it on the overloaded hooks near the door, covering up someone else's leather jacket. I paused. Wait a sec. That jacket looked familiar.

"Surprise!"

Hand over my heart, I faced the kitchen, where Shannen, Faith, and Chloe were all gathered around the table, filling bowls with snacks. Shannen wore a dark green minidress with a black lace overlay, Faith was sporting a floor-length pink gown, and Chloe had donned her silver maternity dress from Christmas. I froze.

"Um, Annie, are you aware that there are three Cresties in your house?" I said under my breath.

"I'm aware. The things I do for my best friend," Annie said. Then she leaned toward my ear. "I already booked a HazMat team to come delouse the place tomorrow."

I laughed, but I was touched. Annie had allowed her three most hated enemies into her house just to cheer me up. Either she was the best best friend ever, or I was in a sorrier state than even I thought.

"Ally!" Faith walked over and threw her arms around me. She had on so much perfume that my mouth filled with the sour, flowery taste of it. "Ohhhh! It sucks to break up right before Valentine's!"

"Hey!" Annie smacked the back of Faith's head. Hard. "We don't say the *V*-word on Guys Suck Day, remember?"

"Ow! God! Sorry!" Faith said, rubbing her scalp.

"So what *do* we do on Guys Suck Day?" I asked, joining the others at the table.

Trying to get into the spirit, I took a handful of M&M's and started to munch on them. But even chocolate couldn't chase away the gray cloud that had settled all around me ever since I'd driven away from Jake's house three nights ago. For the last time. My heart clenched every time I thought about it—the look on his face, the effort it took not to turn around. But I knew I was doing the right thing. Jake was no good for me anymore. He wasn't even good for himself. I just wished I could get my heart to believe it.

"We watch girl-power movies," Chloe said, fanning out a selection on the table, including *Soul Surfer*, *Bridesmaids*, *John Tucker Must Die*, and *Whip It*.

"Cool," I said, nodding.

"Eat tons of junk food and drink tons of wine," Shannen said, producing a bottle from behind her back.

"And, if we get drunk enough, we call all the boys we hate and tell them to suck it," Annie said, grabbing the wine and pouring herself a glass.

My stomach turned over at the thought of drunk-dialing Jake and making an ass out of myself. "Let's not get drunk enough," I said, taking the bottle and setting it aside.

"Buzz kill," Annie muttered as she started gathering up some of the bowls of junk food. The rest of us helped and we all headed into the living room.

"Where are your parents, anyway?" I asked.

"Not here," Annie replied.

"There's also dancing, apparently," Chloe said over her shoulder as she sat down on the larger of the two mustard-colored couches. She dropped the movies onto the coffee table and leaned back, arms around her belly. "But after what happened at my birthday I think I'll sit that part out."

"Oh, no!" Faith said. "There's no sitting anything out on Guys Suck Day!"

She walked over to a cabinet on the far wall, opened it, and clicked on the stereo. A pounding dance beat filled the room, and Faith started to dance, kicking aside the throw pillows on the floor to make room. It was odd, watching her act so at-home in Annie's house. I still couldn't believe the two of them were actually ever best friends.

"Let's go, Chloe. On your feet." Faith took both Chloe's hands and hauled her off the couch, almost tipping them both over from the effort.

"All right, all right!" Chloe said. She stepped from side to side carefully, and when Faith spun her around, she cracked a smile. "Hello? If I have to dance, you have to dance!" she shouted, pulling me into their circle.

"Fine," I said, rolling my eyes.

Annie whipped out her Flip to tape us, and I found myself giggling nervously. As soon as the camera went on, Faith started hamming it up, rolling her shoulder back and kissy-facing the lens. Then Shannen joined us, half dancing, half posing for the camera.

Hmm. Perhaps Annie hadn't invited them here for me, but so that she could film them doing embarrassing stuff she could use against them later.

"Oh, yeah! Work it, ladies! Work it!" Annie directed, climbing up on the couch to get an aerial view. Chloe and I cracked up laughing, more than happy to fade into the background as Faith and Shannen jockeyed for camera position.

"So where's Will tonight?" I asked.

"He wanted to do something, but I said cheering you up was more important," Chloe told me, tucking her brown hair behind her ears.

"Chloe! You didn't have to do that!" I said.

"Whatever. We'll go out for dinner tomorrow night," Chloe said, lifting a shoulder. She reached around me for some chips and almost got her arm knocked off as Shannen attempted a twirl. "My dad says all the restaurants rob you blind on V-day anyway."

Like Chloe had any sort of problems with money. But I guess Will was conscious of that stuff.

"Make love to the camera, girls. Make *love*!" Annie wheedled.

"Shannen! Get out of my dance space!" Faith whined, shoving Shannen aside.

"Don't make me show them your bad side," Shannen shot back.

Faith squealed and ducked her head as Shannen chased her around the room, Annie in hot and gleeful pursuit.

"This is actually kind of fun," I commented, stuffing some more M&M's in my mouth.

"Yeah. I'm not even thinking about all the things I don't want to be thinking about," Chloe replied as Shannen jostled her aside, trying to cut Faith off.

"Me neither," I added.

Then we both just stopped. Because saying we weren't thinking made us both start thinking.

"Let's make Annie dance!" I suggested.

"Most definitely," Chloe agreed.

We turned and grabbed Annie by the wrists, tugging her onto the makeshift dance floor as she screamed in protest. The rest of us made a circle around her, and Annie threw her hands up in surrender, probably experiencing her worst nightmare as the gooey center of a Crestie doughnut. I wrestled the camera away and turned it on her.

"Hey! This was your idea, remember?" I said with a laugh. "Dance, Goth Girl! Dance!"

"Okay, but you guys are so not prepared for the ferocity of my moves," Annie said. And then she launched into a full-on lawn-sprinkler the likes of which I've never seen. Shannen tried to mimic it, badly, and before long all five of us were doubled over laughing, gasping for breath, and best of all, not thinking.

march

I can't believe Ally and Jake actually broke up.

What? You've been saying all year that they
should break up.

I know, but they got this far. Like, why break up now?

Totally. She should've at least stuck it out till
the prom.

OMG, I know. You don't just give up the chance
to go to the prom with Jake Graydon. I don't
care what he did.

Or who.

ally

"You girls look so beautiful!"

My mother took a step back to admire as Quinn and I stared at our reflections in the wall of mirrors in front of us. I had to say, for bridesmaids' dresses, these were not half-bad. My mother had chosen basic, black, satin, strapless, tea-length dresses with a slim waist and an A-line skirt. There was no lace, no sequins, no tulle. Quinn looked pretty and slim, and I looked tall and sophisticated. It was a win-win.

"Are you sure you want black?" Quinn asked, turning to the side. "It's kind of depressing for a wedding."

"I'm going to brighten them up with some funky jewelry and maybe have you wear jewel-toned shoes," my mother explained, reaching over to fluff my skirt.

Quinn frowned thoughtfully. "That could work."

"Of course it's gonna work," I said, kind of nastily, I'll admit. "It's her wedding day. Anything she says will work."

My mother shot me an admonishing look as Quinn raised her hands. "Okay, okay. Sor-*ree!*"

Quinn walked over to a pink velvet chair in the corner, sat down, and pulled out her phone. Probably texting someone about what an ass her soon-to-be stepsister was. Maybe even Hammond. In a disturbing new and somehow incestuous-feeling twist, the two of them were now officially a couple. He'd sent her two dozen red carnations in the Valentine's Day flower sale fund-raiser, and she'd spent the rest of the day telling everyone who would listen that she now had a senior boyfriend. Last night I'd caught them making out on the couch in the living room and I'd almost lost my dinner.

"Honey?" my mom asked, smoothing my hair. "Are you okay?"

"Why does everyone keep asking me that?" I asked, heading to another pink chair on the opposite side of the huge dressing room. When I dropped down, the skirt poofed up against the armrests like a black cloud. Classical violin music played through the speakers overhead, and the whole room smelled of lilacs and roses. I wondered if the people who worked here ever felt like they were going to OD on romance. "I'm fine, okay? *I* broke up with *him*. And it was, like, a month ago already."

Actually, it had been three weeks and one day. A torturous three weeks and one day. Three weeks and a day of Jake walking past me in the halls without so much as a glance. Of watching him flirt with every underclassman blessed with two X chromosomes. A month of second-guessing myself, of thinking he looked happier without me, of wondering if I had somehow been the problem. So no, I was not okay. But it had been long enough that I felt like I *should* have been by now, so I kept pretending I was.

"I have an idea," my mother said, perching on a stool next to the chair. "How about tonight you and I go out to dinner? Just the two of us?"

"Really?" I said, brightening slightly.

"Yeah. You pick the restaurant. Anywhere you want."

I smiled. I knew she was busy with work and wedding planning and everything, so the offer meant a lot.

"Thanks, Mom."

"Aw, sweetie." She kissed my temple and gave me a quick squeeze. "Everything's gonna be okay. You'll see."

My phone rang, and the seamstress returned to the dressing room with her clipboard. My mom got up and I grabbed my phone to answer it. Annie's tongue stuck out at me from the screen.

"Hey," I said, smoothing my skirt out. "What's up?"

"Don't shoot the messenger," Annie said.

My already-tentative smile died. I sat up straight. "What?"

"The Evites to Jake's birthday party just went out," Annie said grimly. "He invited every single person in the entire senior class and half the juniors. I even got one."

I swallowed hard. "Everyone except me."

"Everyone except you, Chloe, and Will."

I drooped back in my chair and stared. I didn't even know what to feel. For the millionth time in the past month, my vision blurred. I picked at a string sticking out of the cushioned part of the armrest as the store's soundtrack flipped to the classic wedding march.

"I guess I'm not surprised."

"He sucks, Ally. I'm going to form a protest. I'll get every Norm in town to stay home."

I snorted a laugh. "Like I'd do that to you."

This party was like a jackpot for Annie. Usually she had to sneak into Crestie parties to do her anthropological research. Now she was actually invited. Besides, keeping the Norms home wouldn't exactly hurt Jake. All of his close friends were Cresties. In fact, with the way his brain had been working lately, I had to wonder if he'd only invited the Norms to make me, Chloe, and Will feel even more left out.

As the music swelled to its crescendo overhead, I couldn't help remembering Jake's birthday last year. When he'd gotten his car and the first thing he'd done was zip right over to the Orchard View Condominiums to see me and we'd driven up to the country club and we'd kissed. For the first time.

"You know you did the right thing breaking up with him, right?" Annie said. "The strong thing."

"Yeah." My voice was thick. "I know."

"Are you okay?" Annie asked.

"Ugh. I wish people would stop asking me that," I replied, swiping one tear off my bottom lashes. Mercifully, the wedding march had ended, and my mom started motioning to me to wrap it up. "I'm fine. Thanks for letting me know, Annie, but I've gotta go. We're doing final measurements."

"Cool. Well, have fun."

"I will," I said.

I hung up the phone and forced a smile onto my face as my mother and the seamstress approached with their measuring tape and pins. For the next fifteen minutes I was turned and poked and prodded and appraised, the whole time just trying as hard as I could not to burst into tears.

jake

My party was the party that kicked every other party's ass. As I did a lap around the game room, I actually started to think that every single person I had invited had shown up. At least it seemed like it. There were dozens of people gathered around the pool table, faces I barely recognized hunched over the pinball machines, and the Idiot Twins had drawn a crowd at Ping-Pong, jumping and flailing and hitting backhands like they were on the court at the US Open or something. The music was loud, the beer was flowing, and everyone was having a kick-ass time. I was on top of the world.

I half wished Ally would try to crash, just so she could see how not affected I was by the fact that she'd dumped me.

"I can't believe your parents actually let you have this thing."

Shannen strolled over to me and rested her crooked arm on top of my shoulder. She looked fucking hot in the skinniest jeans I'd ever seen, with a wide-necked top falling off her shoulder. And no bra strap. So was she commando under there, or wearing some insane, strapless bra? Did girls know how much the not knowing drove us crazy?

"Yeah, well. Dad's still psyched I'm not a baby daddy and he has friends in high places, so no one's gonna be shutting us down." I turned toward her and put my beer cup on the top of the billiards cabinet. She was standing so close, I could almost see down her shirt and get my answer. When I realized I was looking, I almost gagged. This was Shannen. She used to be my best friend. If I was thinking about getting a peek, then I was definitely seriously drunk. "I'm glad you came," I said, looking away.

"Me too," she replied.

Was it just me, or was that her sultry voice?

"Come with me. I need to talk to you."

She took my fingers lightly and tugged me toward the door. My heart pounded. Whatever this was, it was probably not a good idea. But I couldn't think of a reason not to go—she had no boyfriend, and I definitely had no girlfriend—so I went. Shannen led me out into the kitchen, past the dozens of bowls of snacks and hundreds of forgotten cups, and over to the foyer. She was heading for the stairs. I glanced down at her ass and instantly felt myself stiffen. This was Shannen. This was not good. This was very not good.

But then she turned around and sat down on the bottom step. I glanced up toward the second floor in confusion.

"Have a seat." She patted the space next to her. I sat.

"What're we doing?" I asked.

Shannen looked down at her beer cup, held lightly between her fingertips. "We used to be best friends, right, Jake? We used to tell each other everything?"

Suddenly I didn't like where this was going. I leaned back, resting my elbows on the steps behind me. The music was dull from in here, and I was already starting to lose my buzz.

"Yeah," I said.

"So for old times' sake, I just want you to tell me one thing," Shannen said. She placed her cup aside and leaned back next to me. "Are you ever going to talk to Chloe again?"

I balked. "That's what this is about? Shit."

"I'm serious. I just want to know," Shannen said. "Because this torture stuff you've got going on? It's not you. And I think if you talk to her, you might stop doing it."

I felt like my eyes were on fire. "Why does no one seem to get what she did to me was not even close to being in the realm of forgivable?"

"I didn't ask you to forgive her," Shannen said simply. "I asked you to hear her out."

"Why should I?" I demanded.

"She fucked up." Shannen shrugged. "Everyone fucks up." She picked up her cup again. "You fucked up last summer and everyone kept right on talking to you. Even Ally."

The sound of her name squelched the buzz completely. My chest felt hollow, but heavy somehow. "Yeah. And look how long that lasted," I shot back.

Shannen laughed. "It lasted a long frickin' time," she said, her eyes dancing. "She stuck with you even knowing you banged her best friend. She stuck with you even though you were at Chloe's beck and call for months. And she stuck with you even after you became the loud-mouthed asshole from hell you've been for the past two months."

"Wow. Tell me how you really feel," I said.

She took a swig of her beer and held it in her mouth for a second before swallowing. "I'm just saying. That girl stayed with you longer than I would have. She stayed with you longer than most people would have. Because she loves you."

Something was welling up in my throat. I tried to swallow it back, but it wouldn't go.

"But back to Chloe," Shannen said. "You should talk to her. You're going to do it eventually anyway, right? I mean, look. You hated me last summer, but here we are."

She nudged me with her shoulder and I sat up straight, rubbing my hands together. "Yeah. How did that happen?"

Shannen's eyes narrowed. "I'm not sure. . . ." She sat up too. "Somewhere in there we just started talking again. But the thing is, you don't have that kind of time with Chloe. You can't just let it happen. Five more months and we're outta here. Everyone's either gonna go off to college remembering you as a cool guy with awesome friends"—she paused and gestured modestly to herself—"or as the complete and utter prick who tortured a pregnant girl."

Over in the game room, one of the Idiot Twins whooped over a win and everyone applauded. Meanwhile, I felt the full weight of what Shannen was saying. I felt the clock start ticking on my senior year. On life as I knew it. On any scrap of a chance I had left with Ally. To me the future had always been this kind of hazy blur. Something fictional that the future me would have to deal with, not the *me* me. But now here I was. Having to deal. Shannen got up, hooked one thumb into the back pocket of her jeans, and tipped her cup in my direction.

"Just something to think about."

"Says the girl who spent last year torturing Ally Ryan," I said, trying to get in the last word.

Shannen slowly smiled. "Haven't you heard, Jake? I'm reformed."

"Or maybe this is just a prank like everything else, right, Shan?" I said, pulling myself up by the banister. "I go over to apologize to Chloe and she, what, throws a pie in my face?"

Shannen laughed, shaking her head. "First off, pie? That is *so* beneath me. And secondly? You wait long enough and the real joke will be that *she* won't even listen to *you.*"

Then she turned and walked away to rejoin the party, casually ignoring the fact that she'd just obliterated my night.

jake

Cars were parked at every imaginable angle. On my driveway, in the cul-de-sac, down the street. Half the population of OHH was passed out inside my house, and from what I could tell, the morning traffic jam was going to be worse than the first half hour after a Giants game at the Meadowlands. I squinted in the darkness as I tried to make my way through, but it was like a maze. It took a good five minutes to cross over to Chloe's yard, a trip that would usually take ten seconds. Five straight minutes of second-guessing myself and almost turning back.

First of all, it was two in the morning.

Second of all, what was I supposed to say?

Third, was I doing this because I wanted to, or because Shannen had basically forced me to?

But no. I had decided this on my own. For the past two hours I had sat in my room, thinking, while everyone else had the time of their life downstairs. That was what Shannen had forced me to do—what I'd been avoiding doing forever. And even though I hadn't stopped being pissed off, I realized I *had* been acting like a dick. I knew how hard the pregnancy was for Chloe. I knew because I'd been there. And for the past few weeks I'd mocked her about the things that were worst for her. Her weight, the rumors, the slut thing. Her situation already sucked. She didn't need me making it worse. I could've been the better guy and just let her be, but I didn't. I took my anger and hurt out on her—the stuff that Ally had said had changed me—and it had only made me feel worse. It wasn't until I imagined apologizing that the weird pressure I'd been feeling around my heart since September finally went away.

I looked up at Chloe's house and swayed on my feet. I was very drunk. Was that going to be a good thing or a bad thing? Whatever. There was nothing I could do to change it.

Carefully as possible, I made my way over to the trellis attached to the deck attached to Chloe's room. I got a grip with my hands and started to climb, but two steps up, the world started spinning around me. I gritted my teeth and tried to keep going, but the toe of my boot slipped on the next step, something gave, I lost my grip, and suddenly I was weightless.

My back slammed into the cold dirt. The trellis crashed down on top of me.

Ow. Mother effing ow.

A light flicked on overhead. My heart stopped. This was where Mr. Appleby came at me with a baseball bat. It was finally going to happen.

But then, suddenly, Chloe was hovering above me, her light brown hair tumbling over her open robe.

"Jake? What the hell are you doing?"

I coughed as I shoved the flimsy trellis aside and struggled to my elbows. "I was coming to talk to you. Here. I'll climb the other one."

"Omigod. No. Don't move." She glanced over her shoulder toward her room. "Actually . . . meet me at the front door."

"Okay."

The inside of my head felt crooked, like my brain had shifted sideways or something. I shook it, like they do in the movies sometimes, but that just made it worse. Groaning, I shoved myself to my feet, dusted my jeans off, and staggered toward the front door. When I got there, Chloe was standing at the open doorway, her pink, fuzzy robe tied around her big belly.

Huge belly, actually. Ginormous.

"What're you doing here?" she demanded in a whisper. "Don't you have guests?"

"Party's over," I told her. "I came over to say . . ." I paused and cleared my throat. "I came over to say . . ."

Wow. This was harder than I thought. I wanted to say it, so why couldn't I say it?

Chloe rolled her eyes. "Come inside, it's freezing out here."

I swallowed hard, her dad with a baseball bat flashing through my mind again, but I went inside. The marble-floored foyer was a lot warmer than the driveway. She shut the door quietly and hugged herself.

"Okay. What?" she demanded.

I closed my eyes and just did it. "I wanted to say I'm sorry. For everything. I mean, for everything *I've* done or . . . or said, or whatever, to make you feel . . . bad about the . . . the—"

I gestured at her stomach, and her hands moved to cover it.

"Anyway, I'm sorry." I cleared my throat again. "I do think what you did sucked, but I maybe shouldn't have been such an asshole about it."

Chloe let out a small laugh.

"What?" I asked defensively.

"Nothing, it's just . . . Nothing. I'm sorry too. I tried to tell you that back in January, but you wouldn't listen," she said. "And now it just seems so pointless. I'm gonna have this baby any day now and it'll all be over."

I pressed my lips together and looked her up and down. "Can I just ask you one thing?"

She took a deep breath. "Sure."

"Why? Why did you do it?" I asked.

Chloe sighed and walked over to the living room or parlor or whatever her mom called it. She leaned against the back of a couch and sighed.

"I think I just . . . I wanted it to be you," she said, glancing up at me quickly. "I wanted it to be yours. Will and I were broken up and it wasn't pretty," she said, shaking her head. "The idea of going to him and telling him . . . I just couldn't. And you were my friend. You were a good guy. . . ."

My chest sort of swelled when she said that. Because I didn't feel like a good guy. Not right now.

"My parents knew you. My friends were your friends. It just would have made everything so much easier. So I said it was you, and once I said it . . . it felt impossible to take it back."

She paused and took in a broken breath. "And you were so amazing, Jake. You were obviously just as scared as I was, but you were always there. I needed that. I needed someone on my side. And you were always there."

Out of nowhere, my eyes stung. "I'm sorry. I'm so sorry." I turned away from her and brought my hand to my forehead. "God, I suck."

"You don't suck," Chloe said. "You just . . . *shit*."

"I know. I know. I'm a shit. I—"

"No. No, Jake!" Chloe said, panicked. I turned around and she was staring at the floor. Standing in a puddle. "I think my water just broke."

I took an instinctive step back. Because, gross. "Omigod."

"I know!" she said.

"What do we do? Call an ambulance? Should I get my car?"

Even as I said it, I saw my car blocked in by four thousand other cars.

"No, just . . ." She paused for a second and her brows came together. "Ow. I guess that's a contraction."

Now my pulse started to slam. My already shaky head went fuzzy.

"What do I do? Tell me what to do," I said.

"Get my parents!" she cried, holding on to her stomach with one hand and the back of the couch with the other.

I looked over at the stairs. "If I go into your parents' room right now, your father is going to blow my head off."

"Jake! Just go!"

I turned and sprinted up the stairs. The only reason I knew which of the two dozen doors was her parents' was because of the time I'd taken High-Maintenance Tori up here at one of Chloe's parties sophomore year. Just thinking about a random hook-up right now made me sick. I was about to just open the door, but instead, I decided to knock. It was flung open in about two seconds, and there was Chloe's mom. Thank God.

"Jake?" She shoved her hair out of her face. "What the—"

"It's Chloe. She's downstairs. Her water broke. She's having, like, contractions."

Mrs. Appleby's face was white. Her husband appeared out of nowhere, jamming his feet into shoes and his arms into a sweater.

"What the hell are you doing here?" he growled at me as he passed by.

His wife was inside the room now, shoving things into her purse and throwing clothes on over her nightgown.

"I just . . . long story. I—"

But he was already gone, barreling down the stairs.

"Is there anything I can do?" I asked Chloe's mom.

She stood up straight, her eyes darting around the room. "Um . . . get Chloe's bag! She packed a bag for the hospital. It's purple and it's at the foot of her bed."

"Okay!"

I sprinted down the hall, grateful to have a job. I grabbed the bag from the floor. As I turned toward the door, I noticed the teddy bear in the center of her bed and grabbed it. I don't even know why.

Downstairs, Mr. Appleby was helping Chloe into her coat. I walked over with the bag and the bear, and her mom snatched them out of my hands. Chloe was panting, scared out of her mind, from the look on her face.

"Let's go," Mr. Appleby said.

Chloe took the bear and clutched it to her chest. We started out the door.

"Not you," her dad grunted at me.

I froze.

Chloe shot me a helpless look. "But, Daddy—"

"No! I don't want that kid anywhere near you or me or the baby," he said gruffly. "No arguments. Now let's get in the car. We're wasting time."

I stood in the open doorway as Chloe was dragged off by her parents and helped into the car. I wanted to go with them, but at the same time I wanted to stay here and not have to deal. Right after her door was closed, Chloe lowered the window and stuck her head out. I took a step forward, ready to give her whatever she wanted.

"Call Will," she said. "Tell him to meet us there."

I tasted bile in the back of my throat. I couldn't think of one thing I'd rather do less. But I nodded.

"Okay," I said, my voice harsh.

Then her dad took off, peeling out of the driveway and slamming on the brakes as he saw the mess on the street. He managed to maneuver his way out somehow, but I imagined he was cursing me the whole way. One more reason for him to hate me.

I tugged my phone out of my pocket and opened my contacts, then stopped. Who was I kidding? I didn't have Will Halloran's number. I tipped my head back and groaned at the sky. One thing. She asked me to do one thing and I couldn't even do it.

I imagined going back to my house and waking up some Norms to see if they had the kid's number, but that might take too long. I could have driven to the hospital and asked Chloe for it, but her dad wouldn't let me near her, plus I was drunk, plus my car was blocked in, plus Chloe was a little preoccupied right now. I pressed the heels of my hands to my forehead.

"Think, moron, think," I said to myself. Who did I know who would have Will Halloran's number?

And then it hit me. Just like that. I hit the speed-dial button. Ally answered on the fourth ring.

"Jake?"

She was half-asleep.

"Ally," I said, warmth rushing through me at the sound of her voice. "I know you hate me right now, but I need your help."

ally

Will and I ran into the emergency room entrance at the hospital, out of breath from our sprint across the frigid parking lot. For the middle of the night, there sure were a lot of cars parked out there. It had taken us the ten longest minutes of my life to find a spot, and the whole time Will had been rocking forward and back in his seat, muttering something under his breath that sounded like a prayer.

"Whoa, whoa! Can I help you?"

A skinny, redheaded nurse in pink scrubs stopped Will before he could get through the next doorway. From the twigginess of her freckled arms, I wouldn't have thought she could stop a kitten, but she somehow held him back.

"My girlfriend. She's in labor," Will said, panting. "What room is she in?"

The woman shot me a curious and kind of judgey look over Will's shoulder.

"Her name's Chloe Appleby," I said.

"Hold on. Let me check."

She moved over to the desk at roughly the speed of spilled pudding and tapped a few keys on her computer.

"Here it is," she said. "And what's your name, son?"

"Will Halloran," Will said.

"You're on the list of approved friends and family." She looked me up and down as she slowly wrote out a pass for Will. "And you?"

"Oh, I'm not going up," I said. "I'm good."

"She's Ally Ryan," Will blurted, wiping his palms on the butt of his jeans. "Allyson Ryan."

I shot him a look like *What the hell?* And he shrugged. Panic was coming off of him in waves and I got the feeling he was just terrified of going anywhere alone.

"Is she on there?" Will croaked.

The woman's eyes flicked over the computer. "Why, yes she is. It's your lucky day, kids. You get to witness the miracle of childbirth." And then she snickered.

My heart, which was just starting to calm down from the midnight cardio, started to pound anew. The woman handed over two passes and nodded at the door. "Elevator's that way."

Will started through the door, but I hesitated, shifting from foot to foot. "Is she . . . like, did she have the baby yet or is she still—"

"In labor?" the woman said, clearly amused. "I don't have that kind of information, kid. You'll have to see for yourself."

Right then an ambulance came tearing up to the glass doors, sirens blaring, and Will yanked me through the door and into the hallway. His finger trembled as he hit the up button for the elevator. Suddenly a wheelchair slammed through the door we'd just come through ourselves, with a hugely pregnant woman panting like a dog. An orderly pushed the chair in our direction, while a beefy dude—her husband, I guessed—shoved a Flip camera in her face.

"How're you feeling, hon?" he asked as they barreled toward us.

"I'm feeling like I'm going to take that camera and shove it up your ass!" she shouted back through her teeth.

Will and I gaped. The elevator pinged and opened. The orderly shoved the woman inside, while her husband, now looking a tad green, trailed behind her.

"You two coming?" the orderly asked.

"We'll wait for the next one," I heard myself say.

As the doors slid closed, the woman started screeching.

"Um, I don't think I want to go up there," I said, clutching my pass with both hands as Will hit the up button again.

"Don't make me do this alone," he replied.

His plea was so sincere, so childlike, so not-manly-three-varsity-letter-athlete, that I couldn't turn him down. The second elevator pinged and we stepped inside. Mercifully, it was empty.

On the fifth floor, a nurse directed us to Chloe's delivery room. Mrs. Appleby met us outside. She looked freaked, but determined. Like she was steering an out-of-control bus full of kids.

"Good, you're here," she said to Will. "She keeps asking for you."

Will glanced warily at the closed door. "Is she okay?"

At that moment, the door opened and a nurse stepped out. Chloe's cries of pain filled the hall. Will looked like he was about to fall over.

"She's doing fine," Chloe's mom assured him. "Come on. I'll take you in."

I shifted uncomfortably from foot to foot. "So I should just . . ."

"You can wait out here, Ally. Thanks for bringing Will."

"Yeah, thanks for driving me. I don't think I could have—"

"It's not a problem."

I waited until the poor guy was through the door, then sat down in one of the waiting area chairs. My knees were weak. My hands were quaking. I felt both tired and completely alert at the same time. Figuring our friends would want to know what was going on, I sent a quick text to Faith and Shannen, telling them to come by in the morning. Then I settled back to wait. And think about the last half hour.

Jake had called me. I'd woken up in the middle of the night to see his face on my phone for the first time in over a month. I didn't even know what I thought he might have been calling to say, but I did know I grabbed the thing and answered it so fast I clearly wanted to hear whatever it was. I hadn't been prepared for the panic.

He'd told me Chloe's water had broken. Why he'd been there when it happened, I had no clue. He'd asked me for Will's number, and I'd said I would call Will, but Jake had insisted. He had to be the one to do it. I'd hesitated. What if he said something awful to Will? I wouldn't have put it past him. But Jake had begged, and he'd sounded so plaintive that I'd given in. And two minutes after we'd hung up, Will had called me and asked for a ride. Something about his dad being out on an emergency job and him not being able to find the keys to the other car.

And now here I was. But where was Jake? Clearly he was once again a part of this. Clearly he'd somehow come around to the fact that he cared. Should I let him know what was going on?

I stared down at my phone. There was a distinct flutter of hope around my heart. Hope that maybe Jake hadn't changed beyond recognition. Maybe I should just try. Maybe I should just see. I typed a text.

WILL & I @ HOSP. CHLOE STILL IN LABOR. TNX 4 CALLING US.

I hit send before I could rethink it, and his text came back almost instantly.

GLAD U GUYS R W/HER. KEEP ME POSTED.

I leaned back in my chair and sighed. This night just could not get any weirder.

jake

I could hear voices inside Chloe's hospital room. The door was cracked, but I couldn't see who was in there. Was I supposed to knock? Walk in? Wait for whoever it was to leave? A nurse walked by me and shot me a sort of disturbed look, like maybe I was there to steal a baby or something. I flashed my visitor's pass at her and knocked on the door.

God, please don't let it be her dad in there. Or Will.

"Come in!"

Chloe and Ally both looked up. I froze and almost dropped the vase full of lilies. Ally was here. Oh, shit. Ally was here.

"Hi," Chloe said.

"Hi," Ally said.

I looked over my shoulder. "Um, I can come back."

They exchanged one of those looks. Those looks between girls where it's like they have an entire conversation without saying anything.

"It's okay," Chloe said eventually. "Come on in."

I approached the corner of her bed awkwardly. She looked pretty good, but tired. Almost, like, droopy. Her hair was back and she had no makeup on and there were dark circles under her eyes. It seemed like forever that I just stood there with no clue what to say. There was only one chair in the room and Ally was in it.

"Here. Put those on the windowsill," Ally said finally, standing up so I could slide by. My arm brushed hers and I felt like I was having a heart attack.

I put the flowers down next to the other ones—there were a lot—and Ally sat down again. If I wanted to get out of the two-foot space between me and Chloe's bed, I would have to step over her knees. I cleared my throat and leaned my butt back against the windowsill. I hadn't been this close to Ally in ages. It was torture.

Ally and Chloe both stared at me.

"So," I said finally. "Um, how was it?"

Chloe scoffed and looked past me out the window. "It sucked."

I nodded. My collar prickled. My palms were slick. Ally was looking at me like she'd never seen a guy before. Was she surprised I was here, or did she think that I shouldn't be?

"Did you . . . I mean, did you get to see the baby?" I asked.

Chloe shook her head and a tear slipped down her face. Shit.

"She doesn't even know what she had," Ally told me quietly. "Boy or girl. She told them she didn't want to know."

I nodded again. My heart felt four times as heavy as usual. What was I doing here? What was I supposed to say? I looked at Ally. I just wanted to grab her and pull her out of here and go do something normal with her. Like get a burger or go for a walk or see a movie. But I couldn't do that. Because we weren't together. Because she hated me. Because there were huger things going on right now.

"Is there anything I can do?" I asked.

"You've done enough," Chloe said.

My insides dropped. Was she mad at me? Again?

"I'm sorry. That didn't come out the way I meant it," Chloe said. She wiped her eyes with both hands and grabbed a tissue from a cart next to her bed. "You guys, thank you so much for last night. For getting Will here. I mean it. I'm sorry I'm such a mess."

She blew her nose noisily and the tears came faster. I clenched my hands. I'd never been more uncomfortable in my life.

"It's okay. You don't have to apologize." Ally got up and went over to Chloe's bed, sitting down right next to her. She put her arm around Chloe, and Chloe leaned into her, crying.

Ally stared at me. I turned up my palms like *What should I do?*

She kind of jerked her head toward the door. I didn't think it was possible to feel any worse, but that did it. That killed me. I stood up and wiped my palms on my jeans.

"Um . . . Chloe, I'm just gonna go," I said quietly. "But if you need anything—"

She nodded, sobbing, and pressed her eyes closed. On my way to the door, I shot one look over my shoulder at Ally, hoping for something, I don't know what. But she wasn't looking at me. She had pulled her knees up onto the bed and turned toward Chloe completely. It was like I was already gone.

I heard it was a boy.

I heard it was a girl.

I heard she had twins. One of each.

No! It wasn't twins. It was a baby with two heads. One looked like Jake and one looked like Will.

Okay. You have been reading way too many supermarket 'zines.

What if, like, neither one of them was the father? What if it came out looking all, like, Asian or something?

Omigod. Do you think that's why she hasn't come back to school? Is she afraid Will and Jake are gonna gang up against her?

She probably just doesn't want to come back until she's lost all the baby weight.

Well, let me just tell you, I saw her at Scoops last night and she's not gonna be losing an ounce if she keeps ordering up Monster Brownie Manias.

No. Freaking. Way. Her ass must be the size of North Dakota!

More like South Dakota. Because it is most definitely moving in that direction.

Oh my God, you are so bad!

Just telling it like it is, ladies. Chloe Appleby as we knew her? Definitely done.

ally

I felt like I was slogging through fog. Everything around me was hazy and shapeless. I could spend entire class periods staring at the leaves on the trees outside, watching them tossing around in the breeze, focusing and unfocusing my eyes. At lunch, Annie and David and Marshall, who was now Celia-free, just let me be. Every day I ate quickly, then went outside to the courtyard to read. Suddenly I couldn't stop reading. Every weekend I was at the bookstore picking up the latest new releases in the teen section. Anything with a romantic cover. Anything about being star-crossed or forbidden or on-again-off-again. I didn't know why, but I couldn't stop myself. If I was awake, my face was pretty much buried in a book.

And then there was Jake. Always talking to some new girl, always smiling at some adorable face, always messing around with his friends. It was like he didn't miss me one bit. It was like I'd never even existed.

The thing was, nothing in my world seemed to matter. Not my mom's wedding, not the upcoming prom, not graduation. Everything seemed so dull. So ordinary. I couldn't look forward to any of it.

"I think I'm depressed," I said while rain pelted the windows of the cafeteria. I'd been sitting quietly at our lunch table for ten minutes, not eating, not reading, just dipping my straw in and out of my soda can.

David, Annie, and Marshall looked up, surprised, like until that moment they'd thought I'd lost the power of speech.

"Well, yeah," Annie said, pushing her laptop aside.

"What? You think so too?" I asked, sitting up straight.

"Let's see. You walk around school like a zombie, you never talk to anyone, and no one's seen you eat a non-carb in a month," Marshall said, glancing at my tray full of mashed potatoes and gravy. "It's pretty obvious."

"Agreed," David said, popping a chocolate chip cookie into his mouth.

"Also, Sarah Dessen has obviously replaced me as your best friend, which is just not healthy," Annie added, shaking her head.

"Good to know I'm so transparent," I said, miffed.

"You want to spill?" Annie asked, leaning into the table. "Because we already have, like, five good plans to snap you out of it."

Marshall and David nodded in this sort of disturbingly eager way. Suddenly my face began to burn.

"You guys have been *talking* about me?" I asked.

Their gaze darted this way and that. At least they had the decency to look guilty about it.

"Cookie?" David offered, opening the Famous Amos bag toward me.

I narrowed my eyes at him and took one.

"Okay, plan number one, the sugar high," Annie said, holding up a pinkie. "We go into the city and snag passes to the Candy Expo, pretend we're up and coming confectioners, and just go to town sampling everything. Plan number two, shopping spree, on Gray, in his car, on Fifth Avenue. Plan number three, the kidnap plot. We snag Jake Graydon out of the locker room after lacrosse practice and—"

"Hi, guys!" Faith dropped into an empty chair at the very

end of our table. She was wearing a frilly pink top, and her blond hair was back in a ponytail that she'd somehow styled into one very long curl down her back. Annie's mouth snapped shut. Marshall and David shifted warily in their seats, as if an alien had just crash-landed in our midst. "Ally, I have the hugest favor to ask you."

I blinked. Ever since Jake and I had broken up and Chloe had had the baby and Faith had snagged the lead in the spring musical, we'd barely spoken. Just seeing her right now seemed out of context. Like part of some former life gate-crashing this one.

"What kind of favor?" I asked.

"You have to join prom committee," she said, lowering her chin, the better to give me a serious stare.

All four of us cracked up laughing.

"Yeah. That was *not* one of our plans," Annie said, reaching for her lemonade.

"Talk about depressing," David added.

I took my first bite of food. Eating that Famous Amos had made me hungry. Or maybe it was simply laughing that had made me feel better. "Thanks, but no thanks."

"Please?!" Faith begged, grabbing my arm. "Shannen won't do it and Chloe's MIA. Without a good Crestie contingent the Norm crazies have taken over!" She glanced around the table at my friends. "No offense."

"Isn't it interesting how people only say that when they've already caused offense?" Annie said.

Faith scrunched her nose at Annie, who stuck her tongue out in response. I sighed and pushed my potatoes around on my plate. It had been almost a month since Chloe had given birth and she hadn't returned any of my calls. Hadn't returned *anyone's* calls. Shannen's mom had told her that Chloe's parents had hired a district-approved tutor so Chloe could finish the year out as a home-schoolee. As far as Orchard Hill High was concerned, she'd pretty much dropped off the face of the Earth.

But not entirely. Because people were still gossiping about her. Still telling bad jokes. Still making up stories. And every time I overheard something, I got even more depressed. This was Chloe Appleby. She was supposed to be living up her senior year, running the prom, planning a huge graduation party, walking at the front of the class as valedictorian. But instead she'd become one big joke.

"Anyway, please do it?" Faith begged. "It'll help you take your mind off things! Maybe it'll even knock you out of this weirdo daze you've been in."

My jaw dropped and Marshall hid a laugh behind a cough—very badly. Even Faith had noticed?

"Honestly, someone *has* to help me or I'm not gonna have the votes to kill this insane idea they have for the theme." Faith sat back in her chair and crossed her slim arms over her chest.

"What insane idea?" I asked.

She lifted her hands wide. "A Postapocalyptic Prom!"

I gagged on my mashed potatoes.

"Sweet!" David squeaked.

"Yeah. Very romantic," Faith said sarcastically. "They want the backdrop for prom pictures to be one of those nuclear bomb mushroom-cloud things," she said, shuddering dramatically. "So. Will you help?"

"You just convinced me," I said.

Not that I thought I was going to be having my prom picture

taken, considering the fact that I was dateless, uninterested, and uninspired. But that didn't mean I shouldn't help the rest of the senior class avoid having their memories look like something out of the *Hunger Games* movie. And maybe Faith was right. Maybe this would help knock me out of my daze. Something had to. If everyone was noticing it and talking about it, it must have gotten pretty bad. I tugged out my phone and opened it up to the calendar.

"When's the next meeting?"

Faith squealed and clapped her hands, bouncing around in her seat. "Omigod! Yay! You are so *not* going to regret this. Throwing yourself into a new project is always the best therapy. Right?"

She looked to the table for confirmation. David shrugged and ate a cookie. Marshall shrugged and ate a chip.

"Just for the record? I liked the kidnapping Jake idea," Annie said, lifting her pudding spoon.

Faith shot her a wary look as I typed into my phone. As if on cue, Jake's laugh rose up from a table two rows away, and when I looked over, some sophomore with too much cleavage was gazing up at him like he was a god.

"You know what?" I said, glancing over at Annie as I hit save. "Let's go back to the shopping-spree plan. That definitely sounded like something I could get behind."

jake

This was my last chance. My last shot at an athletic scholarship. I'd been wait-listed at Rutgers, Ramapo, and William

Patterson, and almost everywhere else had flat-out rejected me. The Richmond lacrosse coach was holding on to my application because he hadn't finished recruiting yet, just like Rutgers, and both schools had sent scouts out to see me today. I had to show them my skills. I knew this. I knew my life basically hung in the balance.

I just couldn't seem to actually care.

On autopilot, I ran upfield at a sprint, grunting as my legs pumped beneath me. The sun was warm on my face. I could feel the dirt under my fingernails. Sweat prickled my skin and slipped down my back. In the stands, Shannen and Hammond and even Quinn screamed my name. My brother shouted with the rest of JV. This was actually happening. I was actually here. It just didn't exactly feel like I was.

Connor passed me the ball and I made a clean catch. That was when I saw Ted Langer barreling down on me. First team all-state last year. Bigger than the biggest guy on our football team. His tree-trunk of a forearm was gunning for my chest. If I didn't move, I was pancake.

I glanced at the scouts. The one from Rutgers had his hand over his mouth, like he was already imagining my gruesome death.

Fuck that. I still had some pride somewhere in me.

I juked left and spun right. Langer threw himself at me and caught air. Shannen screeched so loud I felt it in my spine. I half tripped, half lunged toward the goal and hurled the ball. Saw the net punch out. Heard the whistle.

"Score!" Connor shouted, racing toward me. He almost tackled me to the ground, but I managed to stay on my feet.

The whole team was grinning and slapping me on the back.

I'd basically just won us the game and I couldn't even put on a smile. I ducked my head and jogged back upfield. Saw the scouts making notes on their clipboards. Saw this girl Lucy I'd been stalked by for the last two weeks jumping up and down with that look on her face. Like I could go over there right now and tear her clothes off and that would be fine by her. She'd been dropping hints about the prom for the past two days, and everyone was telling me to ask her. She'd look hot in a prom dress, and she was more than willing to do whatever I wanted after. Score and score. Just like my life was supposed to be. Just like it was before Chloe, before Ally. I was back to being what everyone expected me to be.

But Ally wasn't there. She wasn't there and I couldn't smile.

It was amazing, really. Amazing how everything could look so perfect and normal, when everything was so very not.

ally

Someone was going to get strangled with a roll of black tulle. I wasn't sure whether it was going to be my mom, who'd gone into full-time bride mode; Faith, who had somehow gotten the prom theme changed from Postapocalypse to the equally cheesy, though far less dark, Springtime in Paris; or Quinn, who had convinced my mother that we should both wear pill-box hats with our bridesmaids dresses. Apparently they'd started studying the Kennedy years in her history class and now she was obsessed with Jackie O. Why that meant I needed an old lady hat and a veil in my wardrobe I had no idea, but my mother had decided it was just retro-funky enough for her tastes, and now I had an actual hatbox in my closet.

Sigh.

So when my mother dropped off forty bags of custom M&M's in my room and told me it was my job to fill hundreds of tiny boxes with them and tie them with bows and tags for favors, you can imagine what I wanted to tell her to do with them. I mean, she didn't even say "please," which was basically the number one lesson she'd drilled into my brain my entire childhood. But instead of pointing out this hypocrisy, I took a deep breath and allowed her to leave my room unharmed. She was, after all, my mother. And I had basically no speech prepared for her wedding, since I'd thrown out my two-thousand-five-hundredth version yesterday. As maids of honor went, I was already turning out to be a huge disappointment.

I leaned back on my throw pillows and sighed, staring at the cardboard crates full of yellow and white ribbons, waxy plastic boxes, and bags of candy. This was going to take me hours. Why couldn't my mother have just gone high-end and ordered Godiva boxes instead of trying to be cute? Maybe I should ask Quinn to help. She was very into this bridesmaid thing. But that would mean spending hours alone with the princess of pep herself, and I was just not in the mood. I needed to call in reinforcements. Someone who wouldn't happily chat my ear off. Someone on my wavelength.

I sat up straight. I knew exactly who to call.

Twenty minutes later, Chloe and I were sitting on her bed, facing each other over a pile of plastic boxes, quietly munching on yellow and white M&M's that read MELANIE & GRAY and TRUE LOVE and attempting to tie the slippery silk ribbons.

"Thanks for doing this," I said. "I would have lost it if I had to do this by myself."

"No problem." Chloe added a box to the "done" pile. "I do tie a kick-ass bow."

"It's always been one of your special talents," I replied with a smirk.

Chloe reached for another box and held it between her thumb and forefinger. She looked better than I had expected. Her baby weight was almost gone and she wore the tiniest bit of mascara and lip gloss. Her room was another story, though. It looked like she hadn't left it in weeks. Her laptop was open on her desk, surrounded by teetering piles of books and papers, and a line of empty water bottles. The garbage can was full of college brochures, and the chair by the deck was covered in a mound of rumpled designer clothes. Workout DVDs were strewn on the floor in front of her TV, and an exercise ball, mat, weights, kettleball, and running shoes were tossed in the corner near her closet.

So at least she was working out. Depressed people don't work out. Right?

"So, I have news," she said suddenly, starting to fill the next box.

"Yeah?" I tied a ribbon, badly, and tossed the box in the done pile. Chloe fished it right out and started to retie it. "What's up?"

"I got into Brown," Chloe informed me.

"Omigod! Really?" My eyes widened. "That's your dream school!"

"I know." Chloe's lips twitched into a small smile. "I actually got the letter back in March, but I wasn't really opening mail then. I got into Duke, too. And Dartmouth."

"Chloe! That's unbelievable!" I said. I leaned over all the crap between us to give her a half hug. "You must be so excited."

Even though she didn't look it.

"Yeah," she said, lifting her shoulders and letting them drop. "I guess life really does go on."

She tossed my now perfectly bowed box in the done pile and sighed. My heart felt heavy against my ribs. This was just not right. When someone worked their ass off as hard as Chloe had her whole life, she should be able to enjoy getting into all these amazing schools. But instead, she looked like she'd been rejected ten times over.

"Chloe," I said, ripping open a new bag of M&M's. "You have to come back to school."

She chuckled and shook some M&M's into a box. "Why?"

"Because . . . you have to," I said lamely. "What are you getting out of locking yourself up in here twenty-four-seven? You should be hanging out with us, planning the prom, going to graduation practice. You're missing out on the best part of senior year."

I felt fake even as I said it, because it wasn't like I was exactly enjoying myself. But Faith had been right about joining the prom committee. It might not have entirely snapped me out of my funk, but it had been distracting. I was no longer focused on Jake and lost love and feeling sad for Chloe. That crapioca was still there, yeah, but it wasn't running my life anymore.

"I don't know, all that stuff . . . the prom and everything . . . it just feels so, like, shallow now," Chloe said. She pushed her hands into her hair, then hugged her knees. "I'd feel like a poser or something, pretending I actually cared." Her gaze flicked up tentatively. "Besides, I can just imagine what everyone is saying about me."

She had a point there. Making up lies about Chloe Appleby had become the number one pastime at Orchard Hill High. But that was mostly because she wasn't there to defend herself.

"Who cares what they're saying?" I replied. "How great would it be to go to the prom with Will? I mean, he's, like, one of the hottest guys in our class. You could get some sick prom dress that'll make everyone salivate and show them how totally fine and *not* fat you are. Don't even try to tell me that wouldn't feel good."

For the first time, Chloe smiled for real.

"It would actually be kind of nice to see Will in a tux," she said, blushing.

"See? There you go!" I reached for a box and filled it with candy. "So . . . you'll come back?"

Chloe bit her lip and narrowed her eyes. "I'll think about it."

"Cool," I said.

As I slipped another ribbon from the pile, something inside my chest seemed to loosen. For the first time in a while, I felt like I'd done something good.

jake

When I drove past Ally's house for the third time, I saw the curtain on her window shift. Fuck. I floored it and took the turn at the end of the street like a NASCAR driver. Had she seen me? Was that the first *time* she'd seen me? Did she think I was just driving over to the Twins' place or did she know I was basically stalking her?

I lifted my fingers from the wheel, trying to give my sweaty palms some air. This was totally effed up. I couldn't be one of those guys who drove by a girl's house just to see if she was home. Those guys were pathetic. They were the guys who wrote poetry in the back of their Trig notebooks and got their asses tossed into that gross shower stall at the dark end of the locker room with the cold water turned on and the door jammed closed with a broom handle. Definitely not me.

I headed toward town and tried to think. The problem was, Ally's birthday was coming up. Her mom's wedding, too. I didn't care so much about missing *that*, but the idea of missing her birthday . . . I couldn't deal. Last year that had been the day I'd turned it all around. Shown up at her house with the perfect gift. Gotten her to say she'd go out with me. I didn't know if it was because of that or what, but lately I'd started feeling like her birthday was kind of a deadline. Like if I didn't find a way to get her back by then, I never would.

But was it even possible? How many times could I make some "grand gesture" as Chloe had once called it, and get my sorry ass forgiven? Besides which, I was out of ideas. Getting her championship ring for her last year had been genius, if I do say so myself, but this year, I had nothing. Not a clue. And I was desperate.

I stopped at the corner of Orchard Avenue and Elm. Up ahead, the lights of the strip mall where Ally worked were all on. My jaw clenched. There was one person who could definitely help me. I just wasn't sure if she would. And I also wasn't sure if I could stomach the idea of groveling to her. But then, I'd already decided I was desperate.

The light turned green. The car behind me honked. I hit the gas and lurched through the intersection. Five minutes later I yanked open the door of CVS. Annie Johnston was behind the counter, her black hair sticking out from under a black-and-white-checkered visor, and she was blowing the most massive gum bubble I'd ever seen.

"Hey," I said.

The bubble popped. She stared at me as it deflated over her chin. Her eyes were round. I could tell she was trying to come up with something rude to say.

"I need your help," I blurted.

Very, very slowly, Annie peeled the gum off her chin and stuffed it back into her mouth. Then she did something that almost knocked me over. She smiled.

"It's about freaking time."

I just heard that Chloe Appleby is coming back to school.

What? I thought her mother sent her away to a convent.

Do people really do that?

I heard it was Catholic school.

Right. Because Catholic school girls never hook up.

Can we focus, please? I cannot believe she's coming back!

Do you think she's still with Will?

Maybe she'll get back together with Jake.

After the way he treated her? Please. Girl has some pride. I don't know. She's probably hella huge. And her stock has definitely dropped. Jake Graydon could turn that right around.

God. Sometimes I'm glad I'm not popular. It sounds like a pain in the ass.

I heard that.

ally

"These are your order forms for your caps and gowns," Dr. Giles announced, walking up the aisle in the auditorium the first Friday in May. He handed a stack to the person at the end of my row and the forms were passed along. "They are not difficult to fill out," he shouted, his voice filling the room. "You simply supply your name, your homeroom, and your size. Therefore, when I say that the deadline to hand these in is this coming Monday, I expect to receive each and every one of your completed forms this . . . coming . . . Monday."

"Wow. Someone's in a good mood," Annie whispered to me as she picked at her chipped blue nail polish.

Behind us, a few girls kept snickering and texting. I glanced sideways at Chloe, who sat on my left. It was her first day back and already her cheeks were red with embarrassment. So she thought that snark fest was about her too. She noticed me looking and tried to smile.

"I'm just glad we don't have to wear maroon like the guys," she said nonchalantly. "No one looks good in maroon."

"Too bad they don't have a double XL in the girls' column," someone said in the row behind ours. "*Some* people might need it."

My heart plummeted and I glanced at Chloe. Her expression darkened and the order form crumbled in her fist atop her thigh. Part of me wanted to grab her and just walk out of there. But then she lifted her head and turned around with a bright smile, hooking her arm over her seat in a casual way.

"Excuse me, Denise, but have you actually *seen* this body

I'm rocking lately?" she said, flicking her fingers in an up-and-down motion. "Because I happen to weigh less than I did before I got pregnant."

Denise Zeldina turned momentarily white. Clearly she had not been expecting a comeback. But she recovered soon enough.

"I wasn't talking about you," she said. "God. Self-absorbed much?"

"Oh, really?" Chloe's eyebrows shot up. "Then who were you talking about?" she asked loudly. "I'm just curious which one of our classmates you think is in need of a double XL graduation gown. Because I'm *sure* that whoever she is, she would *love* to hear your opinion on her body."

Everyone around us swiveled to stare at Denise. She turned beet red and sunk down in her seat.

"Yeah. That's what I thought," Chloe said.

"I think that's enough, Miss Appleby," Dr. Giles said as he strolled by.

Chloe crossed her legs casually, smoothing her skirt over her knees, not the least bit thrown by the vice principal calling her out.

"Oh, I'm done," she replied. She fished a pen out of her leather bag and put a big check mark inside the SIZE: S box.

I couldn't stop smiling. Looked like Chloe Appleby was officially back.

"All right, that's it for today," Mr. Giles announced. "Next week we'll start practicing the processional, but for now you can go to the cafeteria until first period is over."

The room filled with voices and laughter, everyone giddy with an overwhelming sense of entitlement. The casual way in which we'd just been dismissed said a lot. It said we were out of here. That it didn't entirely matter what we did from here on out. Thirty minutes of hanging out in the caf instead of going back to class? That was a gift only the seniors could be given.

"I'll be right back." Chloe slipped out of her seat and jogged up the aisle ahead of us. I assumed she was going to catch up with Will, and I almost tripped when I saw her grab Jake's arm. The two of them turned and walked out into the lobby together, talking quietly. I would have basically killed to know what they had to say to each other. I mean, had she seriously forgiven him for everything? Had he finally forgiven her? I'd been wondering about it ever since he'd called me to get Will's number that night, ever since he'd shown up at the hospital the next day. What, exactly, had gone on between those two?

"Please tell me you're not paranoid about them coupling up again," Annie said under her breath. "Because that is so not happening."

"I know," I replied, feeling warm all over. "And even if it is, who cares? We broke up, remember?"

"Yeah. Right. Who cares?" she said, flicking a blue nail polish chip at Denise Zeldina's hair.

As we approached the doors, Jake walked off and we caught up with Chloe. "What was that all about?" I asked casually, even though my heart was pitter-pattering with curiosity.

"Nothing." She lifted her shoulders. "He texted me this morning that he wanted to help decorate for the prom, so I was just telling him I'd e-mail him the meeting schedule."

My brow knit. Jake had volunteered for prom committee? When? And why volunteer to help Chloe? She hadn't even attended a meeting yet. Not that I thought for a second he'd come to me, but he could have talked to Faith. She was, after all, in charge.

"Um, okay." We turned and walked slowly toward the caf with the throng. "So you two are, like . . . okay?"

Chloe tugged open the door and let Annie and me pass through first. "Pretty much."

I couldn't take it. She was talking about this way too simply. I stopped by the bathrooms and she and Annie stopped with me, letting the rest of the senior class file by.

"Seriously? Even after everything he did? Everything he said? That crap he—"

Chloe lifted a hand. "He apologized for that. That's why he was at my house when my water broke," she added under her breath.

I felt like someone had just spun me around five times fast and left me to try to focus. How had I never heard about this before? This was monumental. "Wait. He apologized? What . . . what did he say?"

She looked down at the floor and shrugged. "He said he was sorry. For everything. Like, everything he'd said or done to make me feel bad. He said he still thought he had a right to be mad, but that he shouldn't have been such a jerk about it."

I leaned back against the cool cinderblock wall, trying to process this information. Jake had apologized. He *had* realized he was wrong. Finally. This was amazing. He had actually dropped the negativity. Which meant that maybe, just maybe, he was still the Jake I'd known and loved.

So why wasn't I more relieved? More excited?

I glanced across the cafeteria to where Jake was sitting with the rest of the guys, and my heart felt sick. I knew why I wasn't relieved. Because he hadn't apologized to me. If he was back to his old self, and he knew I'd broken up with him because I missed who he'd been, then why hadn't he come to me?

Because he was really done with me. He didn't love me anymore. When I'd ended things with him, I guess I'd really ended things. For good.

"I mean, what am I supposed to do, hate him forever?" Chloe continued, following my gaze. "I was scared, so I told a lie and totally ruined his senior year. Then he was pissed and he mocked me out for a couple of months. Honestly? I don't even know if we're even."

"Man," Annie said.

"What?" Chloe snapped, expecting an insult, I'm sure.

"You are just *way* more enlightened than I thought," Annie said.

Chloe and I both blinked. "Um, thank you?" she ventured.

I shook my head and started walking again, but my steps were slow. My heart felt like a cement ball inside my chest. I couldn't think about the fact that Jake was ignoring my existence right now. If I did, I would cry right in the middle of our free period, which was so not cool. Instead, I decided to focus on Chloe.

"I just don't know if I could do it," I said. "Forgive someone after something like that."

Not that anyone felt the need to *give me a chance.*

"Right," Chloe said, sliding into a chair at the end of a table and pulling out her laptop. "And who was the first person around here to start talking to Shannen again?"

Annie laughed and dropped into a seat at the opposite end. "She got you there."

"Who got who where?" Shannen asked, shrugging out of her denim jacket as she and Faith arrived.

"Long story," Chloe and I said at the same time.

Shannen narrowed her eyes at us. "Okay. I'm getting us all doughnuts now. I'll be back."

"Just a banana for me!" Faith shouted. "Gotta fit into that prom dress." She started pulling out her prom planning notes and catalogs, laying them out on the table.

"What're you doing?" I asked.

"We've got to catch Chloe up on what we've got planned," Faith replied.

Chloe sighed as she watched the materials pile up in front of her. "I'm just saying, Ally, if we can all forgive Shannen for what she did to us last year, then you can forgive Jake for what he did to me."

"Omigod! Are we getting back together with Jake?" Faith squealed, clasping her pink pen between both hands.

"Shhhhh!" we all admonished her. I looked around quickly, but no one seemed to have noticed her outburst.

"No one is getting back together with anyone," I whispered.

Annie cracked open a can of Pringles and popped one into her mouth with a smirk. She muttered something under her breath that sounded a lot like "Or so you think," but she was too far away and her mouth was too full for me to be sure.

"What?" I asked.

"Nothing," she said with a shrug.

Then Faith dragged Chloe and me down into Springtime in Paris hell, and by the time the bell rang, Annie was long gone.

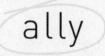

ally

On the morning of the wedding, I woke up facing the bay window at the back of the house. The sun was predictably shining, the sky a perfect, cloudless blue. I could only imagine the pure insanity that had taken over the first floor, but I couldn't make myself move. I just lay there, gazing out that window, motionless, until my eyes started to sting.

My mother was getting married. Today. To someone who was not my father. My family was officially over.

And Jake wasn't even going to be there.

I sat up straight the second I thought about him. Why couldn't I stop thinking about him? He'd barely even blinked when I'd broken up with him, and that had been months ago now. He hadn't bothered to tell me he had a change of heart and had apologized to Chloe. He hadn't called me, hadn't texted, had barely looked at me in the halls. And everyone was talking about the slutty sophomore he was apparently taking to the prom. So why did I care? Why could I not stop caring?

Sometimes I wished Chloe had never told me that Jake had finally said he was sorry. Maybe then I could still be so mad at him I wouldn't care what he was doing. Or who he was doing it with.

I looked over at my laptop, the screen playing my slideshow screen saver. At least I'd finally finished my speech last night. Ironically, thanks to Jake and his advice.

"Ally? Are you up?" Quinn shouted from down the hall. "Our stylists are here!"

"I'll be down in a few minutes!" I shouted back.

I took a deep breath and held it. This was not about Jake. This was not about my dad and our former life as a family. It was about my mom. And as heavy as my heart and head and limbs felt at that very moment, I was going to put on a happy— no, a jubilant, ecstatic, blissful face—and be the best maid of honor ever. I flung the covers off my legs and hit the showers.

As I lathered my hair and scrubbed my face, I recited my speech over and over again in my mind. It was short and sweet, per Jake's tips, and I had it down—flawless—but even so, I felt panicked every time I thought about getting up there in front of the crowd. One more reason to wish Jake was going to be there.

I groaned and yanked on my hair extra hard as I rinsed it. Suddenly I remembered that song Quinn had spent half of last summer practicing, getting ready for this year's musical auditions: "I'm Gonna Wash That Man Right Out of My Hair." If only that were possible.

Twenty minutes later, I was sitting in an actual salon chair set up in front of a huge mirror in the middle of the room that used to be Quinn's mom's gift-wrapping room. Quinn, at least, didn't seem to care that my mother had taken over the space. She sat at a manicurist station behind me, wearing a short pink robe, her blond hair already styled into a classic bun. Some dude with a Mohawk worked on the nails of her left hand while she chatted on her cell phone in her right.

"So, you want it exactly like we did your other daughter's?" my mom's stylist, Marta, asked her.

My heart sort of stopped. My eyes met my mom's in the mirror. Her hair was long and natural down her back and her makeup had yet to be applied, as Marta insisted that the bride should have the last turn in the chair. There were little frown lines around her mouth, and I could tell she was waiting for me to correct Marta about Quinn's status.

"Whatever my mom wants," I said with a smile.

I felt her sigh of relief on the back of my neck. "You can wear it down if you want to, Ally," she said. "Or in a ponytail." She looked at Marta. "She practically lives in ponytails."

"No, it's fine," I told Marta. "Do it like Quinn's. It'll look better in pictures."

My mom gave me a proud look and kneaded my shoulders. Then she grabbed a chocolate croissant off a tray of food near the door and handed it to me. We exchanged a smile, and as Marta began to tug and yank and curl I chomped into my breakfast.

"Hang on, Lindsey. I just got a text," Quinn said.

As she turned her phone to look at it, it slipped from her palm and bounced along the carpet toward my feet. I couldn't move to get it, since half my head of hair was clutched in Marta's iron fist grip, but I looked down. The screen read:

ANNIE J.

I blinked as Quinn pounced on her phone. I couldn't have just seen that right. There may have been some odd relationships popping up over the last year, but Quinn and Annie? I was pretty sure they'd never even occupied the same airspace.

"Who's that?" I asked as she perched onto her chair again.

"Just a friend. Someone from ballet," she said, texting back quickly.

When Quinn was done, she told Lindsey she had to go and she set the phone aside, giving her manicurist both hands. She didn't meet my eyes again, but that was nothing new. But the longer I looked at her, the harder she started to blush. What was going on here? Were Quinn and Annie talking? And if so, why?

"Face forward, please," Marta said, giving my hair a yank.

"Ow!" I complained with a wince.

"Price of beauty, hon!" she trilled.

Once Marta was done making my scalp feel so tight I thought it might start to tear off, she affixed Quinn's pillbox hat to her head. I cringed, just watching the thing go on. I was going to look ridiculous in that. Like, Halloween-costume ridiculous. As Marta removed the white tissue paper from my own hat, I caught my mom's eye in the mirror. She was chewing on her lip like she hadn't eaten in days.

The hat floated down toward my head. I closed my eyes and told myself it was just one day. Just a few hours . . .

"Stop!"

Everyone jumped. I turned and looked at my mom. "No. I can't do it to you, Ally. You don't have to wear that."

"But, Mom—"

"No." She turned around and plucked a couple of yellow gardenias from one of the flower arrangements decorating the room, then handed them off to Marta. "Use these," she said. "They're more her."

I was touched, but still. I didn't want her to change her wedding just for me. "Mom, it's okay," I said. "I'll wear the hat."

"Yeah. What about the pictures?" Quinn put in, turning in her chair.

"Ten years from now when I look at the wedding album, I'm not going to care what you girls were wearing," my mom said, looking into my eyes. "All that's going to matter is that you were there."

I smiled up at her, my eyes filling with tears. Maybe this day wouldn't be so bad after all.

jake

I was so nervous walking up to the church, you'd think I was trying to crash an NFL draft party or something. There were

tons of people milling around outside. My eyes darted to anyone wearing a dark suit. Were any of them bouncers? Was there
a guest list? If there was, I bet the words "Keep Jake Graydon
Out" were written across the top.

My shoes crunched on the brick steps. Some guy who looked
a lot like Dr. Nathanson, but wasn't, gave me the stink eye. I
attempted to smile and somehow tripped myself in the process.

"There you are."

Annie grabbed my arm. She was wearing a dark blue dress
with a wide neck, black fishnet stockings, and high heels. With
her hair back from her face, she actually looked kind of . . .
pretty.

"Get inside. They're gonna be here any minute."

Pretty but WWE-wrestler strong. She yanked me through
the double, arched door and shoved me into a corner. The
church was small and white with lots of stained-glass windows
and a ton of flowers. She pushed me half behind a tall vase with
sticks and blooms coming out of it in every direction.

"Stay there until they're pronounced man and wife. Then go
out that door right there, get in your car, and wait until Quinn
gives you the signal. Got it?"

"Yeah! Yes. Got it," I whispered, smoothing my suit jacket.
She was so intense there was no point questioning her.

"And do *not* let her or her mother see you," she ordered,
lifting a finger at me.

"I won't." I raised my hands in surrender.

"Good." Annie turned to walk away.

"Hey, Annie," I said, stopping her in her tracks.

She gave me this exasperated sigh as she faced me again.
"What? Do you need me to write it down for you?"

I shook my head. "No, I just wanted to tell you . . . you look really nice."

Annie's mouth fell open slightly. Her face turned pink. "Um. Thanks?"

"You're welcome," I said.

She turned and slowly walked away, and I swear she swung her hips a little bit. I laughed to myself. Over the past couple of weeks I'd finally sort of started to get why she and Ally were friends. Even I kind of liked hanging out with her. Which maybe I'd get to do more. If everything went like it was supposed to.

Please let it go like it's supposed to.

Suddenly people started filing into the church in a crowd. My heart started to pound and I ducked in farther behind the flowers. Before long, the music started and Dr. Nathanson walked down the aisle with two people who must've been his parents. Next up was Quinn. She totally milked it, walking as slowly as possible, giving little flirtatious smiles to the people in the pews. She got to the front. I held my breath.

And there she was. Ally looked gorgeous. She was wearing more makeup than I was used to, but in a good way. Her lips were red and shimmery and her eyes looked huge. The dress was black, and she wore yellow flowers in her hair. On her feet were these red high heels—pretty much the sexiest shoes ever.

She paused inside the door, right across from me. She was, like, ten feet away, and for a split second I was terrified that she was going to turn and look right at me. But instead, she lifted her chin and walked down the aisle with a smile on. I knew that part of her was sad about this. That her heart was breaking right now, knowing her parents were never going to get back together. But you never would have known it.

And in that moment I felt this whole new respect for her. I felt proud. I felt unworthy. Like maybe I didn't even deserve to be here. Like maybe she was way too good for me.

I glanced at the doors as the pastor welcomed everyone to the wedding of Melanie and Gray, my toes itching inside my socks. What if I ruined her day just by being here? What if she said, "no"? What if this whole thing was just one giant mistake?

Annie sat near the front, her back to me. Quinn stood next to Ally, watching the pastor. Before I could double-think it, I walked quietly to the door and slipped out.

ally

So that was it. My mom was married. And she had such a smile of pure joy on her face as she and Gray walked up the aisle together, I was, shockingly, almost happy. Quinn and I trailed after our parents along the velvet runner as the people in the pews clapped and tossed rose petals and cheered. Before long even I was smiling.

Then we got to the door. Quinn looked outside and threw her arm across the opening, blocking my way.

"What're you doing?" I asked.

Behind us, the guests were starting to crowd the aisle, headed toward the exit. I could feel them starting to clump up behind me.

"Um, your mom! She left her makeup bag in the dressing room. You should go get it," Quinn said.

"And you can't go get it because . . . ?" I asked.

The guests were starting to breathe down my neck or angle to try to get around us. My fingers were slick as they clutched my bouquet. Quinn glanced over her shoulder at the street, then rolled her eyes.

"Fine." She grabbed my gloved hand. "We'll both go."

Before I could point out that it made no sense whatsoever for us both to go retrieve a tiny bag, she had dragged me back into the church and toward one of the side aisles. We twisted through the laughing, chatting throng, headed for the door that led to the church's offices and the bridal dressing room. Everything back here smelled dusty and waxy, like the scent of the two million candles that had been lit in the church over the years was clinging to the carpet and drapes. Quinn opened the door to the dressing room and practically shoved me inside, her bouquet crunching against my back.

"Ow." I craned my neck trying to check down my back for scratch marks. "Do they have you doing weights at cheerleading practice now?"

I dropped my bouquet on the coffee table and started to search the room, beginning with the vanity table and its drawers. There were a couple of half-drunk glasses of champagne, a crumpled tissue, and a bit of spilled powder, but no bag.

"We've *always* done weights," Quinn groused. "Do you ever listen to anything I say?"

She walked to the window facing the front of the church and pushed the drapes aside to glance out. Then she placed her own flowers aside, whipped her phone from her tiny purse, and quickly sent a text.

"I don't see a makeup bag," I told her, checking the couch

cushions and the chair. "Are you sure she left it in here?"

Quinn stared down at her phone.

"Quinn?"

She looked at me, startled, like she'd forgotten I was there. Then someone knocked on the door and Annie stuck her head inside.

"Did you find your mom's purse?" she asked.

"It's not her purse," Quinn said through her teeth. "It's her makeup bag."

"No. It was her purse," Annie shot back through her teeth, shoving the door open wide and crossing her arms over her chest.

"Okay. *What* is going on?" I demanded.

"Nothing!" Quinn replied shrilly. She brought her hands to her head and her pillbox hat shifted to the side. "I just— I can't—"

She grabbed her flowers, pulled Annie out into the hall, and slammed the door behind them. I groaned in frustration. This was ridiculous. Whatever was going on, I was missing my mom and Gray drive off, and Quinn and I had to get in our Town Car and get our asses over to the country club, stat. We were in the wedding party. We had pictures to take and we were supposed to be announced at the beginning of the reception. If we weren't there when we were supposed to be, my mom would freak. I was about to yank the door open when I heard Annie whispering furtively.

"But he's not there yet!" she hissed.

"Well, you were supposed to talk to him, not me," Quinn whispered back. "Where is he?"

"I don't know! He's not answering my texts!" Annie said, frustrated.

I had no clue what they were talking about, but a foreboding chill went down my spine and I felt goose bumps pop up along my arms. I opened the door. They both went silent and stood up straight.

"What's going on?" I asked.

"Nothing," Annie said.

"Nothing," Quinn echoed.

"Good. Then I'm leaving," I told them.

I pushed right between them and headed back inside the church. The worship space was almost empty now, only the florist and her assistants running around, dismantling the flowers so they could be brought over to the club. I walked down the side aisle and turned purposefully toward the door.

"Ally, wait!" Annie called out, jogging to catch up with me.

"You can't go out there yet!" Quinn added.

"Why not?" I said suspiciously, quickening my pace. I glanced over my shoulder at them and they were both gunning for me, like a couple of well-dressed bounty hunters. I gripped my bouquet, prepared to fight them off with it, if it came to that. "What's going on out there that I'm not supposed to see?"

"Nothing. There's *not* something out there that you *are* supposed to see," Quinn replied, so desperate and frustrated she was turning pink.

Even Annie looked confused by that one. She made a final lunge, but there was no stopping me now. I ran outside into the bright afternoon sunshine and saw . . . nothing. Nothing but a bunch of cars full of wedding guests clogging the narrow street.

Annie stood next to me, panting for breath, and looked around. "Shit."

"Where *is* he?" Quinn whined.

"Where's who?" I asked, throwing my hands up and letting them slap down at my sides. Petals showered from my bouquet. "My dad? Because in case you haven't noticed, it's too late for him to swoop in and stop the wedding."

"No, not your dad," Quinn said, like I was just so stupid. "We've been trying to help—"

"Wait," Annie said, touching Quinn's arm. "There."

Her brow crease flattened, replaced by a victorious kind of smile. I turned to look where she was looking. An Escalade edged forward in the traffic, revealing an army green Jeep parked across the street. And leaning back against the Jeep, his legs crossed at the ankle, his hands pushed casually into the pockets of his suit pants, was Jake Graydon. He looked breath-stoppingly gorgeous in a slim-cut suit and light blue striped tie, his hair gelled up a little bit in front.

Jake smiled slowly. I didn't know what to do with myself. I felt this weird, tingling mix of excitement and apprehension, of hesitation and pure giddiness. I laughed, I couldn't help it, and Jake pushed himself off the car, crossing the street to meet me at the bottom of the steps. Annie gave me a nudge and I tripped my way down there. Up close, the color of Jake's tie made his eyes look almost impossibly blue, and he smelled clean and freshly shaven. I could feel my pulse thrumming in my wrists.

"Hey," he said.

"It's *Sixteen Candles*," I blurted.

Jake nodded. "Annie made me watch it, like, ten times before she agreed to help me."

I glanced over my shoulder, but Annie and Quinn had already disappeared. "I knew those two were up to something."

"Ally, listen." Jake paused and looked down at my flowers. For a second I thought he was going to take my hand, but he changed his mind. "I've been a total jerk," he said, gazing into my eyes imploringly. "You tried to tell me, but I wouldn't listen. It was like I didn't . . . almost like I didn't want to let it go. I just wanted to be mad at Chloe. I wanted someone to, like, hate for everything that had happened. I don't know."

He rubbed his brow with his hands, like making this speech hurt his brain.

"But you were right," he continued after a moment. "And I only realized it after I told Chloe I was sorry. I just felt better, you know? And then I felt like an ass again, because you knew. You knew that it would work that way and I didn't listen."

I stared at him, my heart welling with something that felt like pride. Then he ducked his face and shook his head.

"This sounded a lot better in my mind," he told me.

"You're doing okay," I encouraged him.

"Really?" he asked. "Because I wouldn't blame you if you never wanted to talk to me again. But I . . . I just wanted you to know that you were perfect. You were amazing, actually. And I know I didn't appreciate it. I treated you like crap."

I swallowed hard. Part of me wanted to argue, but I couldn't. Because in a lot of ways it was true.

"I almost didn't come here because, I mean, how many chances am I gonna ask for, right?" His voice was throaty and his eyes were hopeful as he looked at me. "But then I realized it was too important . . . that I . . . loved you too much not to try. So is there any way, I mean . . . could I have a third chance?"

My heart pounded in my chest. I looked carefully into his eyes. This was the Jake I knew. The Jake I loved. But how was

I supposed to know that he wouldn't change again? That the guy who'd tortured Chloe and seemed to take so much pleasure in it wouldn't suddenly come back? I vividly remembered that darkness that would come over his face whenever he saw her. The memory of that transformation still made me shudder.

"Jake—"

"Oh. Shit," he said, just hearing my tone. He started to turn away. "I'm such an idiot."

"No! I mean, don't go . . . yet." I closed my eyes, trying to figure out how I felt, what to say. "I just . . . I can't do this right now. I'm supposed to be at the country club already. My mom . . ."

"So blow it off," he said with a tentative smile. "Like in the movie."

In that moment he looked so vulnerable, so open, it made me want to just take him up on the offer. Go somewhere and be alone with him and cuddle and kiss and talk and kiss some more. But I couldn't. I didn't entirely trust him. And not only that, I'd made a promise to myself that this day was not going to be about me.

"I have to make a speech, remember?" I told him. "My mom would die if I blew it off. Well, first she'd kill me, and then she'd die."

Right then, the silver Town Car that was supposed to squire me and Quinn to the reception zoomed past, Quinn gazing up at us from the back passenger seat.

"And there goes my ride," I said, lifting my flowers.

"So I'll drive you," Jake said.

My eyebrows shot up. Jake was technically not invited to the wedding. And if I brought him into the reception, I'd have to explain it to my mom. Something I didn't remotely know how to do.

"It's just a ride. I won't even come inside if you don't want me to," Jake said, as if he was reading my thoughts. He took out his keys and twirled them once, catching them in his palm. His eyes danced. "Your limousine awaits, princess."

Then he held out his free hand to me. And after only a moment's hesitation, I took it.

ally

The note card on which I had written my speech—just in case—was starting to go soft in my hands from the disgusting amount of sweat my palms were producing. I stared at it under the table, my salad untouched, keeping one eye on the band director for the signal that I was up. Ever since we'd arrived at the Orchard Hill Country Club, I had been unable to relax. Even in the moments I wasn't consciously thinking about my speech—like when I was inhaling mini crab cakes at the cocktail hour, posing for the ten billionth picture with my mom, Gray, Quinn, and her uncle Mason, or dancing to awful renditions of Britney Spears tunes with Annie, my heart was still pounding with nervousness. I just wanted to get this over with. Then maybe I could enjoy myself.

"If I may have your attention, please!" the bandleader suddenly announced.

My knee bounced up and knocked the underside of the table, causing everyone's china to jump. Mortifying. Totally mortifying.

"We'll now hear from the maid of honor and the best man!"

There was a smattering of applause. I rose slowly, rubbing my knee under the tablecloth. On the other side of the table, Mason buttoned his tuxedo jacket and strode purposefully to the front of the room. Why couldn't I be that confident? And why hadn't Gray made *his* daughter the best man and forced her to get up in front of hundreds of people and make a stammering idiot out of herself?

I glanced at Quinn as I passed her by. She was laughing in a totally carefree way at something Hammond had just said to her. Lucky.

Somehow, I arrived at the bandstand without tripping. The gazebo room of the country club looked like something out of a modern fairy tale. The ceiling was draped with a canopy of white lights, and every table was adorned with colorful swags of floral garland. Flowers burst from the glass centerpiece vases like fireworks, and the windows looked out over the lake, where hundreds of yellow, red, and orange paper lanterns bobbed in the setting sun. I took a deep breath and looked at my mom, seated at the sweetheart table with Gray directly across the dance floor. She was giving me that look. The one that said I could do no wrong. Damn, I hoped she was right.

"Ladies first," Mason said, handing me the microphone.

My jaw hung open. Was he kidding? He was, like, forty something years old. He couldn't give a kid a break and lead off?

"Uh, hi," I said into the mike.

"Go, Ally!" Shannen shouted, earning a round of laughter.

I tried to shoot her an *I hate you* look and instead found myself looking at Jake. At the last minute I'd decided to let him come inside, and the maître d' had said there was no problem squeezing him in at my friends' table. My mother hadn't even seemed to notice he was here, and now I was beyond glad he'd come. However stupid or weak or wrong someone on the outside may have thought I was, this day just hadn't felt right without him in it. And besides, he was the one who had advised me on my speech. Now we were about to find out if he was right.

Jake lifted his chin and gave me a confident nod. I squared my shoulders and began.

"I'm Ally, daughter of the bride," I began. My voice sounded weird and nasal, coming back at me through the speakers. And loud. Way too loud. I held the microphone farther away from my lips. "I was really psyched when my mom asked me to be her maid of honor . . . until I realized I was going to have to do this," I joked. The laughter was more wholehearted than I expected and I felt my confidence rise. "But honestly, it made sense. Because my mom and I have always been best friends."

"Awwww!" the crowd cooed.

I smiled. Who knew they were going to be so effortless? I could have written any kind of crap and they would have eaten it up.

"I'm sure you can all imagine that it's not the easiest thing, watching your mom marry someone who's not your dad," I said, my stomach clenching a bit. "But if she was going to marry someone, I'm glad it was Gray, because it's obvious to the world how happy he makes her, and anyone who makes my best friend that happy has to be pretty cool."

I glanced at Gray and he smiled, nodding his head in thanks. My mom kissed his cheek.

"So thank you, Mom, for giving me the distinct honor of making this speech," I said, with a touch of sarcasm that made everyone laugh. "And thank you, Gray, for being the guy who makes my mom's face look like that," I said, pointing.

My mom's eyes shone and her cheeks were all pink with happiness. I earned another "aw" from the crowd, then turned to pick up my champagne glass.

"To the bride and groom!" I shouted, my relief at being done pouring through every last speaker in the room.

"The bride and groom!" the guests replied, lifting their glasses.

Then there was a round of applause and it was over. Just like that. After months and months of worrying. I handed the microphone to Mason and stepped back, so very happy that I was done. For a while I watched my mom and Gray react to Mason's speech, but as it went on longer and longer, people started to get antsy and squirmy, including me. Looked like Jake had been right about the speeches. Short and simple was the way to go. I turned, just slightly, to see if he was still paying attention. I figured he'd be eating his salad or laughing it up with the Idiot Twins or something. But he was just sitting in his chair while my friends chatted and ate around him, watching me. I felt the intensity of his stare from my scalp all the way down my arms and into my fingertips, along my spine and down to my toes.

And just like that I knew. Whatever fears I still had, whatever distrust, whatever disappointments or questions, I knew that this wasn't over. Not by a long shot.

jake

"Your mom seriously knows how to throw a party," I said, gripping the Jeep's steering wheel.

Oh, nice. Bring up her mother. That's romantic. Jackass.

"As long as I don't ever have to give a speech again, she can throw whatever parties she wants," Ally replied.

She was sitting in the passenger seat, but as far away from me as possible. Across the water, the lights of the country club glowed. The gazebo room was full of dancing guests. Every once in a while a laugh could be heard through the open car windows. But the only thing I could think about was that this was where I'd kissed her the first time. How I'd kill to do it again. My pulse pounded in my ears. Would she ever let me do it again?

"I thought you were awesome," I said.

"Please." She rolled her eyes and flicked the window controls back and forth. Which did nothing, since the car wasn't on.

"No. You were," I protested, maybe a little too loudly.

"Well, I couldn't have done it without you," she said.

I felt a rush of pride. Maybe all wasn't lost.

"Seriously, if it wasn't for your advice, I would've rambled on longer than Mason did."

"Yeah. That guy crashed and burned," I said with a laugh.

Ally laughed too. She rested her elbow on the armrest and her temple on her hand and looked over at me. I suddenly felt like some awkward dork with bad breath and no clue.

"What're we doing?" she asked.

"What do you mean?" My fingers curled around the wheel so tightly, they hurt.

"Jake—"

There it was. That same tone she'd had outside the church. Like I was pitiful and she was about to let me down easy. I couldn't let that happen. I couldn't hear that right now. I closed my eyes and gritted my teeth.

"Will you go to the prom with me?" I asked.

The moment of silence that followed was the longest moment of my life. The crickets chirped outside. Something surfaced in the lake, then went under again, leaving ripples that went on forever, making the paper lanterns bounce and sway.

"I thought you had a date for the prom already," she said.

I blinked. "What? No. Who?"

She lifted her shoulders, looking out the window. "I don't know. Some sophomore? That's what I heard."

"Yeah, well, don't believe everything you hear," I said. I cleared my throat. Pressed my right hand against my thigh. "Do you have a date already?"

I held my breath until it felt like my lungs would burst.

"No," she said slowly. She looked down at her hands, picking at her painted nails. She almost never had painted nails. "I wasn't planning on going."

"So go with me." I turned in my seat. "Come on. Remember last summer? We used to talk about it all the time. How we'd make up for last year this year?"

Last year I'd screwed up by asking someone my friends wanted me to ask, and Ally had gone with Marshall Moss. It had been one of the most pointless nights of my life. And torturous, watching her flirt and dance with that dude like he was the only guy there.

"Come on, Ally. Just say yes." I pleaded. "I'll make everything up to you, I swear."

Ally's hands dropped into her lap and she sighed. That sigh took the air right out of me. She was going to say no. This was it. This was where she let me down easy. This was the real end.

Then she looked up at me and bit her lip. "Can I think about it?"

Think about it? Was she kidding? Like this wasn't torture enough, now she was going to drag it out? My neck burned. Here I was, basically begging her, and that was her response?

But then I looked into her face and instantly cooled off. Of course she wanted to think about it. I was her asshole ex-boyfriend. What did I think I'd done to deserve a quick "yes"? Stage one scene from one stupid old movie, which wasn't even my idea? Not enough. Clearly there was more work to be done.

"Sure," I said, my heart heavy. How was I going to fix this? What was I going to do? "Yeah. Just . . . let me know."

ally

My birthday. This was my eighteenth birthday. Was I doing something fabulous, like hanging out at a day spa with Shannen, Chloe, and Faith or hitting a few clubs in the city? No. Was I doing something quaintly low-key, like having dinner out with Annie and David and my parents and laughing while the waiters sung their off-key version of happy birthday? No. Was I sitting on the couch in the living room, watching *Cake Boss* with Quinn while she texted with Hammond and waiting for my dad to show up to take me out for a $9.99 special at Chili's?

Yes. Yes I was.

I shifted in my seat and let out a sigh. My father was fifteen minutes late and hadn't called. I wondered if he was going to stand me up. That would just be the icing on the cake. Pun very much intended.

"I wonder what Mom and Dad are doing right now," Quinn

mused, checking her watch before absently shoving a piece of popcorn into her mouth.

She'd started doing that lately. Calling my mom "Mom." It was just weird.

"Probably sipping wine, watching the sunset over the beach, being totally, disgustingly, in love," I said flatly.

They had called earlier that day to wish me a happy birthday and tell me they were bringing me back a killer surprise when they got home. But I didn't even care about presents. I just missed my mom. I'd kept her on the line for way too long, talking about nothing, just because I didn't want to hang up.

"Wow. Someone forgot to take her happy pills this morning," Quinn said, nudging my leg with her socked foot. "Maybe if you'd've talked your dad into taking you somewhere cooler than *Chili's*—"

"Hey, my dad's not made of money like some people," I shot back.

Quinn raised her hands in surrender. "Sorry. Sheesh. Cheer up already. It's your birthday."

"Yeah, yeah," I replied, sinking into the couch.

"You never know, you know," Quinn said. She set the popcorn aside, grabbed the remote, and turned off the TV abruptly. "Maybe something unexpectedly fabulous will happen."

I rolled my eyes at her. "I think you take too many happy pills."

She was opening her mouth to retort when the doorbell rang. I grabbed my bag as I jumped off the couch. "See ya!"

"Have fun!" she shouted after me.

I ran through the kitchen, down the hall, and through the foyer, psyched to finally be getting out of the house. But when

I flung the door open, it wasn't my dad standing there. It was three people in ski masks. Shannen, Chloe, and Faith. I could tell by the hair sticking out around their necks. Behind them, Faith's car idled in the driveway.

"What're you guys—"

"No talking!" Shannen said, pitching her voice superlow. Then Chloe and Faith yanked a pillowcase over my head and led me toward the car.

"You guys. What're you doing? My dad's gonna be here any minute to take me to—"

"I said, shut up!" Shannen barked. "This is a kidnapping."

I sighed as someone ducked me into the backseat of the car. "But my dad—"

"Shut up or you won't get your present," Faith ordered as a couple of car doors slammed.

I rolled my eyes under the pillowcase as the three of them started to whisper, but suddenly I couldn't stop smiling. Whatever these three crazies had in mind, I was in. Maybe Quinn was right. Maybe something unexpectedly fabulous *would* happen.

ally

At first I tried to keep track of where the car was headed by counting turns, but it took about five minutes for me to get completely confused. I attempted a few questions, but Faith, Shannen, and Chloe just kept telling me to shut up, so I finally bagged it and just settled in for the ride. For a while they sang along to the stereo while I sat there and nodded my head to the beat. It felt like we were in the car forever. So long that I started to wonder if they really were taking me into the city to club-hop. If so, I was definitely not dressed appropriately.

Finally, the car skidded to a stop, tires squeaking. I was thrown forward, then back, and I felt my neck crack.

"Oops! Sorry!" Faith said, killing the engine. "Girls, get the prisoner."

I waited for the door to open next to me and put my foot out onto asphalt. There was no street noise—no honking or voices or random music playing—so we were definitely not in the city. Two of my friends took my arms and steered me around. We walked up an incline and then made a right. Suddenly I could hear voices. Lots and lots of voices. And music being played from speakers that sounded like they were everywhere. Had they taken me to some kind of outdoor concert? And if so, were people disturbed by the sight of a girl with a bag over her head?

"Where the hell are we?" I whispered.

Then we stopped. Someone whipped the pillowcase off and a thousand voices shouted, "Surprise!"

I blinked in confusion, trying to focus. We were standing under one of the baskets on my basketball court. Well, Jake's basketball court. We were in Jake's backyard, which used to be my backyard. And pretty much every one of my friends from school was crowded onto the court under a big white tent. David's band was set up in one corner, and a huge spread of food was placed along the opposite side of the court from the bleachers. Annie stood at the front of the crowd, her Flip camera trained on my stunned face. My dad broke out and came over to envelop me in a hug.

"Are you okay?" he asked me.

"Um, yeah," I stammered out. "Just . . . shocked. You were in on this?"

"Like I'd really let you spend your eighteenth birthday at Chili's?" my dad said incredulously. "But no, your friends planned it. I was just the cover."

I turned to look at Shannen. "You guys did this?"

"Nope," Shannen said, shaking her head and knocking her fists together. "This one was all Jake. The whole thing was his idea."

Just then, Jake emerged and tossed something at me. Something blue and silky and crumpled into a ball. I caught it against my chest and unfolded it in front of me. It was a basketball jersey with my number and the words BIRTHDAY GIRL printed on the back.

"Happy birthday," he said, standing in front of me with his hands in the pockets of his jeans. He'd gotten his hair cut, and he wore this light blue Lacoste polo that made him look like a model. So not fair, having an ex who looked like that. And I hadn't even had a chance to get changed out of my distressed jeans and green-and-white-striped T-shirt.

"Um, wow. I—"

I didn't know what else to do or say. I was so overwhelmed, there were no words.

"Did we miss it?"

"Mom?" I blurted.

I whirled around to find my semi-tan mother, and a super-tanned Gray, striding through the gate with Quinn right behind them. My mother's shoulders drooped when she saw me.

"Oh! We missed it!" she pouted.

"You're here!" I shouted.

I threw myself into her arms and she kissed the top of my head to a round of teasing "awww"s. I felt like a complete dork, hugging my mommy like I hadn't seen her in years, but I couldn't help it. She wasn't supposed to be back for three more days. And besides, I had all this pent up Jake-related emotion inside of me and I had to hug it out somewhere.

"Happy birthday," she said, cupping my face as she pulled away.

"Told you something fabulous could still happen," Quinn chided me.

She sauntered over to the drinks table and joined Hammond and some of her friends. I couldn't believe she'd actually managed to keep this a secret from me. I couldn't believe any of them had.

My mother and Gray went over to say hi to my dad and Jake's parents, and everyone else started to mill around. A bunch of people came up to tell me just how hilarious my face was when they'd whipped the pillowcase free, and the music started up again full-blast. The faces whirled by so quickly, accompanied by happy birthdays and hugs and kisses, but through it all I kept searching the crowd for Jake. Where had he gone? Was he upset I hadn't said anything? Was he hiding out in his room or something?

But then, as I was hugging Marshall, I caught a glimpse of Jake over his shoulder. He was directing one of the waiters on where to set up the cake, like a true party planner. He must have felt me watching, because he looked over at me and our eyes locked. I stared at him for a good, long minute, my heart so full it was taking up my entire chest.

"Thank you," I mouthed to him.

He smiled. If possible, he looked hotter in that moment than he ever had before. "Anytime."

jake

When people began to leave, I started to get tense. I tried to keep an eye on Ally, but there was so much going on. The cake, the pictures, the dancing, the good-byes. I just wanted her to stay. If she left with her parents or one of her friends . . . I didn't know what I was going to do. Honestly. I didn't know.

But then I saw her dad hug her good-bye. And a while later her mom and Dr. Nathanson left with Quinn. Annie snagged a ride with Marshall, and David's band started packing up. There was a scary second there when it looked like she was planning to hit the diner or something with Shannen, Chloe, and Faith, but they left without her too. Soon the court was almost empty. Ally stood near the gate with a couple of Norms, laughing about something, but her eyes kept trailing over to me. I pretended to help some of the worker guys clean up, but I didn't even know what I was doing. Every inch of my skin tingled. It was like I was about to get on a rollercoaster, but I couldn't see where it was going.

Please just let me get her alone. Please, God, just let me get her alone.

Finally, I heard her say good-bye to her friends. She walked over to me slowly, her hands behind her back, crossing one foot over the other. It was a flirt walk. This was promising.

"Hey," she said.

She must have been able to hear my heart pounding. It was obvious to the world. "Hey."

She smiled and hugged herself, looking around at the tent, the decorations, the gift table. "And you thought my mom threw a serious party."

I cracked a grin. "I'll admit it. I had some help."

"I figured," she said. "But thank you. I can't believe you did all this."

"Really?" I said, stepping closer to her. "Can you really not believe I'd do this for you?"

My voice sounded throaty and my chest was warm with hope. Because I meant it. I'd do anything for her. She just had to believe it. She gazed up at me, searching my eyes, and I leaned in closer. My lips actually tingled. For a second, her eyelids went heavy, and I swore she was going to let me kiss her. Finally, finally, finally. But then, suddenly, she pulled away. I felt like I was going to die. Seriously. Right then and there.

She turned around and walked slowly away.

"Where're you going?" I said.

"Just getting something." She popped open the door of the shed that held all the sports equipment and came back with a basketball. "How about a little one-on-one? It could be your present to me."

I smirked. "Oh, so the party and the jersey weren't enough?"

She looked me in the eye and very, very sexily shook her head, her hair falling forward in front of her face. I swallowed hard.

"Okay," I said, clapping my hands together. "I'm in."

We decided to play to eleven. Ally took the ball out first, being the birthday girl and all. As I crouched in front of her, I

realized that my goal for this game was just to not get humiliated. There was no way I could beat her. This had been proven
before. And besides, I didn't *want* to beat her. It was her birthday. And yeah, I was still hoping to get that kiss. Losing probably wouldn't put her in a kissing mood.

"Ready?" she said, dribbling between us.

"Ready."

Instead of cutting right or left, she came right at me. I
backed up fast, almost tripping myself, but she still slammed
her shoulder into mine. I felt myself blush as her body grazed
past me. She took the ball to the hoop and hit an easy layup,
then retrieved the ball and tossed it back to me.

"One—nothing," she said, taking the defensive position.

I just watched her, tossing the ball from hand to hand. Had
she made contact like that on purpose? Was she just messing
with me? I decided to test it.

I took the ball just a few steps away from the midline, stopped
moving, and lined up the shot. As the ball arced through the
air, Ally jumped for it, and missed. When she came down, she
tripped right against me. The ball swished through the hoop.

"One—one," I said, my breath short, even though I'd barely
moved.

She looked up at me with those big brown eyes, her chest
pressed against mine. "Nice shot."

Then she took her time moving away, her hand trailing
across my pecs.

Yeah. She was definitely doing that on purpose. The rest of
the game was pretty even, both scoringwise and flirtingwise.
She took the ball up and I grabbed her hand, holding her back
as she strained against me. She still made the shot, tossing the

ball underhand at the hoop. I raced forward to try for a layup and she bent down to tackle me at the waist. By the time she got to eleven, we were both giggling like idiots and flushed from contact as much as the exercise.

"Nice game," I said with a laugh, reaching out to slap her hand.

Her fingers slipped against mine. "Nice game."

We both sat down on the bottom bleacher. Our knees were touching. I turned toward her, my shoulder grazing hers, and placed my hand on her back. She didn't move. I slipped it up slowly, trailing my fingers under her hair. She closed her eyes and tipped her head back into my hand. Her whole neck was exposed and I wanted to kiss it so badly I started to salivate. But I controlled myself.

The kissing, as much as I wanted it, was not the ultimate goal here. One step at a time.

"Hey," I said.

She opened her eyes and looked at me.

"Go to the prom with me," I said, holding my breath.

Ally slowly smiled. She bent forward, grabbed the ball, and stood up. My hand dropped down. What the hell was she doing now?

She dribbled the ball methodically to center court, lifted it, and hit a sick and perfect three. The ball bounced back toward her and she stopped it with her foot.

"Hit that shot, and I'll go to the prom with you," she said.

I rolled my eyes. Man, she was really toying with me tonight. I shoved myself up off the bench and lifted the hem of my shirt to quickly wipe my face.

"Here."

I held my hands up for the ball. She popped it up with the toe of her sneaker, then tossed it at me. I adjusted the ball a few times, spinning it between my palms. My pulse was racing. I had to make this shot. I had to. My pride, my prom—hell, my chances with Ally—were on the line. I walked over to her. She inched away so I could stand right where she had been standing. I lifted the ball, bent my knees, said a silent prayer, and took the shot.

The ball crashed against the backboard with a loud rattle, and bounced off into the night. My heart sunk.

"Ouch," Ally said, grimacing.

In that moment I honestly thought she was pure evil.

"Guess that's that," I said, irritated.

Then she jogged over, picked up the ball, and brought it back. She held it out to me.

"Did I not mention you get unlimited chances?" she said, arching one eyebrow.

It took a second for what she was saying to sink in, but when it did, I smiled. And suddenly I didn't even care that she was toying with me. I had my answer. We were going to the prom. Ally Ryan was going to be my date. Ally Ryan was going to be mine again.

With a grin, I took the ball from her, turned around, and let it fly.

june

O.M.G., you guys, Jake Graydon didn't get into college.

Come on! Not possible.

Not even one?

Not. Even. One. I just overheard him talking to his counselor. He was practically in tears.

Please. Couldn't he, like, charm his way in?

He's not a vampire, okay? He's just a normal, very hot guy with zero powers of mind control.

I don't know about that. He does have a way of talking girls into—

That's different. Hot guys are, like, a dime a dozen to college admissions boards.

Did I tell you guys my school has a three-to-one ratio of guys to girls?

Yes. You've told us. Hello? This is not about you and your future sexcapades.

You're right. You're right. So what's he gonna do?

I don't know. But I heard they have an opening for a janitor here next year.

ally

The prom was completely amazing. Thanks to Chloe's intervention, Faith's pink, black, and white color scheme had been dropped, and now everything was blues and purples and greens. One side of the country club ballroom was decorated to evoke Paris during the daytime, with colorful flowers bursting from baskets, a carefully constructed Pont Neuf over a glimmering fake Seine, and Notre Dame painted on a mural that took up one entire wall. The food was laid out on graded tables, so it felt like browsing an outdoor market, and the waiters, with their trays of hors d'oeuvres, wore black cropped pants, white T-shirts, and berets. The other side of the room was decorated to look like Paris at night, with a huge Eiffel Tower lit up by twinkle lights and glittering fireworks painted onto the mural of the nighttime skyline. Prom photos were taken in front of the iconic tower, which in my humble opinion was way better than a toxic, nuclear mushroom cloud.

But the best part about prom? Jake hadn't stopped holding my hand since we'd arrived.

"So what do you think? Should we do the formal pose thing and face each other or do the arms-around-you-from-behind thing?" he asked me as we stood on line to have our picture snapped.

I leaned back into his chest, savoring the feeling of having his body so close to mine again. "Arms-around-me-from-behind thing. Definitely."

Jake grinned, and for a second I thought he was going to kiss me, but then the photographer called us up and the moment passed. I was kind of stunned that he hadn't gone in for the kiss yet. Not at pre-prom pictures at Chloe's house, not in the limo, not once at the table. I knew I'd thwarted a couple of attempts at my birthday, but I was still wary then, and yeah, maybe having some fun with him. But had I totally screwed it up? Was he never going to try again?

We stood together on the square of black velvet in front of the Eiffel Tower and toed the tiny masking-tape line. Jake slipped his arms around the waist of my deep purple, one-shouldered dress and I put my hands on top of his.

"All right, say '*fromage!*'" the photographer requested with a flourish.

Jake and I just smiled. The flash went off and we walked over to the computer screen to see how it had come out. Jake looked so happy, standing there with his arms around me. So giddy, almost. And I looked even giddier.

"That's it. That's our senior prom picture," I mused quietly.

Jake squeezed my hand and rolled his eyes. "You're not gonna get weepy on me now, are you? Because we've only been here an hour. It's not over yet."

Just then the pounding dance music switched over to a slower song. I looked up at Jake and grinned. "No, it's not."

I tugged his hand and we strolled slowly to the center of the dance floor. My arms slid up around his neck and he held me close around my waist. So close I turned my head and rested my cheek against his chest. Nearby, Chloe was dancing with Will, David twirled Annie around as they laughed, Quinn and Hammond were practically melded together as one. Faith was just leading her date, some guy from Valley we'd never heard of until last week, onto the dance floor, and Shannen, who had decided to come solo, had momentarily snagged some other girl's date. Lincoln was even there, dancing with Marni Burt, whose mother—perfectly—owned the homemade-candy store over in Westwood. I watched each of them for as long as they were in view, trying to solidify the moment in my mind. In a few weeks, we were going to say good-bye. After graduation, we might never be in the same place together again. Watching them now, it felt like they were already fading away.

"Hey," Jake said.

I felt the word rumble through his chest. I leaned back to look up at him.

"Yeah?" I asked.

"There's something I've been wanting to do for a while," he said.

My feet stopped moving. "What's that?"

He smirked. Like I didn't know. "Just promise me you won't move this time."

I smiled and tightened my grip around his neck. "I promise."

"Good. Because you're not getting away from me again," he said quietly.

"No. You're not getting away from me," I replied.

But I felt the sting of it even as I said it. Because who knew where Jake was going to be next year? Who knew if we'd be able to make a long-distance relationship work? But I didn't want to think about that now. I wanted to think about this. This moment. And what Jake had been wanting to do.

Ever so slowly he smiled that sexy smile of his and slid his hand under my hair. I tilted my head back, my eyes fluttered closed, and he kissed me. It was a kiss that felt like something

I'd been waiting for my entire life, not just the last few months. It felt like we were the only two people who had ever kissed and that no one else could ever understand how completely, mindblowingly perfect it was.

And whatever fears were poking around in the back of my mind, whatever doubts about the future my heart was clinging on to, it really did feel like it was never, ever going to end.

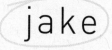

jake

The call was from a 732 area code. My mouth went completely dry. I glanced across the kitchen at my mom and she stood right up from her stool at the island. The terror and hope must've been written across my face.

"Well? Answer it!" she cried.

At that moment the doorbell rang.

"Jonah!" my mom shouted. "Get the door!"

"But it's not for me! It's Jake's *girl*friend!" the twit shouted back.

"Just *getthedoor!*" my mother yelled through her teeth.

I picked up the phone. "Hello?

"Hello, is this Jake Graydon?" The voice was familiar. Male. It was a person I had only spoken to once before, but who I'd kind of pinned all my hopes to.

"Yes," I said, turning toward my mother. We faced each other over the kitchen island. She pressed her fingers flat against her lips. Behind her, Ally walked in with Jonah, looking perfect in a green dress with her hair back in a ponytail. She shot me this look like *What's going on?* But I couldn't even respond.

"Jake, this is Coach Turbeck from Rutgers Lacrosse," the man on the other end said, his voice booming. "How you doing today, son?"

"Good," I said, then cleared my throat. "Fine. How're you?"

Did I sound like as much of a tool as I thought I did? I turned away from my audience. I couldn't take them staring on top of everything else.

"Well, I'm great, son," he replied. "I'm always great on a day that I get to deliver good news."

"Good news?" I repeated.

I put my free hand over my eyes. I did sound like a tool. But I couldn't take this. My heart was in my throat. I was sweating so bad I was going to have to change my shirt before we left for Shannen's birthday party.

"Yep. I'm calling to let you know you've been accepted at Rutgers University, and you've got a spot on my team next spring, if you want it."

My knees buckled and I turned around. Every last ounce of uncertainty and anguish, disappointment and anger and fear . . . everything negative I'd felt over the past year . . . was obliterated with that one sentence.

"I'm in?" I said.

My mother squealed and hugged my brother. Ally's eyes widened.

"You're in. Not only was I impressed by your skills on the field, but everyone in admissions loved your essay. That was what really put you over the top."

I glanced at Ally, loving her more than ever right then.

"Whaddaya say, son? Want to play Scarlet Knight lacrosse?"

the coach asked, sounding like he was stifling a laugh.

"Of course! Yes! Definitely!" I replied. "Coach, thank you so much," I said, gripping the phone to my ear. "I swear I won't let you down."

"I had no inkling that you would, Jake," the coach replied. "You'll be getting your official acceptance letter and forms in the mail next week, but I wanted to let you know as soon as I could."

I swallowed a tremendous lump in my throat. "Thank you."

"You're welcome, son. And welcome to Rutgers."

"Thank you. Thanks again, sir," I babbled.

"Anytime. I'll talk to you soon, Jake. Have a good night."

"Bye!"

I hung up the phone, dropped it on the counter, and screamed. "I'm in!"

My mother let out a shriek and hugged me so hard I thought she was going to crack my ribs. Jonah slapped my hand.

"In where? Who was that? What's going on?" Ally asked.

I walked around to her side of the island, grinning the whole way. She took one look in my eyes and her jaw just sort of dropped.

"No," she said, her fingertips touching my arm. "Not— Really?"

"Yep," I said. "I'm going to Rutgers too."

ally

I gazed out across the ocean, the sun hanging low over the horizon. Jake put his arms around my waist from behind and rested his chin on my shoulder.

"Four hours," he said.

I glanced back at him. "What?"

"Four hours ago, we were still in high school."

I laughed, turning to look at him. "Wow. Who's getting all weepy and nostalgic now?"

"Why? What'd he say?" Shannen asked, twirling her graduation cap between both index fingers.

"He said, 'Four hours ago, we were still in high school,'" I mimicked, pitching my voice low.

"God. Who knew the 'coolest guy in class' was actually a dork?" Annie chided. She still had her graduation cap on, and tugged the tassel down in front of her face, crossing her eyes to look at it.

Jake's face reddened and he yanked me toward him, so hard we both staggered backward in the sand.

"I'm just saying, thank God it's over," he announced.

The Idiot Twins cheered and lifted two champagne bottles they'd already swiped from inside Faith's house.

"Hey! Some of us still *are* in high school," Quinn complained.

"And we feel sorry for you," Hammond replied.

Quinn shoved him away from her and he chased her, making her yelp as they kicked up sand on their way down the beach. We'd all driven down to LBI together in a long caravan as soon as all the picture-taking had been done and the parental tears had been dried. Chloe and Will meandered toward us through the sand, still in their graduation gowns, their fingers entwined. Faith was inside her house, opening windows and airing the place out.

Two years ago, if anyone had told me that I would be standing here, on this beach, in front of these houses, with these people, I would have told them to have their prescriptions checked. Yet here we were.

"So. What do we do now?" Shannen asked, leaning her elbow atop my shoulder and staring out at the water.

I blinked, fully realizing for the first time that there was no school tomorrow. For real. School as I knew it was over. No papers to write, no tests to study for, no practices to attend. There were also no babies to worry about, no prom to plan, no wedding to stress over, no scouts to impress, no SAT to take, no applications to fill out. I had nothing I actually *had* to do, and the parents wouldn't be arriving for another few hours.

Never in my life had I felt so free. So happy. And so exactly where I was supposed to be.

I turned around, my white graduation gown, open over my light blue dress, billowing behind me in the breeze. Jake squeezed my hand and I felt the endless possibilities of summer unfolding in front of us like a huge, warm beach blanket in the sun.

"We do," I said with a grin, "anything we want to do."

Acknowledgments

I can't believe the trilogy is already over! It seems like I just pitched the idea of Ally and Jake and the world of Orchard Hill, and now here it is, drawing to a close. A lot of people helped this little trio become what it is, so I'd like to take this opportunity to thank them.

First of all, for helping me make this particular book all it could be (which is something I rather like), I'd like to thank Zareen Jaffrey, Julia Maguire, and Jenica Nasworthy. To those who believed in *She's So Dead to Us* and its sequels from the very beginning—Justin Chanda, Emily Meehan, and Sarah Burnes—thanks for EVERYTHING! And to Paul Crichton, Lucille Rettino, Elke Villa, Krista Vossen, and Logan Garrison, you guys kind of rule (but you knew that).

Big thanks to my family and friends—especially Matt, Mom, and Erin—for letting me bounce ideas off of you and listening to me go on about my fictional characters. And thanks to Jeff Palkevich for sharing my books with your friends.

As always, I want to thank all the fans of the He's So/She's So Trilogy for keeping me inspired and letting me know you're with me. Whether you're a Facebook friend, a Twitter follower, a librarian, blogger, teacher, or a few of the above, I so appreciate your support. I hope you guys like this last installment and will check out whatever I come up with next!

Finally, I have to thank my little guys, Brady and Will, for making everything worthwhile.